PRISONER
of CAGE FARM

PRISONER
of CAGE FARM

Cecelia
FREY

UNIVERSITY OF
CALGARY
PRESS

OPEN SPACES

Published by the University of Calgary Press
2500 University Drive NW, Calgary, Alberta, Canada T2N 1N4
www.uofcpress.com

National Library of Canada Cataloguing in Publication Data

Frey, Cecelia
    The prisoner of Cage Farm / Cecelia Frey.

    (Open spaces, ISSN 1705-0715 ; 2)
    ISBN 1-55238-116-1

    I. Title. II. Series: Open spaces (Calgary, Alta.) ; 2.
PS8561.R48P74 2003   C813'.54   C2003-911205-5

We acknowledge the financial support of the Government of
Canada through the Book Publishing Industry Development
Program (BPIDP) for our publishing activities.

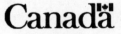

Canada Council
for the Arts

Conseil des Arts
du Canada

Printed and bound in Canada by Friesens
♾ This book is printed on Eco Book, acid free, 100% post-consumer

Cover design, page design and typesetting by Mieka West.
Cover illustration by Ryan Rayner.

I would like to thank the Alberta Foundation for the Arts for a grant which enabled me to take this novel to the Sage Hill Writing Experience. My gratitude and thanks go to Robert Kroetsch and the Novel Colloquium for providing direction and to Sage Hill for providing a safe place in which to work. Thanks also to Willie Fitzpatrick and Christine Mains for discerning and helpful editing suggestions and to George Melnyk and Elona Malterre for inspired solutions of specific problems. Finally, I would like to thank the people at the University of Calgary Press: two anonymous assessors for agreeing to read the novel, Walter Hildebrandt and John King for support of the project, and Peter Enman for his hard work.

chapter 1

Dear Vera: Okay, Toots, I admit it. You were right. This must be the most thoroughly abysmal spot on this or any other planet. Why didn't you nail me to the wall? Tie me to the chesterfield? But you tried to warn me. I can still hear your voice shrieking in disbelief, "You've never been out of Toronto!" and me, saying, "Maybe it's time I was, I'm getting close to thirty," and you saying, "You don't have to go to such an extreme. Just apply for a job at a different school." But, as I told you at the time, that wouldn't have put enough distance between me and Bradley. Something more drastic is required when the person you've been going with for five years calls up out of the blue and says he hopes you're not going to be upset with him, but the fact is, he just got married.

Emiline Thomas shifted her position against the pillow. It was an old pillow, with alarming brown stains on the casing. Filled with chicken feathers, it had a smell that made her think of the bottom of a birdcage. Trying not to breathe deeply, she looked down at what she had written.

She heard again the apologetic tone coming through the telephone receiver. She heard again the clink of glasses in the background, the laughter and merriment. Bradley was speaking from the telephone at the cashier's desk of the restaurant where the celebration was taking place. Everyone was having a good time, except her. She was pierced with loneliness and disbelief. At first she thought he was joking. Then she remembered that they never joked with each other. Earlier that week, he had begged off going to the Saturday night movie because he had to study for an exam. As it turned out, he spent the evening getting married, although later he swore that he had not had a preconceived plan.

What had she done wrong? Had she presumed too much? True, he had never actually asked her to marry him, but he had spoken sometimes as though they were to have a future together. And, while he had always been romantically lukewarm, she simply assumed that was his nature. If their physical contact lacked intensity, well, that was one of the things she liked about him, that he was not demanding in that way. She knew very little about such matters, she assumed that *that* part of the relationship would fall into place after marriage. How could she have assumed so much, as it turned out, wrongly? How could she have been so unaware? Presumably, he had also been keeping company with the other lady. But five years!

She had so relied on Bradley. They had met at the school where they both taught. He had just gotten out of the army and through the VRA plan was working toward a university degree at night school. She assumed that was why he did not propose. He talked a lot about money, the shortage of it, and most of his evenings and weekends were spent attending classes and studying. But she did not mind waiting. "Bradley wants to do everything the right way, in the right order," she told friends. She did not have a family. She had been adopted at birth by a lovely old couple who, unfortunately, had been of an age which prevented them living to her maturity. She had felt some guilt at their deaths, as if she had not loved them enough to keep them alive. Was it the same self-flagellation which caused her to feel the loss of Bradley as her fault? This was only one of the questions that tortured her mind during those long black nights following his announcement.

For weeks she had stumbled around in a daze. She constantly felt that she was falling, that the ground beneath her feet had given way, leaving her unbalanced and confused. Two months passed and still, in the middle of doing something ordinary such as teaching a class, her mental processes would come up against a sudden insurmountable, inescapable wall of deprivation and hopelessness. She knew that she had to do something to escape her thoughts.

Reflecting yet again on the details of her deception, Emiline found her mind slipping into a familiar repetitive pattern. She took herself in hand. She must not think about being abandoned and alone in the world. She must not think about Bradley. That was why she had come here—to erase him and those words from her mind.

The writing pad on Emiline's knees was held at an angle so that her words could be illuminated by a small disc of yellow light beamed onto the page from a flashlight held tightly between her ear and the Chantilly lace of her new nightgown, bought especially for this occasion, the entry into her new life.

She had taken the flashlight from the back shed. She had not mentioned this to anyone. She was not sure why, except it might be against the rules. She had been told about smoking, not to do it in the house. She had been shown where the matches were kept, high up in a kitchen cupboard. She could understand that there was a terrible fear of fire in the country. But why, when the lord and master retired for the night, was it necessary for everyone else to do so, too? It was either that or sit in the dark, since he extinguished the lanterns. The first evening, she had asked for a candle. "We don't burn candles," Mrs. Cage had informed her in a shocked tone. Now, three evenings later, she was shocked at herself for even asking for a candle. If a fire got started here there would be no way to stop it. But why hadn't she asked for the flashlight instead of scooping it into her sweater when she had spotted it on a shelf on her way in from the outhouse? Well, she would borrow it only until tomorrow. Tomorrow was Saturday. That was the day they said they went to town. She would buy her own flashlight tomorrow.

She adjusted the pad.

I hope you can read my disjointed penmanship—I'm writing by flashlight, secretly in the night. There! if that doesn't sound melodramatic and sinister. But, the fact is, there isn't any electricity! Can you fathom it? Well, I suppose you can, having come from Gravelbourg. But that was ten years ago. This is 1952! Isn't post-war prosperity supposed to be sweeping the land? As for the clandestine nature of my activity, I'm sure no one here cares that I'm

writing a letter to my roommate back in Toronto, but
they might object to me using up the flashlight batteries.
Anyway, no one knows. They're all asleep. And it's only
shortly after nine p.m.! Here, they go to bed with the
chickens and, I might add, get up with the roosters.

Emiline's hand paused, pen suspended over the page.
Why was she telling Vera all this? Vera was the one who had
told *her*. Having grown up in a landscape very much like
this one, Vera had left home as soon as she could to join the
WACS, which was no hell, either, as she said, but anything
was better than Gravelbourg. Emiline thought with longing
of how she and Vera had sat about and chatted long into
the night in the cozy little apartment they had shared, how
they had listened to all the latest tunes on the radio while
polishing their nails. Here, no one listened to the radio
except for the weather report and grain prices, and there
wasn't much point in doing one's nails.

Right up to the moment of Emiline stepping onto the
train, Vera had tried to discourage her from coming out
here. "You don't have to do this," she had said. "It's not too
late to change your mind."

"I have to do it," Emiline said. "I'll go mad if I can't
escape."

Emiline considered Vera—level-headed, forthright
Vera. She was telling Vera this because she had to. Now that
she had decided to stay, she needed a strategy of survival.
She must keep the connection to her old world, to the real
world, to Vera. She must write. As long as she could write,
as long as she could document her existence, she would be
all right.

Hand and pen resumed motion.

You may get more than you bargained for when you made me promise to write. Now I know why you wouldn't take no for an answer. One has to be seen or heard by someone else in order to exist, and here the people don't even look at each other. I may find myself running off at the mouth, putting reams onto paper—the necessity of relating my activities to somebody so that I know I'm alive. As for the landscape, it's positively annihilating. When I looked out of that train window day after day (if April is the cruellest month, March certainly must be the bleakest), I was struck with the thought that people here must be very strong to survive, stronger than the place itself, stronger than the circumstances that this place might put upon them, and what an enormous act of will such strength would take. When I got off the train, the thought became an overwhelming feeling.

Emiline raised her head abruptly and the flashlight fell onto the grey woollen blanket at her side. Staring into the shadows at the corner between dresser and outside wall of her small room, she recalled the scene at the station. She heard her own voice, very small, squeaking out of what she had felt at the time to be a very small insignificant person. "Is this it?"

"What's that?" The station master shuffled forth from a maroon shack.

"Kneehill. They told me to get off at Kneehill Station. But there's no sign."

"Blew away in the wind."

"This can't be it." Had her voice revealed her dismay?

"Bad winds last November. Blew an automobile clean off the road."

"They said it was the next stop after Bitter Lake."

"Did a flip-flop right inta the ditch."

"But this can't be a real stop."

"Snapped Olaf Johnson's neck like a toothpick."

"Someone's supposed to meet me," she tried.

The man's eyes were so pale a blue, they were almost white. The pupils were small, scarcely perceptible in the dull light. One eye was smaller than the other, giving him an off-slant appearance. Perhaps his vision was unbalanced. Perhaps he was blind. Surely they wouldn't have a blind station master. He was looking at her, but he didn't seem to see her. It was as though she had stepped between his eyes and the distance. She remembered her manners, which helped her to recollect her resolve. She straightened. "Emiline Thomas," she said and put out her hand. But he did not appear to see it, either.

"I'm for Cage Farm." She firmed her voice and tried to look him in the eye. "They said someone would meet me."

Taking a step closer, he stuck his face near hers. He had a peculiar odour. "You don't look like that other girl," he said with a foolish, loose-lipped grin.

"What other girl?"

"They had another girl there once." Saliva glistened in his stubble of beard. His teeth, what he had of them, were yellow, sharp.

It struck her that she was alone with him, completely alone, in an alien environment where she did not know the rules, or even if there were any. She stepped backward, tripping over her suitcase. She was at the edge of the platform.

"I have the letter." She began to root around in her purse. Proof. For she was beginning to doubt herself. Perhaps she had taken a wrong turn, gotten onto the wrong branch line, gotten off at the wrong stop. She scrabbled frantically amidst tissues, unpaid bills, notes she had written to herself. Where was the blasted thing? "I'm sorry ..." She looked up.

But he had shifted his gaze, up across her shoulder. "There he is now," he said.

Emiline's eyes followed his, but they could see nothing to break the monotony of the expanse of unbroken flatness—field, horizon, sky. When she turned back to question the man, however, he was no longer there.

The memory of that arrival into her new life caused an oppressive grey gloom to settle heavily onto Emiline's spirits. She decided that she had overreacted to the strangeness of it all. Vera was right, she was used to a big city. However, had she not come out here partly for the adventure? Admonishing herself, she picked up the flashlight and set it on her night stand, an orange crate covered with a white threadbare cloth. She bent toward the light.

Remember that Saturday night I got up the nerve to tell you about answering the newspaper ad? We drank two bottles of Chianti, which by the way I cannot think of now without shuddering, and I got so blubbery about Bradley, as if I hadn't been crying on your shoulder for

*two months already, and you crawled under the bed and
found an old map in your box of things and we found
Gravelbourg but we couldn't find Kneehill. Now I know
why. The branch line from Edmonton deposited me
unceremoniously in the middle of nowhere with only a
maroon shack and no sign. For a wild moment I thought
of running after the shabby little train choking its way
into the vanishing point of the eastern horizon, its smoke
settling close to the ground like the tail of a beaten hound,
its whistle sounding increasingly distant and forlorn.
Wait, wait for me, I wanted to call. The unheated cars
and straw-filled seats which I had disdained a short time
before seemed like a sanctuary.*

Emiline looked at what she had written. Her eye
was fastidious. She couldn't help it; she was an English
teacher. After careful consideration, she thought that her
letter sounded all right so far. The part about survivors
having to be strong would pass. What she did not want
to convey was that, for a moment there on the platform,
she had doubted her strength. She didn't want to alarm
Vera. She recalled Vera, at some point, saying, "You have
no idea what you're getting into, poor baby," and her
reply, "What've I got to lose?" and Vera's, "Your sanity,
for starters." She didn't want Vera to think she'd lost
that valuable commodity even before her adventure had
properly begun. Vera was quite capable of hopping on a
train and coming out here and rescuing her. That was the
last thing she wanted. Standing on the station platform,
gazing into that relentless distance, watching the swirl of
dust from the Cage vehicle come inevitably closer, she
had spooked herself. That was why, by the time she made

out the shape of a truck through the dust clouds raised
by its wheels, by the time she could see the scraped and
rusted metal through the red paint, by the time the truck
sputtered to a stop against the edge of the platform, she
was possessed by a fear which she had to restrain from
becoming panic. No matter who was driving that truck,
she would have to get into it. She had no choice. She
could not stay on the platform. Nor could she go into the
station where that man was waiting.

She had done it to herself, Emiline could see that
now. She had let herself get carried away. She had always
had an overactive imagination. Things were better now.
Curling herself more firmly toward the single beam of
light, she took up her task.

*I'm afraid, all in all, I've made a rather bad beginning
(and beginnings are so important). Upon my arrival at
the farm, I asked about a hot bath, which request was met
with total incredulity. I can understand why, now, since
there is no bathroom and no hot water, indeed, no water
of any sort unless it is hauled from the well. To compound
my errors, I couldn't eat supper. Whether it was my
physical inactivity while travelling or my nervousness
upon arrival, I simply could not force a morsel of food
down my throat. Besides, you know me, supper is half a
sandwich and a cup of tea. Here, I was faced with this big
slab of roast beef, mashed potatoes, mashed turnips, buns,
baked fresh, I suspect, for me. Dessert was a raspberry
pie which looked absolutely delicious, made from special
preserves, but the whole thing simply stuck in my throat
and even though I apologized profusely and Mrs. Cage
kept saying, "Quite all right, I'm sure," I could tell that*

I had committed a real faux pas. And I felt miserable about hurting her feelings. Anyway, subsequent suppers have gone better. I try not to eat much during the day so that I'll have an appetite. But the meat they consume! It's incredible. And the cream and eggs and butter. I shall surely return a butterball.

But let me relate events in a somewhat linear order (the teacher coming to the fore). Dane Cage met me at the station, if "met" is the right word. Our introduction was of the "Me Tarzan, You Jane" variety. In fact, he would have said nothing, would have simply grabbed up my bags, thrown them into the back of his truck, climbed into the driver's seat and left me to follow. But I had no intention of getting into that vehicle without knowing who I was getting in with. "I'm Emiline Thomas," I said, sticking out my hand, which he ignored. "Are you Victor Cage?" I asked. I knew he wasn't because he was much too young to be the father of the horde of children I presumed I was hired to tutor, but I had to start somewhere. His eyes flashed across my face like swords, not stopping long enough to let me see into them but giving me the impression of startling clear blue.

He mumbled his name and left me to climb up into that high truck myself, hobbled with my tight skirt, hampered by those ankle-strap pumps I bought just before leaving. Remember? You hooted when you saw them (how right you were, likely I'll never put them on again while I'm here). Obviously, I was overdressed for the occasion. (I had even put on that new hat, the one with the veil and feather.) The only solution was to hike the skirt up above my knees and hope he wasn't looking.

Dane Cage turned out to be a sullen, ill-humoured, not to mention unkempt and odoriferous, travelling companion. He looked and smelled like he had just come from working in the barn, which he might very well have done since he was wearing overalls and boots, both of which were in a filthy state. We would have spent the entire half hour from station to farm (during which time we saw only one farm house!) in complete silence if I hadn't tried once or twice to start up a conversation. In an attempt to get some idea about the family I was brought here to try to educate, I asked him if he was the eldest. After several tries, due to the loudness of the motor and the clatter of that old truck on those pit-ridden roads, I learned that he was "more like youngest, 'cept for Maggie." He seemed so angry, I had no idea why. But I've since learned that he's always angry. And he was ordered to fetch me, a task he did not relish for a variety of reasons, one of which being, I suspect, that he's shy with women.

During the journey I made various hints and suggestions trying to find out about the family's size and makeup and his relationship to it (I thought he might be uncle to the children I was to teach), all of which was met with silence or a response which did nothing but add to my confusion. So I gave up on this line of conversation and tried the weather (appalling), the landscape (appalling), the road conditions (appalling). Long before we rattled into the farmyard my spirit was beaten into silence by his impenetrable manner and the constant "Whats?" back and forth because of the racket. I decided to utilize my time in planning a way to get out of that damn truck now that I was in it, but as I stared out the window at the endless empty fields patchy with crusted leftover snow,

I felt my mind stupefied and doom settling heavily onto my soul. There's no place for people here. I had already felt this on the train, as we clicked and clacked through immense stretches of wilderness and desolation, but there it was like looking at a picture with a frame. I didn't have to think of it as being real. Here, I was in the picture, part of it. I would have to live in it. And I felt that I was travelling ever more deeply and tightly into a maze. We turned off the first road, turned again and turned again, circling in, it seemed, although about halfway along, my sense of direction, not great at best, suffered an absolute collapse. If you were to ask me where I am, I would not know!

Finally, we came upon the house and buildings. They seemed to crouch like prehistoric giant sloths on the flat flat land. As we drove into the yard, the house was to our left, the barns and outbuildings to our right. A few scraggly skeletons of brush huddled against the walls of the house and behind it was a grove of bare branches. These sporadic groupings of trees and bushes that mark the landscape are windbreaks planted by early settlers, the land around being unable to conceive on its own anything but tall grasses. (I know you know these things, but please bear with me. I have to get it all out of my system. And I want you to "see" where your beloved best friend has landed.) By now it was late afternoon and heading toward dusk. Striated layers of various shades of greyish brown hung heavy and unmoving in the metallic light.

Dane shut off the motor and complete silence surrounded us. I thought I had gone deaf. Then the dogs came barking around the truck. You know how I am about dogs. These ones looked ferocious, bracing

*themselves solidly on all fours, sharp teeth clipping the air.
That cinched it, I had made a terrible terrible mistake in
coming here. I resolved to stay where I was in that truck
until someone could take me back to the station and
the return trip home. But when Dane jumped out and
mumbled a word to the dogs, they immediately calmed
down and slunk off to the barn. So I got a chance to
try my disembarking strategy, which was to swing myself
around on the seat and take a leap meant to land me
solidly on both feet. This manoeuvre was successful,
except my hat also took a leap, landing in two feet of ooze
and excrement beyond a low wooden-railed fence. For
all I know, it may be floating still amongst a family of
pigs who were having a great time snorting and snuffling,
snouting each other out of the trough, which must have
recently been replenished with chop. Chop is a new word
I've learned, which I'm sure you already know, so I won't
go into detail about it.*

*We entered at the back door of the house (I suspect
the front is never used. The porch there is grown over
with vines, bare at the moment, and the knob has almost
disintegrated with rust) into a lean-to or shed (where I
discovered the flashlight). The first thing to hit me was
the smell, sweetish-sour mixed with mould. This is where
the milk is separated. Unfortunately, the slop pail (horrid
term) kept for the pigs is also at that door. At this time
of day and year, it made for a dark, cold passage. Then
we were into the kitchen proper, lit by a lantern, bright
by lantern standards, I suppose, where the smell of roast
meat and vegetables came from a large black iron cook
stove that dominates the room and throws a good heat.*

There I met Mrs. Cage, the aforesaid mother, who looked at me out of the side of her eyes in a quite suspicious manner and only nodded before going back to her pans. It seems there is no husband, which is a taboo subject, which I will let you know about as soon as I find out myself. I referred to him at the supper table, one of those general vague comments which could be taken up and developed if anyone cared to but no one did. Rather, it was met by stony silence.

Mrs. Cage is in her sixties, I'd judge, a short, stout woman, brownish-greyish frizzy hair, smallish face with small beaked nose, slobbery around the mouth, slow and heavy and stompy, in floral housedress and badly stained apron. But how unflattering and unfair, although true, is what I have just written. I now realize that her hair was frizzed from the heat of the stove and her efforts at preparing the meal, that her dentures don't fit properly, likely because she doesn't have access to a decent dentist or lab, and that she has a serious case of phlebitis, which I understand in ancient times was called milk leg, ghastly term. More about the Mrs. later.

I was steered immediately to an eating area just beyond the kitchen (how I hated to leave that stove), when what I wanted was a hot bath and a private hour or so to gather myself together. But supper is eaten early here, perhaps because of evening chores, which include milking cows and feeding livestock. Personally, I would rather get the chores over with and then dine. But when in Rome do as the Romans do, as they say. In any case, I have no choice.

I asked about washing my hands and was directed to a basin by the back door half filled with scummy water.

Beside this was a pail full of icy water and a bar of soap in a rather muddy looking soap dish. I managed to dip some water over my hands, get a bit of soap on them and pour a bit more water over. The towel was a grey rag of a thing which had been used so often before me that it was as damp as a used dish rag, so I more or less shook the water from my hands and let it go at that. I didn't have the nerve to ask about the facilities, but after supper I had to, in low tones to Mrs. Cage when she was doing the washing up and the men had gone back outside. I was directed down the garden path, literally, to a place close to the trees, a distance of about a hundred feet. And this, you are simply not going to believe—an old catalogue is used for toilet tissue! I'm sure, even in Gravelbourg, they do better than that. Even a telephone book would be superior to those glossy pages. (I've added tissue to my personal shopping list.) I shuddered, and shudder, to think what people here do in winter. But that definitely will not be my worry as I won't be here then.

The family assembled. I kept expecting to see children, but none materialized. Dane, of course, was already there, having come in with me. Maggie came in from the yard where I believe she had been doing chores. From the smell of her, she may very well have been slopping (new term) the pigs. And would you believe that they don't change out of their work clothes before coming to the table! They tromp into the house with manure clinging to their boots. They slosh around in the wash basin a bit, which doesn't do much good. I couldn't help but notice that Dane, sitting next to me at the table, had long water streaks in the dirt of his arms. And to think I'd pincurled my hair the evening before, bouncing my elbows on the cramped train washroom walls, so that I'd make a good impression on my new employer!

But to get back to Maggie, she's twenty-three, a tall, rangy, gawky hayseed, if ever there was one. Her hair is short (she hacks it off, herself, with a kitchen knife) and looks like it is never washed, and she has crooked teeth. Her personality, like Dane's, suffers from both the effects of isolation and from feelings of discontent. At least, that's my surmisal after three days of them. Of course, no one thought to introduce us properly, so I introduced myself, although by this time I had given up on the handshake. Instead of telling me her name, her response was; "You ain't as pretty as Amy." "Who's Amy?" I asked, but she didn't answer. I looked at Dane for possible enlargement on the comment but his face was like a thundercloud. I turned to Mrs. Cage. "She was before you," she scowled. I remembered what that awful station man had said to me and the challenging, almost threatening, tone of his voice. Mrs. Cage told Maggie to "shut up" and we stood about for several minutes in an atmosphere that was terribly uncomfortable for me, although the others didn't seem to notice anything out of the ordinary.

I counted six places set and only four of us so far, so I deduced we were waiting for the other two. Needless to say, after the blunted articulation and poor grammar of these people, I was anxious to meet the man who had written well-articulated directions in straight neat black script. Sure enough, a few minutes later in came the Lord of the Manor, Mr. Victor Cage, the eldest son. I tell you, the air grew positively electric. I thought it must be because of a particular circumstance, or even because of my presence. Or maybe it was just my imagining things *again. But, now that I've been here three days, I've learned that the atmosphere is always tense when Victor Cage is present.*

As you know, I was expecting a middle-aged man with a brood of children so that I could dedicate myself to forging intellects out of raw material and all that sort of thing. I cringe to think how patiently you listened to my raving on about a noble farmer attempting to educate his children against great odds. You can imagine my surprise when a man, perhaps in his middle thirties, stood in the doorway! My first thought was that he must have had children at a very young age. But, it was quickly becoming apparent that things at Cage Farm were not as I had thought. My mind was brimming with questions, as yours might very well be.

To describe Victor Cage, he is a tall, powerfully built man, arrogant and strutting. He has black hair and eyes, angular face with high cheekbones, aristocratic nose with a hook at the bridge. He and Maggie are dark like the mother while the other two have the lighter colouring of the father, judging from an old wedding photo of the parents on the sideboard—Mr. Cage stiff and straight in one of those suits that look tight and uncomfortable and the Mrs. unidentifiable, so young and pretty she was.

Victor is the Mr. Cage who hired me and who runs the farm and, it turns out, is one of those people who makes everyone feel uneasy with his presence. I think he knows this but it doesn't bother him one bit. In fact, he relishes his power. I will say one thing, he's the only one at Cage Farm who seems to know how to handle himself socially. He held out his hand, shook mine, said, "You're Emiline Thomas. I'm Victor Cage." Well, in spite of the

*uneasiness he caused, I was relieved to find in this place a
reasonable person of normal intelligence. He could speak!
In sentences! His handshake, as you might imagine, was
firm, his hand, strong.*

*It wasn't more than a moment later, when, as if
on cue, all heads turned in one direction. And, there,
standing in a doorway, was a vision I first conceived,
due to her wild tangled hair and grubby appearance, to
be a mad Ophelia. My second thought was that my eyes
were beholding the most fantastic apparition they had
ever seen. Ethereal, so slight as to appear transparent, it
seemed to float, rather than stand. I tried not to stare, so
all I took in at the time was an impression of small even
features, a great deal of straw-coloured hair and loose
clothing. When she moved into the room I saw that her
feet were bare! And almost purple with cold!*

The force of the memory arrested Emiline's writing
hand. "Come and meet your teacher," Victor Cage had
said. With a graceful little sideways dance the image
came close to where Emiline stood. Emiline turned her
head to Victor. She knew that shock must be evident on
her face. "Hester is your student," he explained.

"She can't be," Emiline responded with the first
thing that came into her head. Then she took herself in
hand. "I'm sorry," she turned to Hester. "It's just that I
expected children, several children."

"I didn't say that in my letter," Victor Cage said.

"Perhaps not." Emiline tried to think. What had he,
in fact, said in his letter? "But the ad said tutor, all subjects,
elementary school level. Naturally, I assumed ..."

"Never assume anything," he said and sat down at the head of the table. Everyone else followed suit.

"You sit here." Mrs. Cage, in her rough manner, pulled out the chair next to hers. Emiline decided to leave things until after supper. She didn't want to discuss the matter in front of Hester. Besides, the focus became food. Immediately, everyone started passing bowls and platters at a great rate. Instead, she took up the task of making pleasant conversation.

She blushed now, pen between her teeth and remembering that first supper, to think what drivel had come out of her mouth ("This food smells delicious." "Farm work must be very demanding." "Do you think it will snow?") before she had realized that no one else was speaking. Rather, they were applying themselves single-mindedly to the meal. She had since learned that the social niceties which she had taken for granted back in Toronto had no function in this place and were considered not only strange but silly.

While the others ate, Emiline rearranged the food on her plate and tried to be outwardly calm. In fact, she was seething underneath, for she had been—not lied to, perhaps, but manipulated. Why, oh why, had she so foolishly answered an ad in a newspaper and travelled across a continent without thoroughly investigating the situation beforehand?

And then she noticed that the meat on Hester's plate, which was directly across the table from her, had already been cut up, presumably in the kitchen, and that there was no knife at Hester's place. Her alarm escalated.

What sort of 'student' was she to have? She made up her mind then and there. Directly after supper, she would tell Victor Cage that she would leave tomorrow, that she had made a terrible mistake, that she would pay back the fare. But why was this thought accompanied by something like fear? Emiline pulled herself up short. After all, this was still a free country. They were not back in the Middle Ages.

Emiline's mind was busy contemplating her predicament, her eyes remaining in a sort of hypnotic trance on Hester's plate, when she saw a slender grubby hand push a pea off a dinner plate and the same hand nudge the pea toward her. Emiline looked up. Hester was regarding her, a conspiratorial little smile on her face. Or was it an idiot grin? Then Hester seemed to become aware that Victor, who, along with the others, had been concentrating on his plate, now had his eyes on her. His look was not disapproving. Rather, he was quietly watching her face with a quiet command in his eyes. Quickly pulling back her hand from the pea, she put both hands in her lap and lifted her head to a high place on the wall, seemingly distracted by something only she could see and hear. She appeared to have separated herself from the situation, leaving the real space of the room and entering another realm, one in which she was fully immersed. She stayed there for the rest of the meal.

"Could be." Victor, apparently, was answering her question of a few minutes before about snow. He pushed his plate away and placed his elbows on the table. Then came the frightful row about loading pigs.

Victor announced that they would load pigs in the morning. He said they would do it a particular way, the hard way according to Dane. "I'm not gonna load any goddamned pigs that way," he grumbled. "I never heard of anything so stupid."

"Stupid or not, that's the way we're gonna do it." Victor's voice merely stated a fact.

Maggie joined in, her protests little yelps between the growls of the men. She sided with Dane. Mrs. Cage sided with Victor. "You just do what your brother tells you," she snapped in a voice, sharp and strained.

Although it did not seem to bother the Cages that their family quarrel was being witnessed by a stranger, Emiline sat paralyzed with embarrassment. As their voices mounted, she kept her eyes down. But then she wondered about Hester. She glanced up, across the table. Hester was still staring at a spot on the wall, but now her eyes were bright. This isn't good for her, was Emiline's first thought. Hester's arms were folded in front of her and her fingers were nervously working the cloth of the sleeves of her shirt.

The quarrel was abruptly brought to an end by Victor announcing, "Enough!" Dane and Maggie clomped outside. Emiline heard the clang of the dipper in the water pail and the back door slam.

Mrs. Cage began the mopping up, Hester returned to her room, and Victor turned his attention toward her.

"I'm sorry," Emiline had been practising through dinner and through the row. She took a deep breath and looked Victor Cage in the eye. "It would be best if I returned on tomorrow's train."

"Can't do that," Victor said.

"I know I'll need someone to drive me to the station ..." Emiline was determined to insist.

"No train tomorrow," he said.

Why did she have the distinct impression of a cat playing with a mouse?

"The next day then," she said.

"No train 'til this time next week," he said.

Consequently, here she was, three days later.

And so, wrote Emiline, *to make a long story short, Hester is to be my student. She's twenty-eight years old (my age exactly) and she has not spoken for twenty years! Can you imagine? Being lured out here without being given this information! Apparently, there was an accident twenty years ago, although I'm not sure what it was. I told Victor Cage straight away that I'm not equipped to teach a person with these sorts of problems, that I've had some dealings with autistic children and with deaf and dumb children, but that Hester doesn't seem to fit into either of these categories. I told him that I'm not qualified and that I intended being on next week's train.'*

"Teach her what you can in that week," he said.

"How am I to teach her anything?" I asked. "She needs specially trained help."

"Let's see how it goes," he said, his lower lip becoming fuller. *I've learned that when Victor Cage is bent on having his own way, which is all the time, or when anyone opposes him, he sticks out his lower lip as though he's pouting, but he's not pouting. He has nothing to pout* about because his will is always done. "Look at it this way," he continued, sure of himself since I was quite helpless in the situation, "you haven't lost anything. I'll pay you what we agreed on for the week, no matter how it turns out." And regarding that subject, right then and there he disappeared into a back room and returned with one week's pay, which I accepted since there seemed little else to do. "Well, then," he said, grabbing up his hat, "let's get on with it. We'll learn the rules as we go along, eh?"

Since I did, truly, seem to be stuck here for the week, I let it go, being too tired to argue that evening but silently vowing to be on the train the next time it came through, even if I had to walk to the station with my luggage on my back.

Victor went outside. I tried to help Mrs. Cage with the cleaning up but she soon discouraged that, giving me to feel that my presence in the kitchen was more trouble than it was worth. I asked her about a bath and was told that baths are taken on Saturdays and that there's a pecking order in the use of the bath water. Well, I'm certain she's having me on about the pecking order, but it's obvious that there is no hot water except what is heated on the stove.

Thank heaven I do have my own room (I had begun to wonder about accommodations) even if it is rather small and bare. It's off the parlour, as is Hester's, but while hers is to the front of the house, mine is to the side. Mrs. Cage and Maggie sleep in a room off the kitchen and the men in a room to the back. Except for the kitchen and dining area, all the rooms are frigid.

Mrs. Cage lit a lantern for me, which I was allowed to take to my room so that I'd have a light for unpacking.

Once there, I flung myself on the bed with the thought of having a good cry. However, this intention was circumvented when I all but landed on the floor, the bedsprings are so unspringy and the mattress threadbare, except where it's lumpy. I thought of writing to you but I was too dispirited to do even that. Thank heavens I had brought some good romances with me. I started in on one but before long Mrs. Cage came for the lantern. Anyway, my eyes were closing.

As they are now. I must sign off before my eyes and my batteries run out.

Emiline had not told Vera everything. It would take a novel to do that, she surmised. But why hadn't she told her about the Massey Harris salesman? Vera would appreciate that story. They might have had a giggle over that one. But, perhaps not. The incident had not been funny after all. The salesman had gotten too drunk and gone too far. Emiline had felt embarrassed, even degraded. He had called her a tease and worse. It had started out innocently enough. He had been sitting across the aisle from her. When he nodded and smiled, she had seen nothing wrong in smiling back. She had been so thoroughly bored with two days of barren landscape and no one to talk to. Besides, she had been thinking about Bradley and feeling unattractive and rejected. The salesman had crossed the aisle and, after a while, brought out a silver flask and offered her a drink. Of course, she would not drink out of the flask but he produced some little silver cups. The evening had ended with her having to defend her virtue, having to actually threaten to call the porter, and the salesman lurching down the aisle of the moving train mumbling obscenities. In the morning she stayed in her berth until she saw him disembark at Winnipeg.

Why couldn't she tell Vera? After all, Vera had been in the WACS. But in thinking again about the incident, Emiline felt a fresh wave of repugnance and shame. She had felt so cheap. And yet she would have thought that she could tell Vera anything, that she did not have anything to hide from Vera. She should tell Vera.

Goodnight, goodnight, dear, dear (and more thoroughly appreciated) friend, she wrote instead.

P.S. As for Bradley, it's as though those five years with him happened to another person. A happy person. I am not that person. I can't connect with that person. And yet that must have been me! It's disquieting. Not being able to recognize my past self. I can't remember, except in a surface way, what that other person thought or felt. That other person was oblivious as to what might be lying in wait for her. That person didn't know pain. This person is in constant pain. I came here to try to get away from the pain. Did I explain that to you before I left? I can't remember.

P.S.#2. Saturday morning. It turns out I cannot go to town after all as I'm to stay home with Hester. I'm entrusting this packet to Dane. I hope you will receive it. Please write ASAP and let me know. Oh, and before I forget, please send newspapers. The only one I've seen here is a month-old Camrose Courier.

P.S.#3. Although my first intention was to leave on next week's train, I've decided to stay, for a while anyway. I'll explain in my next letter.

P.S.#4. *Please, please, answer these letters, so that I do not disappear into the void.*

P.S.#5. *Hester's face has the oddest expression. I cannot tell if she's smiling or bemused. There's something shy in it and yet, at the same time, unyielding and certain. She seems to be far away, off in her own space. But what's in that space, I don't yet know.*

Emiline stood at the edge of the field wondering which way to go. Yesterday, she had turned to her right, two days ago to her left. The day before that, she had struck out through a field, but the rapid activity of mice scurrying frantically to escape her footsteps had filled her with alarm. Although she had never had anything to do with mice, instinctively she hated them. Still, she thought, I might have to get used to them. For, in the three weeks since her arrival, the roads had already become monotonous.

The first week, after trying to help Mrs. Cage in the kitchen and finding her efforts unappreciated, of venturing forth into the barnyard, which did not seem to have much point, of traversing the path back and forth to the outhouse, which had point but little else, Emiline knew that if she was to hold on to her sanity, she must sometimes escape the confines of Cage Farm. By that time she had told Victor Cage that she would stay the summer. She had dreaded his smirk of victory but all he had said was, "Let's get on with it then," a favourite expression of his, she had learned, and perhaps an indication of his approach to life.

Escape included diversion as well as exercise. In bed at night, not only did her legs twitch, but her brain, after darting about like a pierced balloon, deflated into gloom. Much as she tried to keep her letters to Vera in a cheerful tone, she was wretched, lonely, and perhaps worst of all, undistracted. She had taken for granted the distractions of modern civilization in the form of films, libraries, radio, lectures, restaurants, cafés, clubs. A few of her acquaintances even had television. To suddenly be deprived of all of these and without even a kindred soul with whom she could speak of anything but weather and chores, seemed a harsh prescription for lovesickness, even if she had administered the dosage to herself.

Part of her gloom was due to the fact that she was feeling mentally stupid. She did not know if this was because of the landscape—the monotony, drabness, and immensity of it were enough to turn a person comatose—or to lack of stimulation in the way of conversation with like-witted friends and colleagues. Perhaps, in a curious way, life was too easy. Her living requirements demanded no effort on her part. Her meals were prepared by someone else, she had a roof over her head and, since discovering an abandoned piece of plywood in the machine shed which she had Dane carry into the house, a passably comfortable bed. Her employment, too, was undemanding, a condition which caused her a great deal of frustration. She wanted to do more.

She now realized that she was to be Hester's constant companion, rather than a tutor with defined hours of instruction. When she had first discerned the truth, she had felt herself swell and prickle with indignation. Not that she objected to Hester, who was by far the most, indeed the only, pleasant person at Cage Farm. But she had been brought out here to this ghastly place under false pretences. She was not to use the skills and expertise for which she had been educated and trained, but, rather, to be a babysitter for a ... what? child? invalid? Then, after the first few days, it became obvious that the word 'constant' in the term 'constant companion' would not involve many hours, since she was free when Hester was in her room, which seemed to be most of the time. So as it turned out, Emiline, for the greater part of the day, could do whatever she wanted. The problem was, there was nothing to do.

She had kept herself occupied for several days in getting her small space shipshape. Ignoring Mrs. Cage's scowl of disapproval at being underfoot, she boiled up some water in a tub on the stove and thoroughly laundered every scrap of her bedding. The washing machine was a quaint, half-cylinder tub affair with a stick lever which required her to brace both feet solidly on the linoleum, grab the stick with both hands and swing mightily back and forth. She hung the lot outside on the clothesline, where it froze into large stiff sheets which she then brought in and flung about her room. There it all wilted into damp dispirited rags which were still not dry at bedtime, and she spent the night on a bare mattress huddled beneath her piled-on clothing. Undaunted, she tackled her room. Whisking a pail of hot reservoir water from under the nose of the startled Mrs. Cage, she scrubbed down ceiling, walls, floor and furniture, although after discovering that her night stand was a wooden crate, she discreetly lowered the cloth and retreated.

Since this burst of housewifery, she had inquired about riding but was told that the only horses at Cage Farm were work horses. She wondered if there was a bicycle about the place but there was not. Besides, the unimproved country roads were little more than bumpy ruts and would be difficult to manoeuvre.

Then one Monday morning, she decided that something had to be done about Hester. Emiline had always found Monday mornings to be especially invigorating. That was when she was all fired up and determined about what she hoped to accomplish the coming week. She and Hester were sitting as they usually did over lessons at the dining table. Emiline was watching Hester's hand. Hester had strange hands, so narrow as to appear deformed, as though they had been bound and not allowed to grow to their full proportions. The way they moved, too, was odd. They seemed to drift from one thing to another, directionless, without force or motive, travelling a slow vague route, like a feather picked up and carried by wind. It was as if there was no direct line from brain to hand. And yet they were exquisite, the tapered fingers moving so delicately across the clean page. But what was this? The hand kept sticking to the paper. Was it just this morning's jam or a buildup of several days? Emiline winced. And truth to tell, Hester smelled—a sour, stale, slightly mouldy smell. As Emiline watched Hester's black-ridged fingernails in the light of a Monday morning, she knew that something had to be done.

It took some time. Rome was not built in a day, she kept telling herself. She could not simply jump on the other woman, strip her down and plunge her into a tub full of hot water. No. But by careful coaxing and subtle suggestions, over the course of the following days she managed it, until Hester stood before her looking presentable. It turned out that Hester had clothes in her closet, all in much the same style of loose flowing garments and all with a musty trace of disuse. She did have slippers to put on her feet. Her hair was a greater problem, being in such a state of tangle that, even with Emiline being as gentle as possible, brushing it out brought tears to Hester's eyes. The washing of it took a whole morning. Hester was suspicious of water and would not bend her head forward over a basin. However, Emiline found that by sitting her on a chair and bending her head back, being careful not to splash water on her face, the feat could be accomplished. In fact, Hester quite liked the water being poured through her hair and onto her scalp. It seemed to have a soothing effect. At the end of it all, Hester stood before her dresser mirror. Smiling, she touched her face in the glass. Emiline could not be sure that she knew the difference between her grimy self and her clean self or if, in fact, she made a connection between her real self and her mirror image. Still, the teacher felt pleasure in the student's pleasure.

That chore accomplished, Emiline bravely faced forward. Work and sleep were the two activities engaged in at Cage Farm. To Emiline it was amazing how much these people slept. In addition to their nine o'clock bedtime, they seemed to be continually nodding off during the day. In the afternoons, especially, after the heavy noon meal, she would come upon Mrs. Cage napping at the dining room table with her head propped up in her hands. Once in her explorations she found Dane sprawled in a shaft of sunlight in the hayloft, his face strangely soft and vulnerable, a dust mote dancing on the wet lower lip of his gaping mouth. Another time she discovered Maggie, looking like a scarecrow in straw hat and overalls and with her face askew, propped up in the tall grass against the far side of the machine shed wall, likely where Victor wouldn't see her. Hester spent every afternoon between the hours of one to five in her room, supposedly resting, if not sleeping. Against her will, Emiline found herself netted into this sleep pattern. She couldn't wait to get to her room after dinner for her nap. She was incredulous. She had never in her life napped in the daytime! It was as though she were drugged or as if a spell had been cast upon her. Somehow, she must keep herself from falling into that deadly habit. She took up walking.

And yet she dreaded these excursions. The first time she had tried to go for a walk, although she had admitted this to no one, she went only about half a mile down the road. For, standing there exposed on the flat plain she had known terror. She had tried to reason it out. She could see the Cage house. Other shapes, presumably houses, humped up in the flat distance. People lived here. What surrounded her was simply earth and sky, features of the planet which was her home. But her terror was not subject to reason. Her feeling was similar to that of claustrophobia, with attending confusion, loss of one's bearings, a sense of suffocation. Yet how could she suffocate? Out here in the open. How could she be confused? Here, all was straightforward, the fields squared, the roads running north/south and east/west in a perfect grid. She could stand here and, by turning her neck, view three hundred and sixty degrees. Maybe that was it, she decided. Exposure. There was nowhere to hide. Anything might come swooping out of that space. Anything could pounce from that relentlessly huge sky, a low grey sky which seemed to be growing darker by the minute. A terrible, unnatural silence sat on the land. There was something uncanny about it, as though unknown presences were lurking.

She turned and started running, fast, faster, back to Cage Farm. Her heart was bolting wildly in her chest. The running itself seemed to charge her anxiety and yet she couldn't stop even though she heard her raw, hoarse breath in the silence and felt her chest heaving painfully. She turned in at the lane. The cold and the running had affected her tear ducts. Her eyes were streaming. She could not see. She ran smack into something. Wildly, she thought it was the monster from whom she was running. She felt she was being smothered. She struggled to break free but a strong force held her.

"And where are you going in such a rush?"

It was the voice of Victor Cage. Her face was tight against his large solid chest. She was aware of his smell and of the rough wool texture of his shirt.

"I'm terribly sorry," she panted, her mind casting about for some excuse for her behaviour. "I didn't want to be late for supper."

"You've got lots of time," he said wryly. "It's the middle of the afternoon."

Her elbows were up against the wall of his chest. She turned her head to the distance. "I thought I was lost," she said.

"How could you be lost?" His tone was slightly mocking. "What would you be lost in?"

"Yes. You're perfectly right." She steadied and strengthened her voice. She freed herself from his hands. Still confused in her sense of direction, she started to go around him toward the barn. With one hand on her shoulder, he steered her toward the back door.

"It's a matter of using your common sense," he said, releasing her shoulder. "You can see Cage Farm for miles away."

"Yes."

"And choose your weather." He looked up at the sky. "We're in for some snow. Sometimes, visibility can get bad."

She felt that she must make some defence of her actions. "I guess I'm used to the city," she said.

"Just do what you're told," he said, "and you'll do fine."

Since that episode, while she still did not feel comfortable while walking, she was able to manage the feeling better. In essence, she did what Victor Cage had told her to do. She used her common sense. She kept track of her path, going so far as to keep a stub of pencil and scrap of paper in her pocket, noting her turns. And he was right about being able to see the farm for miles. It was actually difficult to lose sight of it. The only problem was that, from a distance, the other farms around looked the same. She told herself that it didn't matter, any farm would be all right. Any farm meant that she was not lost. Any farm would give her directions back. But that thought did not comfort her. She did not want to approach a strange farm. The Cages were bad enough. Who knew what sorts of frightful people might inhabit the other farms around here? Who knew what wild animals might be about? She had already heard coyotes in the night. And she found the domesticated ones, snorting bulls, barking dogs, equally terrifying.

Today was different than that first day. April was now established. Hours of daylight were longer and the weather was milder. The snow had disappeared from all but the shadiest sides of the fields and ditches. Trees were starting to swell. Foals had dropped. Two new calves tottered splay-legged and curly-haired in the barn. A great whirr and clatter of machinery was heard in the early mornings now.

Today, the sun shone gloriously, the sky was pure azure blue. Emiline could hear sounds of life all around her. Bird melodies came out of the ground beneath her feet. She thought she must be imagining things. But no, there it was again, a clear melodious trill. She took a deep breath of air, fresh with the smells of grain and damp earth. There was something about these smells that affected her sensibilities. She thought of Bradley. But she had never had quite these feelings with him. She and Bradley had been comfortable cozy companions. These present sensations were uncomfortable, disturbing. She didn't know what to do with them.

Across the field, she could see a few bits of straggly brush which lay in a straight line and evenly spaced poles which indicated a wire fence. There seemed to be a second line of brush just a little farther distant, which suggested a road between the two. To get to that road by way of roads, as she figured it, she would have to walk a few miles around. She decided on the short cut.

She looked at the field of stubble before her and tried to decipher its rodent population. She couldn't see any movement. Still, she knew it must contain mice, all the fields were full of them. This she knew already from experience, and Dane had confirmed the fact. That was why, today, she was wearing high rubber boots borrowed from Maggie and had her slacks tucked firmly inside the tops.

It was early afternoon. After the inevitable gigantic midday meal, the others had returned to their work, Dane to the machine shed where he was repairing a tractor, Victor to town for parts, and Maggie to clean out the barn. Mrs. Cage was already starting the evening meal.

Emiline was still astounded by the way these people ate. After platters of meat and basins of vegetables at noon, they still came in at five like starved ravens. A typical day started with breakfast at six. On her first morning, she had arrived in the kitchen at eight, having waited in her room until she heard everyone leave so as not to be in the way. There was no sign of anything resembling breakfast, including coffee. "I just got it cleaned away," Mrs. Cage said in sullen tones from the cupboard counter where she was elbow deep into something in a gigantic mixing bowl. The realization came as a shock to Emiline—the older woman did not want her there. Emiline was not used to being disliked, and even though Mrs. Cage meant nothing to her, she could not help but feel a bit hurt.

"Let me make my own," Emiline offered. "Just tell me where things are."

Making a piece of toast involved moving a heavy washtub full of water to the side of the black iron cookstove, getting bread from a tin box which Emiline found impossible to pry open, hauling out a cutting board from some obscure corner of a dark pantry, finding the toaster rack, holding the rack above the hot stove lid until both bread and cook were crisp, finding the butter in the back shed where it was kept in a cooler on the outside wall and, in general, causing a total interruption of Mrs. Cage's time and task. For, in the end, Mrs. Cage made the toast, heaving great sighs and hobbling about in what appeared to be extreme bodily pain. To Emiline's protests, she replied, "It's easier."

Emiline sat meekly at a small kitchen table with her toast. She watched Mrs. Cage's back as her arms plunged about in the bowl to which she'd returned. That first morning, Emiline still intended being on the next train out. As she chewed the coarse crusty bread, which she had to admit was rather tasty, she rehearsed how she would broach the subject. She would apologize yet again for her terrible mistake, she hoped that they would forgive her and could someone please take her to the station? I don't have to say it for a few days yet, she decided with some relief. This is only day one of a seven-day week.

However, by noon, the subject of leaving had been put on file in her mind, and by noon the next day, she had convinced herself that the experience of Cage Farm would, after all, be an adventure. It would provide countless stories to relate to her friends in Toronto when she returned. She had given up her place in the school system and likely could not be reinstated until September. She might as well stay here a while longer, catch some spring and summer, see if the place was more bearable during those seasons.

What had happened to change her mind was Hester. After Emiline had eaten up every scrap of toast—what else could she do when Mrs. Cage had gone to so much trouble?—and after she had tried to wash her plate and knife but was told to leave it until the dinner washing up, she inquired of Mrs. Cage about Hester and lessons. As she reasoned, she had an agreement with Victor Cage, he had paid her to teach and she would teach. Besides, she was stuck here until next week, she had to do something with her time. And she was curious, too, as to what might transpire with her student. "Maybe Hester and I should get started," was the way she put it. Mrs. Cage didn't lose a stroke in the rhythm of her plunging. "On a lesson," Emiline raised her voice. Mrs. Cage turned from the waist to frown at her, her mouth in a grim line. "The tutoring,"

Emiline went on. "Mr. Cage spoke to me about it last evening?"

"I know all about the tutoring," grumbled Mrs. Cage. "You don't have to tell me about the tutoring. Waste of time and money." With that and a look of thorough disapproval, she wiped her hands on a tea towel and disappeared into the inner regions. A few minutes later, she returned and without a word went back to her bowl.

And suddenly Hester appeared in the doorway. Soundlessly, she floated into position. Again, as the evening before, Emiline's heart gave a little leap of joy when she looked at Hester's face. It was a small, narrow, perfectly shaped face, fine as a porcelain figurine. Like her hands, there was a strangeness about it, an abnormal delicacy as though the bone beneath the white transparent skin was so thin it might shatter. Later, Emiline wondered about her initial response. She did not think it was because of her need or because of the void left by Bradley. Rather, she decided, she had responded as anyone would upon first viewing a great painting or hearing a masterpiece of music. The perfection in the facial features allowed the viewer to transcend earthly considerations and to escape the self. It's a face, thought Emiline, that for some unfathomable reason gives meaning to the day and makes life bearable.

They sat at the long dining table, their two heads, one dark, one light, bent together. Emiline had brought an assortment of primers, story books, notebooks, pens, pencils, crayons. She did not know what Hester might be capable of doing. She did not know how much speech she understood. She realized that she should have questioned Victor Cage more thoroughly. All she knew was that, as a child, Hester had attended the district school for nearly two years. She may have had other tutors—around that subject was a vagueness mounting to evasion, for although Emiline had asked questions, she had not received direct answers. "I don't know if she remembers any of it," was all Victor had said the evening before. In any case, Emiline's first task was to find out what Hester did remember. She decided to start with first grade material and see how that went.

"What would you like to do?" Emiline tried an encouraging smile. Hester watched Emiline's face carefully. She returned a replica of the smile.

Emiline drew a large circle on the notepad and pushed the pad toward Hester. She put the pencil into Hester's hand. To Emiline's delight, not only did Hester copy the circle, with that delicately shaped albeit filthy little hand, but she did it in such an exact and conscientious manner that the action threatened to break Emiline's heart. Next, Emiline drew the first letters of the alphabet, one at a time, on the paper. After each letter, Hester took the pencil and copied in a meticulous manner. She seemed to be trying hard to please. Emiline was generous in her praise and Hester smiled shyly. That was when Emiline realized that her plan for the next train out of here was in jeopardy. Already, she was starting to feel that her future happiness, her very life, might depend on this fascinating creature.

The next hour was spent with Hester copying the alphabet. They were on 'm' when Emiline was brought back to reality by a voice in the doorway. "How's it going?"

Emiline, so engrossed she had scarcely heard the door slam and the sound of voices in the kitchen, jumped and turned. Victor Cage, his hawk nose lifted and his red lips pursed as though disdaining something, filled the kitchen doorway. Emiline could not help but notice a thick brown neck, a v-shape of dark hair protruding from the top of his khaki shirt, muscular forearms revealed by the rolled up sleeves.

"Fine," Emiline beamed. "Great."

"Good." He looked at her for what seemed to be a long time. Yet there was no regard or consideration in his gaze. It was as though she had gotten between him and something else on which he was focused. Emiline felt something in herself move before, abruptly, he turned and went back out through the porch into the yard. She could see him through the window, crossing to the machine shed. He had a distinctive way of walking, a saunter that was also a swagger. His body moved all together in one motion, like a cannon ball, she thought, yes, a cannon ball coming for you that you can't dodge.

With a start, she realized that she had been staring after Victor Cage for quite some time. As she bent her head back to the table, her heart was thumping so loudly she thought that Hester would hear it. She looked at the paper where Hester was at work. In her distracted state, she did not immediately see or understand that Hester had made a jagged black scar across the neat letters that they had just written. Emiline's eyes leaped from the page to Hester's face, only to be met with a bland, vacant expression.

Emiline took the pencil from Hester's limp hand. "We were at 'm'," she said and drew a neat 'm' on a clean sheet of paper. She handed the pencil back to Hester. But the day's lesson was finished. Though Emiline coaxed and cajoled, Hester sat with her hands in her lap and would not respond. "What shall we do now then?" Emiline cast her eyes about on the table and saw the storybooks that she had brought. "Would you like me to read to you?" she offered. Hester kept her head down and pressed her lips together.

Emiline considered the situation. What had changed a cooperative, pleasant young woman into this brat? It must have something to do with Victor's interruption. Perhaps it was simply that her concentration had been broken. But, no, Emiline detected an air of malevolence. Was Hester disturbed because the focus of Emiline's attention had been deflected from her? Well, Emiline had no intention of giving in to silly fits of moodiness. "Which book shall it be then?" she said briskly, pulling one from the pile. It happened to be a book of Grimm's fairy tales, meant for the children who had not materialized. Emiline started reading about princesses under spells so that all they did was sleep, princesses so sensitive they could feel a pea through twelve mattresses, princesses in high towers who let down their golden hair. Each time she finished a story, she tried to close the book but Hester's hand, that strange small hand, intervened. Growing tired of Grimm, she tried to exchange him for something else on the table, but Hester would not have that either. And so they sat in the suspended air of the close room, with only the sounds of Emiline's voice and a hibernating fly which occasionally buzzed in sporadic fits of renewed life between the panes of glass at the window, as Emiline read on and on. The thought occurred to Emiline—she was reading Hester's own story to her.

That first day, Emiline was enchanted by Hester; the second day she made up her mind that she could not abandon her to Cage Farm. Cage Farm was like being plunged back into the ignorance and superstition of the Middle Ages. And there was something else, too, something about the Cage family. Emiline supposed that every house, every family, had its own particular aura. That of Cage Farm and the Cages was one of darkness. And there was an unpleasant tone to the atmosphere that was curious. She had to admit that she was frightened of Cage Farm, yet she could not put her finger on why. What was there to be afraid of? When she thought about the daily activities, the contact she had with the Cages at mealtimes, there was no evidence of anything particularly sinister. But there was such a lack of sympathy and human understanding. Apart from the quarrels, the family members had nothing to do with each other. They did not regard each other in a friendly way or, indeed, in any way at all. They were not persons to each other. Well, perhaps she was reading too much into the situation. Vera had often warned her of her tendency to do that. Still, there was something unhealthy here, and whatever it was, Hester, so like a child, must be particularly vulnerable to it. With the heightened sense of responsibility of a born teacher, Emiline could not forsake a person who seemed to be so at the mercy of her circumstances and of the people around her who, whether by stupidity or carelessness, had shockingly neglected her potential.

Also, Bradley was still an issue. The pain inflicted by him was still that of an open wound. Perhaps, as she had analyzed it to herself, the mysterious circumstances of her birth and her aloneness in the world explained why she had let herself presume too much where his affection was concerned. In any case, she felt a great empty place inside her. It could only be filled by someone who needed her. She sensed that she, too, was in a vulnerable position, that her heart was primed to respond to this beautiful damaged creature as it might have to a doe caught in a hunter's trap.

Questions tumbled about in Emiline's brain. What had happened to Hester to destroy her communicative abilities forever? What was the secret of Cage Farm? Emiline was sure there was one. Or was her mind already succumbing to what Vera had called the alien influence, the freakish effects of isolation?

Cage Farm certainly fit the definition of an isolated place. Someone by the name of Millie came to get eggs. Al, a man of ruddy complexion and squashed looking face, who seemed to be Millie's husband, came once to buy some gasoline. No one else disturbed the monotony. Was that why the Cages were strange? Did that explain the lack of spontaneity and ordinary human communication between them? No one ever said a kind word, no one was ever generous or encouraging. The image of a pack of snarling dogs that Emiline had conjured up at the first supper had been verified by other scenes between Victor and Dane. Mrs. Cage and Maggie didn't say much during the men's confrontations, but they had their own set-tos. It appeared that Mrs. Cage approved of very little that Maggie did, thought or said. What would start out as Maggie vehemently defending herself would turn into a yelling match in which everything either of them had said or done over the past twenty-three years came up for review. Other than these occasions, Mrs. Cage scarcely opened her mouth. At heart, she was more of a brooder than a fighter. But unlike Hester, her attitude was conscious. It was as though she were hiding in her silence, hiding from attack, from the rudeness of her children, from blame. Yet she was not invisible. Her anger and bitterness, while seldom voiced, were palpable, in her groans and sighs, in her facial expressions, and added to the strained mood. She served the meals with surly precision, plunking the bowls down on the table with an angry thud. No one thanked her for her efforts, except Emiline who made a point of so doing. Mrs. Cage, rather than being appreciative, was contemptuous of such remarks.

Although Emiline had gamely set her mind to the task ahead, she still had times of fear. When she lay in bed at night unable to sleep, staring into total darkness—why had she not considered the absence of streetlights and lights of other houses close by?—she felt herself sinking into a morass of doubt, not only about the reality of her situation, but the reality of herself. Her place on the planet was severely compromised. She had been dispossessed of her former life. She had been dispossessed of love. She could not go back to her place of employment in Toronto. She could not return to the school where she had taught for eight years. On the other hand, she felt out of place in this new territory. She did not know the rules, she did not know the ways of the people, their manners and morals. Sometimes in the middle of the night she despaired of being able to endure. For, along with the sense of being separated from her known world, she still found herself dwelling on Bradley's betrayal and his loss to her. At times she knew such plunging sadness, she decided it must go deeper than mere circumstances or the events of her daily life on Cage Farm. She brooded so often and so obsessively about Bradley, she began to think it was loss of love in the world that she was mourning. Although she had been very fond of her adoptive parents, she had not felt a deep bond with them. Perhaps she had always been looking for that deep bond. She felt herself to be a creature who needed love, who suffered from lovelessness, and there was no love in her life. What was the solution? She could neither go backward to Bradley nor forward with anyone else. She did not feel inspired to seek another love, perhaps she never would. Perhaps love was erased for her from the world. The image of Victor Cage standing in the doorway invaded her mind. Her reaction to that figure appalled her. That's not love, she thought. That was fear. The thought came unbidden but she recognized it as being true. Just like the others, she became tense when he entered a room. Why? she wondered. What was there about the man? Why were they all afraid of him? She worried that it was fear that had influenced her decision to stay. Was she too cowardly to face him? And there was something else, too, something mixed with the fear, something she could not name.

Deeply engrossed in her self-involved thoughts, Emiline looked up and was surprised that she had gotten herself through the field. She had correctly judged the road situation and again found herself standing at a divergent point—right, left or forward. To the west, diagonally across another field and about half a mile away, were some bushes. She was surprised that she hadn't noticed them, but perhaps she had been concentrating on her feet and the mice population. Carefully, crouching between two strands of barbed wire, she eased herself into the field and set her boots forward. As she advanced, she discovered that the land sloped slightly downward so that gradually some of the bushes in front of her became the tops of trees.

When Emiline arrived at the edge of the growth, she beheld an incredible sight—a valley and, at its bottom, a river. The landscape was still the seasonally ubiquitous greyish brown, the trees and bushes a tangle of grey sticks. The river was narrow with dirty snow patches clinging to its banks. The far embankment was rocky, rising to a cliff edge, mottled with a few deformed pines. But to Emiline the scene was breathtaking, the terrain entirely different from that only a mile away. She could scarcely believe that she had not known of the existence of this valley, this river, spread now before her like a banquet. For several minutes, she simply stood and feasted her eyes. The valley bottom was thick with natural grasses on earth which had never been ploughed. Along the slope, several trees were coming into leaf, their green shapes suspended here and there like filmy balloons. To her left and down a bit was a little meadow with a purple carpet and floating above it a gauzy black cloud.

After the past few weeks of sensory deprivation, Emiline felt something inside herself break and come to life, some inspiration, some hope, some lifting of a heavy burden. It was as if her mind and spirit had been shut up in a dim room and now the door was opened. She realized how much she had missed the cheerfulness human beings feel when they are in a place sympathetic to their feelings. Now that this opportunity for freedom was before her, she must pursue it. She must get down to the river.

She looked around for the easiest path down the slope. The way to her left, across the purple carpet, contained more open ground. As she descended the embankment, clutching at spidery branches of trees and bushes to steady herself, she marvelled at each sign of the valley coming to life after winter—the carpet that was a bed of crocuses, the cloud that was a swarm of shimmying aphids.

She was concentrating on the steep slope, walking on the sides of her boots. In places, the grassy ground turned to slime. In other places, patches of ice, the more treacherous because they were hidden and in some cases transparent, had resisted spring temperatures. The boots were old and the tread was worn down. As she let go of one spindly tree trunk before taking the plunge to clutch another, out of nowhere came the dog.

It was large, light brown, with a sharp deep bark. As it closed in on her, she saw thick muscled forequarters and a muzzle pulled back on huge snapping teeth. She clung to the tree, trying to stay on her feet. The beast kept leaping up, nipping both her and the air indiscriminately. Screaming, she rolled the front of her body into the tree, hoping to avoid abrasions to her face. Teeth snapped at her ankles. Rabid barking shattered her ears. She held fast to the trunk, knowing that if she fell she would be a goner.

"Whose dog is this?" she screamed, not really expecting an answer. Likely, there was no other human being within hearing distance. She wondered about climbing the tree but it was little more than a sapling. "Someone come and get your damned dog!" she shouted, more to relieve her terror than in expectation of a response. Later, however, she did not know what she would have done if the man had not come to her rescue.

He came sliding down the slope, bent-kneed like a skier, at the same time calling to the dog. But the dog, sensing her fear and feeling its own power, did not easily back off. The man called again and again. Finally, arriving at the tree, he took the beast's collar in his hand and pulled back, half choking the animal. He took the dog off a few yards. It danced around him, expecting praise for a job well done, but the man spoke harshly to it and sent it packing up the slope. He turned to Emiline. "Are you all right?" he said.

"No, I am not all right!" Emiline felt a startling wave of anger as a reaction to her fright. She heard her voice scream. It sounded to her own ears like the voice of an hysterical female. She was shaking, her knees felt like water. She knew that if she let go the tree, she would dissolve to the ground. "What sort of person would keep a vicious animal like that?" she spat. She put her forehead against the tree.

He came close to her. She saw him out of the corners of her eyes. His face was stormy. "Caliban is not a vicious animal," he said, clipping his words sharply. "He was simply protecting his property."

"They say dogs are like their owners," she shot back. "No wonder he's vicious."

For a moment, he looked like he might respond in kind but then he seemed to change his mind. "We'd better see what the damage is," he said. "Can you stand?" He put his arms around her and pried her from the tree. "Hang on," he directed. She had no choice. Holding on to what she perceived even in her distraught state to be an attractive man, Emiline submitted to being half dragged, half carried up a path diagonal to the slope. And so, Thorncliffe Heights materialized in the life of Emiline Thomas.

chapter 3

"So you're the new girl at Cage Farm."

Emiline sat primly stiff on the edge of a sofa. She wore sweater, slacks and socks, having removed jacket and boots at the door. Her hands held up a cup and saucer as though they were a defensive barrier between herself and the young man. He had introduced himself as Lewis McFadden.

"I'm a certified teacher with eight years of experience in an urban school system and I'm well past the age of girlhood," Emiline snapped in an effort to get a grip on herself. She was not quite over her experience with the dog. In fact, as she realized, she was still shaking. Her cup and saucer rattled together. She set them down.

He regarded her across a low table set with tea cups and a pot wearing a crocheted cozy. He had offered her something stronger but she had shaken her head.

"Sorry," he said. "Bad choice of words. I know you're a person with credentials."

"How do you know that?"

"There are few secrets in the country."

This remark served to add further fuel to Emiline's sputtering temper. Not only had she been physically assaulted but she was the subject of gossip. God knew what else about her life was public knowledge. She felt an irrational surge of indignation at the thought that her essential privacy had been violated. "At the moment," she said, "I am a person who is upset, with just cause, I would think, having been attacked by a very large, very stupid dog, said attack being entirely unprovoked."

"You've just had a shock. Of course you're upset." His voice was determinedly pleasant. She couldn't stomach it or his manner. He sat back in a low chair, one ankle crossed over the other knee, a half-smoked cigarette dangling from a relaxed hand. The smell of his cigarette was infuriating her still further. He had offered her one but she had been too prickly to accept and now she was regretting her refusal.

"Thank you for your permission to be upset by your dog attacking me."

"But you were trespassing." The smooth voice was roughening up, losing patience.

"Surely you don't own the river valley."

"As a matter of fact, we do."

"How can anybody own a river valley?"

"Our land encompasses this section of it."

"Well, how are people to know what you own and don't own? Perhaps you should have a sign."

"We do have a sign. On the road. You must have climbed through a fence."

Emiline opened her mouth to refute the statement but then remembered that she had, indeed, climbed through a fence.

"As for 'people,'" Lewis went on, "anyone from around here knows Thorncliffe Heights."

She looked up quickly. He was not joking. "I'm not from around here," she said. "I'm from Toronto. But I imagine your grapevine has relayed that news, also. Toronto's in the east," she thought to add. "It's the largest city in Canada."

"If you were from the country, you'd know about dogs. Everyone keeps dogs in the country. They're an absolute necessity on a farm."

"Dogs and vicious beasts are two different things."

"Obviously, you're disturbed."

"I am not disturbed!" Emiline lowered her voice. She knew that she was being unduly unpleasant but it was either that or fall apart. She did not want to burst into tears in front of this stranger, but she feared that the dog might be the last straw. The encounter had crumbled the emotional and mental structure that she had been working so hard on strengthening. She wanted Vera. She wanted a steady strong shoulder to lean, if not cry, on. "At least not without good reason." Straightening, she clasped her hands on her knees.

"Caliban didn't really bite you. He just nipped at your ankles. He thought you were a cow. He was doing his job."

"He would have bitten me if I hadn't been wearing boots."

For a moment neither of them spoke. Lewis opened his mouth. Emiline thought two things—he's a man who gives his words thought; he has long thin lips. "If I say 'likely not,'" he said, "then you'll answer in kind and the conversation will continue to be pointless. Perhaps we can talk about something else. How do you like your new job?"

Emiline regarded the tall, lean, dark-haired man. He didn't look anything like the men at Cage Farm or the farmers she had seen at train stops across the country. He was wearing an open-collared shirt and V-necked sweater of fine wool, polished loafers, diamond socks. His slacks were pressed. She guessed he was in his early thirties. With his question, his voice had changed, ever so slightly. It had taken on an offhand tone. There was something false in it now. He couldn't care less whether or not I like my job, thought Emiline. Why would he care? But he's not just making conversation, either. She suspected that he was fishing for information. But why?

"Fine, thank you," she replied, tersely.

"You must find it lonely out here."

"Not particularly."

"And how are things at Cage Farm?"

"Fine."

"Getting settled into the country life are you?"

"Yes."

"Still, it must have been quite a shock, after Toronto."

Emiline could hold out no longer. Her inherent good nature overcame her intention to be difficult. Besides, she was starved for human contact and conversation. "I thought I had arrived on the moon. Oh, I had heard of Edmonton. Vaguely. But I had no real idea what it was like or even where, exactly, it was. Then when I got off the train at Kneehill there was this terrible creature ..."

"Archie Dekker. He was damaged in the war. Dad helped him get that job. It gives him a roof over his head and a few dollars for groceries and tobacco. He can be frightening if you're not used to him. But he's harmless."

"I suppose I overreacted. I was in a rather edgy state by then."

"It all takes a bit of getting used to," he agreed. "You must find it boring, being so far from city lights."

"In Toronto, I used to go out nearly every night of the week. I haven't even been to town yet."

"You haven't missed anything."

"Still, they must have shops. I'm to go this Saturday."

The last was said with some defiance. The town business was becoming a bone of contention between her and her employer. Someone must stay at home with Hester and that someone always turned out to be her. Why can't Hester come to town with us? she wondered. She'd get too het up, was the answer. Why can't she stay alone for a few hours, since she spends every afternoon in her room anyway? she inquired. A great silence met that suggestion. Emiline detected some discomfort, even evasion, except for Victor, who never seemed to feel uncomfortable and who looked her straight in the eye. "We don't do that," he said. "We don't leave her alone. But we'll have to figure something out." It was after supper on a Friday evening. Emiline had tackled them before they dispersed to do chores. Why can't we take turns staying? she asked. What did you do before I came? Maggie, was the answer. Emiline looked at Maggie. She had never seen such a nasty expression on anyone's face in her entire life. She could imagine that if Maggie didn't get her way in this, her bad temper the following week would be unbearable. And, in truth, Emiline did not want Maggie to have to stay at home. The poor girl got little enough pleasure out of life. However, she was becoming desperate for certain personal items. Give us a list, said Victor. The idea was ludicrous. To give Victor Cage a list of her feminine needs? Death would be preferable. She had succumbed now for four Saturdays. But she had wrung a promise out of Victor for the coming Saturday. Maggie was to stay at home. Emiline had already prepared herself for the consequences.

"Oh we have our dramas," Lewis was saying. "People killed, mutilated, by machinery, by animals ... by each other. But most of the time, nothing much happens. Some people think that that's part of the country's charm."

"They couldn't be young people."

"There's the Saturday night dance."

"How would I get there?"

"Dane used to go. Even Victor, sometimes."

"Perhaps I should stick to my walking." Emiline could not, even in her wildest imaginings, see herself going to a dance with Victor or Dane.

"And how about ... your student? What does she do when you're out walking?"

There was that note again, barely discernible. He was good, but his voice became just a little too casual, as if he was feigning indifference. "I believe she sleeps."

"She's well?"

"Oh, yes." Emiline reverted to her formal manner, meant to shut down that line of questioning. She did not wish to discuss a student with anyone and certainly not with a neighbour who could spread gossip.

"I've known the Cage family all my life," he said, as though discerning her reticence and providing an explanation for his familiarity. "To me, Cage Farm is part of Thorncliffe Heights. It's been there all my life, the farm next door."

His tone implied, this is my territory. You're the stranger here.

"Then you must know how things are at Cage Farm," she said.

"I've been away. I haven't really lived here since before the war."

That was it then—his clothes, his voice, his sophisticated bearing. His short haircut had some style and his clean-shaven skin was not coarsened and beaten by weather. His manner was smooth and self-assured. His voice was pleasant, soft and low and deep. Did it have a hint of a British accent?

As if he discerned her thought, he went on, "I've been in England this past year. But I'm based in Toronto," he paused, "same as you."

"Oh," she said, looking up. His eyes revealed amusement, but only slightly so. "You must think me a terrible prig."

"I understand how this country can be quite a shock after a large city. But it works in reverse, too. When I first went to Toronto, I would tell people I was from near

Edmonton, and most of them had never heard of it. Some thought it was in another country. But then, maybe it is."

They were silent a moment. Emiline did feel better after the tea. She moved her leg experimentally. It seemed to be all there. It didn't hurt much. Thanks to Maggie's boots, no skin had been broken. He offered her more tea. She had begun to realize that he might be of some use to her. He must know things about Cage Farm. There are no secrets in the country, he had said.

"That would be lovely," she said, "but I don't want to put you to any trouble."

"Not me. Millie. But Millie doesn't mind."

"Oh," she said, "a Millie comes for eggs."

"That's our Millie. She and Al have worked for Dad forever, it seems. They have a house on the place and look after things when the folks are in Arizona."

"Arizona?"

"They go every winter. They'll be home soon."

"Another cup of tea would be lovely," she said. "You must have a different water supply than that of Cage Farm. The water there has an odd taste, because of minerals, they tell me."

Lewis swung himself easily out of his chair. He had long legs and a loose-jointed way of moving. "Dad had a water purifier installed as soon as they became available on the market. Won't be a minute." He took the teapot into the kitchen.

While he was gone, Emiline had a chance to study the large high-ceilinged parlour. Along the north wall

was a large stone fireplace and an oak bookcase. A set of
windows faced west providing a panorama of valley and
river. Another set on the south looked out onto a sloping
lawn which was stopped by a thick stand of trees. A wide
verandah wrapped around the two outside walls.

The room was attractively, although not
ostentatiously, furnished. Besides the sofa on which she
was sitting, there were several large chairs all covered in
bright fabrics. Tables and shelves in front of the windows
were crowded with plants of every description, some tall,
others trailing vines, and some with flowers, giving to the
room a fresh earthy lightly perfumed air. In the corner
by the bookcase were radio and hi-fi. When Lewis had
brought her into the front through the back kitchen, she
had noticed a piano in the dining room. She looked at
the hi-fi and thought of the parties she used to go to in
Toronto. Oh, how she itched to go through the stack of
records on the shelf beneath.

The floor was of dark, oiled wood. Several colourful
rugs were strewn about, before the fireplace, between the
sofa and chairs. The walls were papered with flowers. The
windows were hung with lacy white curtains which both
let in the light and gave the room an airy appearance.
Everything was clean and orderly, yet the room had a
comfortable, lived-in appearance. Emiline, who for the
past month had resided beneath the dark, low-ceilinged
interior of Cage Farm, felt an oppressive weight lift from
her spirits. To her, this place seemed like paradise, even
before she got up and went to the bookcase.

The books were of an amazing variety—poetry, novels, history of every description, botany, gardening, science, biographies, especially of military figures, but also of literary figures. She pulled out a few. They all appeared to have been well read. She was looking at Brontë titles when Lewis returned to the room.

"Would you like to borrow some?" he asked.

"Oh, could I?"

"I don't see why not. I don't imagine there's a lot of reading material at Cage Farm."

"Not if you discount old Camrose Couriers." She looked again at the shelves. "Such a variety!"

"Dad is an old military strategist. English. He was injured toward the end of the first war and it seemed like a good time to retire from all that. He's into anything to do with the military and history. Mother used to be a teacher. But they're great readers, both of them."

"Let me guess. Your mother taught English literature."

"She taught everything here. But in the old country, that was her specialty. I guess we do have a lot of novels." He glanced toward the bookcase.

"The name Thorncliffe Heights. It's a rather romantic name for a place."

"Yes, I suppose so. And you're right. I think it was mostly Mother's choice."

"Well, nobody reads at Cage Farm." Emiline returned the book to the shelf and herself to the sofa and tea table. She took the cup of tea which Lewis had poured for her. She took the proffered cigarette which earlier she had declined. "They don't smoke in the house there, either," she said. "They're extremely careful about matches."

"They had a fire once," he said. "In one of the out-buildings."

"Ahhh. Of course, that explains it."

Lewis sat back. "Mr. Cage used to read. He'd come over sometimes, especially in winter. He'd borrow books. He and Dad would play checkers and argue about politics. He was from eastern Europe, his name got shortened from Cageny, whether by chance or design I don't know. I believe he'd been some sort of minor civil servant in the old country. He spoke several languages, it's all quite vague, his past. Like so many who came here he thought he was going to make his fortune, but he had no idea how to farm."

"I wondered," she said. "The difference between this farm and Cage Farm ..." She did not want to mention wealth, that would be in bad taste, but he seemed to catch the direction of her thought.

"We have a lot more land. Always did have. Although Victor is buying up land now. He's doing well. He's a much better farmer than his father ever was. Dad helped him quite a bit, after Mr. Cage's death, with farming methods, maybe even more directly."

"I'm surprised Victor would take any help. He seems so ..." She did not want to say arrogant. "Proud," she finished.

"Victor is a shrewd man. He recognizes necessity. And Dad has a manner about him. He wouldn't be overbearing or obvious in his offers."

As he spoke, Emiline studied him in greater detail. He had thick eyebrows. She liked that. They gave a face character. He had lines around his mouth and eyes, deep ones for such a young man. Somehow, he had been made to feel things. And there was something else about him, too, that suggested an emotional nature. His lips, their long thin line every once in a while gave a slight tremor, as though the line was in danger of collapse. And he had nice eyes, kind eyes. Yes, he seemed to be a sympathetic person. She made up her mind to be direct. "Would you mind if I ask you," she said, "just what did happen to Mr. Cage?"

He looked at her quizzically. "You don't know?"

"No one at Cage Farm ever mentions him. Even when I hint."

"Maybe they don't like to talk about it. It was a painful time in their lives. Or maybe it's faded into the past, the way things do. But it's no secret. He died. He had a brain tumour that turned out to be malignant."

Emiline felt let down. She had been so sure that there was some deep dark drama surrounding Mr. Cage.

"It happened suddenly," Lewis went on. "He was having headaches. It was September, he got most of his crop off, then he went to Edmonton to see a specialist. He drove home, went into the house, got out his shotgun, went out to the barn and shot his head off."

That was better, more dramatic, more horrendous. "That explains ... there's something about that house. Some quality ... it's hard to describe, but things are not right." Emiline paused. She was weighing her wish not to be disloyal to the Cages by indulging in gossip against her need to talk to somebody about the circumstances at Cage Farm, to talk it through and try to make sense of it.

As she was trying to decide how to continue, Lewis came to her rescue. "I know what you mean. It's not very cheerful. I suppose nobody puts much thought into making it a home. Mrs. Cage doesn't have the time. As it is, she works herself ragged. And after her husband died she had a bad time of it. It's been an ordeal for her. The neighbours helped them take off the last of their crop that year. Victor was only fifteen."

"He's so ... in charge. One might say domineering."

Lewis looked at her sharply. Had her skin reddened, if only slightly? Had her voice revealed something, a show of emotion? But all he said was, "He's had to keep the place together."

Stop the nonsense, Emiline scolded herself sternly. "Yes, I can see ... he does hold things together." There, she thought that was better.

"He had to become the man of the family overnight."

"You wonder though." Emiline stopped. After all, it was none of her business.

"Yes?"

"If it's worth it. Cage Farm is not a happy place."

"Prisons seldom are."

Of course. Now that he had said it, Emiline realized that it was true. It explained Dane's complaints about farm labour, Maggie's frequent fights with her mother, the general nastiness of the family members toward each other. They were common inmates, forced to associate. "But why don't they leave? Dane and Maggie, at least."

"Maybe they don't have any place to go."

"Any town or city would do. They could get jobs. It would be so good for them. Why, Maggie isn't that bad looking. All she needs is tidying up a bit. If she had a decent haircut and learned how to walk she could be quite attractive. As for Dane ... he was sent to fetch me from the station. I truly believed I had fallen in with a neanderthal."

"Likely he was completely out of his element, having to spend half an hour in a closed cab with someone who looks like you."

Emiline chose not to respond to the compliment. "Anyway, since then I've changed my mind. He might even have brains. But he'll never get close to his potential at Cage Farm. Neither will Maggie."

"Maybe they don't know how to leave."

"Maybe I'll show them."

"And how about you?" he asked. "How do you think you'll fit into a prison?" He smiled. There was something in that smile she did not like. He knew things that she could not know, things she would have to find out.

She smiled back. "By refusing to be a prisoner. My job is to help Hester. As long as I carry out that duty, I'll do as I please."

"What *is* helping her?" he asked.

"Knowledge. Giving her some knowledge."

"Knowledge can be dangerous."

"I have to believe that knowledge is good. I'm a teacher."

"All the same, I'd be careful."

"Careful?"

"She's fragile."

"I would never do anything to harm Hester. I told you, I want to help her."

"You say that Cage Farm is not a happy place. But perhaps it suits Hester. There she can retreat from the world, into her solitude. Maybe happiness isn't the greatest importance."

"What is?"

"Fulfilling some sort of function. Before the war, I might have said, a function that we're put on earth to fulfill. I don't know about that any more. But I believe that we can have a function."

"You were in the war?"

"Yes. It's slowed me down a bit. Got in the middle of a dissertation. That's why I was in England. Research. Now I'm here for the peace and quiet, to hunker down and get the damn thing polished off."

"What's your subject?" She looked at the book case behind his head. "Let me guess. Romantic literature."

"Wordsworth, to be exact."

"Of course." Emiline looked around her again at the room. People would have time here, she thought. Here, people would be pleasant and gracious to each other. "The glory and the dream," she said aloud.

"One of the few places like it left in a post-war world," he said. Was there longing in his voice? Desire?

"Well," she said, "perhaps my function is to help Hester."

"It is an appealing project."

"She so tugs at one's heart."

In some far-off room, the clock chimed four times. She stood up.

Lewis drove her back to Cage Farm. On the way, they chatted about the neighbouring farms, the weather and the fields, as if neither of them wanted to delve further into difficult subjects.

At the same time, Emiline was doing some mental calculations. "When Mr. Cage shot himself," she asked, "is that when Hester stopped speaking?"

"She was the one to find him."

"Ah, then, that explains ..."

"Yes. She found her father's body horribly mutilated by a shotgun blast to his face."

Emiline looked out her side window. The only thing to stop her eye was the horizon. She wondered how far away it was. "They don't let her have knives," she murmured.

"When they found her," continued Lewis, "she was frozen into a trance. She couldn't even blink. It was a sort of living rigor mortis. She was literally stiff as a board. They didn't know how long she had been standing there, five minutes, half an hour at most. They carried her into the house and put her into a warm bath. My parents were called in. Mrs. Cage was hysterical and had to be sedated. My mother massaged Hester's arms and legs for hours. In a way, she was the one who brought Hester back to life, everything but her tongue."

"Have they had her to doctors?"

"Oh yes. This may be the prairie but we aren't medieval."

"I take it nothing could be done."

"No."

"But she was of normal intelligence before that?"

"Oh yes. We went to the same one-room school. She was like anybody else. Although ... no," he said as if to himself, "never like anyone else," and, then, louder, "Do you think she can learn?"

Emiline hesitated. This man knew more than she did about the Cage family. He knew their history. And she owed him an answer since he had been so forthcoming. "She can copy, but then so can chimpanzees. Still, she doesn't seem slow. I'd say the prognosis for simple learning is favourable. I don't know about her ability to reason. She's been so neglected. She has had no opportunity to learn. She's like one of those children you read about, some explorer or archaeologist comes upon in some remote wilderness or jungle, being raised by wolves or apes."

Emiline heard her own voice being coolly professional when what she wanted to do was shout, Yes! Yes, this beautiful creature can learn and will learn. I will teach her!

Fuelled with the information given her by Lewis, she felt newly inspired. She would help Hester to struggle free from the cocoon which she had spun around herself as a protective covering against the world. Through education, through stimulation of her mind and senses, Hester could have a better life.

The car turned from the gravelled road into the two worn ruts in the quack grass that was the Cage driveway and slowed to a stop. Emiline opened the door. "One more thing," she said. "What happened to Amy Somebody?"

"You know about her?"

"Her name keeps coming up."

"Victor hired Amy Boyce to be a companion for Hester. That was a couple of years ago."

"But what happened to her?"

"Nothing."

"Nothing?" Again, Emiline felt disappointment. She had so counted on something sinister, at least bizarre, surrounding Amy.

"As far as I know, she still lives with her parents in town. Why do you think something happened to her?"

"I don't know. Just the way people talk about her, their voices change."

Lewis said no more. He was gazing steadily at the house, his lips set. In the failing light of the afternoon, she thought his face had a greyish cast. He seemed in pain. His eyes blinked quickly several times. It almost seemed he was holding back tears.

There *is* something. Emiline knew it. But she would have to find out what it was another time. They had both had enough for one day.

chapter 4

Not bad, thought Lewis, as he watched Emiline disappear through the door of the Cage house. But not my type. He preferred beauty, and failing that, a certain stylish flair. He recognized his romantic bent.

She's intelligent, he decided. He could not help but admire intelligent people. But when it came to the opposite sex, he liked gentle malleable creatures. He was not at all attracted to women who took that precise, emphatic, schoolmarmish tone of voice. Although, he admitted, to be fair, when using that tone she had been thoroughly upset. When she had settled down, her voice had matched her pleasant looks.

He looked at the closed door. Should I go in? he wondered. I should go in, he thought. Why was he putting off seeing her? He wanted to see her. He always saw her when he came home. That was one of the reasons he came, to gaze upon his heart's desire.

He turned the car around and slowly drove back the way he had come.

I should have gone in, he decided. I should have gotten it over with. I should find out what difference this new girl might make in the story. Emiline Thomas seemed harmless, an outgoing congenial young woman, but she did not understand the situation and, because of that, she might, quite unwittingly, disturb things. He did not want somebody new coming in and changing things that had been the same from his earliest memories, somebody from the outside who was ignorant of the ways of the country and, in particular, of the two families.

Nothing ever changed at Thorncliffe Heights. That was its essential charm for him. That was what he counted on. It would always be here. He could always return. He could regain himself. There had been times, especially during the war, when he had felt lost to himself. But here, his old self, his true self would always be waiting for him in his old room. Here, he knew who he was.

He knew the country. There, in the distance, was the caved-in homesteader's sod house where Bob Priestly's folks had lived when they first came here and where Bob and his six brothers had been born. There, beside it, was the larger shape of the new modern Priestly bungalow where Bob now lived with his wife and children—all the other Priestly kids had left the farm, had migrated to towns and cities. There was the windbreak of poplars Radisson's grandfather had planted. There was the pile of rocks which marked Simpson's Corner.

How often had he travelled this road, both in reality and in dreams, and with what raging emotions in his heart? Before university, before the war, before graduate school, he had taken any excuse—an errand for his father, an inquiry about machinery—to visit Cage Farm. What exquisitely honed reverberations of feeling thrummed through him when, during meals there, he noted Hester's minutest gesture—the breaking of a crust of bread with tapered white fingers, as he memorized the smallest details of her being—the flat fragile rectangle of her wrist bones. In those days, he thought that dreams and reality were the same. Unlike many men who went off to war, he still believed in dreams, but he no longer had confidence in their attainment. He knew where his particular dream resided, but he was reluctant to claim it. Did he fear disappointment? failure? He was not sure. Sometimes he wondered if, in this particular thing, he lacked courage. But no, no, he was waiting, only waiting for the right time, the appropriate time. Sometimes in faraway Toronto, he felt that he had lost touch with the thing in Hester's face which connected him to a world beyond this one, but when he returned he always found it again. At Thorncliffe Heights, he could readily recall her face on the screen of his mind. He did not have to see it with his eyes.

I didn't have to go in, he decided.

How long had he been in love with Hester? It seemed all of his life and all of hers. But that was not true. Before his sixth grade, he had scarcely been aware of her presence on the neighbouring farm. That was when Hester had started school. Although there was only a four-year difference in their ages, she had started late and he had skipped a grade. As he thought of that time now, as he had thought of it so often over the years, he asked himself again, as he had so many times—why? What had prepared him to fall in love with Hester? What facet of his gestation, his birth, his early childhood, had so predisposed him to fall in love with beauty itself? and with a particular kind of beauty, one that in its nature was languishing, ineffectual, almost morbid.

Grade six, when he was eleven years old, had been the apex of his life. It was a time when he knew absolute bliss. He and Hester had sat together on the school bus; they, along with Victor, were the first ones on. He coached her in the Christmas pageant—she was, as might be expected, the angel. In spring he brought her the first crocuses, a speckled bird's egg. The teacher, who was responsible for all grade levels in the one-room district school, often assigned older children who had finished their work to help the younger ones. Lewis more than willingly took on Hester, pulling his desk up beside hers, showing her the letters of the alphabet, the numbers of simple arithmetic. It was such an innocent time, thought Lewis, so terribly, terribly innocent.

And then Mr. Cage had committed suicide and Hester's world had ended, and his along with hers. Lewis recalled the incident in snippets, as whisperings between the adults, as Hester's absence at school, as an announcement by the teacher that Mr. Cage had met with an accident and that the Cage children would be away for a while. The death was in September. Victor never attended school on a regular basis again. Hester did not return until after the Christmas holidays. Lewis vividly recalled her first day back. The school bus made an unexpected stop at Cage Farm and she climbed on. It was a bleak blowing day, and she was bundled up in her familiar coat and scarf and toque. But she looked different, taller, thinner, paler. Lewis immediately jumped up from where he was sitting near the front and took her hand. It felt limp, lifeless. He looked into her face. She looked at him. Her eyes were pure gold, and in that purity was a remoteness, a lack of expression. Something was missing. Life was missing. Her eyes had been ravished. She was contained inside herself. Nothing leaked out. Nothing passed between them. His heart sank. She was lost to him, focused on something that he could not get to unless she let him. She lowered her eyes. That small being standing slumped in the aisle of the bus held for him a desperate appeal. Oh, how he longed to respond to that appeal! But he did not know how. He did not know what she wanted, what she needed. He did not know what to do. To this day, he could bring back the horrifying feeling of standing by helpless and watching a loved one go under. He could still feel his childhood impotence.

It continued for a month. If given pencil and paper, Hester sat with her hands folded in her lap. Sometimes, she looked out the window. His mother, who had substituted at the school during March because the regular teacher left suddenly for a job in the city, said that Hester needed professional help. Mrs. Cage, with the urging of his parents, took her to a special doctor in Edmonton. His father drove them the seventy miles, his mother accompanied them into the office. The doctor made his examination. Nothing was wrong physically. Hester had experienced a childhood trauma, she might grow out of it. The doctor was not a specialist. Child psychologists, or any kind of psychologist, were a rarity in the prairie city in those days. A Depression was happening. Other matters were far more pressing. The doctor seemed to think that Hester's problem was of little importance. She could work on the farm, she would get by. She might even marry if someone would have her. He made a joke about her marriage potential increasing because of her speechlessness. When neither Mrs. Cage nor Mrs. McFadden nor Victor, who had insisted on going along, laughed or even smiled, the doctor suggested that if they wished, Hester could be interred in the provincial mental institution. They rose as one, gathered her up and took her home. Even though his mother tried to convince the Cages that that was the opinion of only one doctor, they never took Hester back to the city. They would keep her at home, they would look after her themselves. She did not need school to get through life.

The death of Mr. Cage became known in the district as 'the accident at Cage Farm.' Before that, Lewis had loved Hester with all of his youthful innocence, with the great surging emotions of childhood, with the totality that only children can feel, when, fully focused, the whole being is concentrated, totally, unreservedly, flamboyantly. He thought that he could not love her more. But after her trouble, her ordeal, her destruction, he found within himself another level of love. The new Hester, the suffering Hester, the spiritual, tormented, yet resigned Hester seemed to be part of him, an extension of him, of his heart, which by some twist of nature was outside his skin. His inner self, in those days he might have said 'soul,' was bound up in her sadness and torment, in her fragility and need. He knew her suffering and was drawn into it. He suffered as she suffered, so that together they had a bond of suffering. His love was greater than hers. He was the one with the undamaged heart, the one who could love, who could sustain love and suffering. Hester was the beloved object. She could not respond as another woman might but she had gradually come back to some sort of life. Her face could convey expressions of pleasure or displeasure. She could become excited or disappointed, although such emotions were not good for her, as was explained to him by Mrs. Cage. She could have 'a turn,' Mrs. Cage said, although Lewis had never witnessed such a thing. When he visited, she always seemed pleased to see him, she always smiled her wonderful smile. Her eyes lit up. Even if she could not love, she could let herself be loved. His greatest pleasure was loving her.

During those years when he was often at Cage Farm, Hester never changed. Victor hinted once that Lewis might try and instruct Hester at home, but Lewis was reluctant to do that, he wasn't sure why. Would he be terribly disappointed if it were hopeless? Or, conversely, if it were not? What if Hester could learn, relearn, to speak? What if she chose to put aside her silence? What if she chose to go to the city and take a stenographer's course and become an ordinary young woman? She would no longer be the chaste fairy princess shut up in her castle tower, waiting for him to come along and bring her to life. Curious thought. Could he really want her to remain as she was? No, of course not. What a monstrous idea.

Still, his worst nightmare was that she was not there. She had disappeared, vanished from the world. He would wake up sweating, staring into blank darkness. He knew that he could not live in such a world. Sometimes, when he was young, if he was at Thorncliffe Heights when he had this dream, he would jump up, slip into his clothes, and stride across the fields to her window. He would cup his hands around his eyes and peer into the gloom the other side of the pane until he could make out an oblong shape on the bed. If it was a bright moonlit night, he could see clearly her hair streaming down across the pillow and the top edge of the bedclothes. What if she had not been there? he would ask himself as he slowly trudged back across the fields, the chill night air sobering his thoughts. What if the Cages moved off the farm? What if Victor decided an alternate fate for Hester? What if, God forbid, she should die before he did? Lewis used to suffer terribly with such thoughts. But he was older now. He knew that if and when these things happened, he would have to deal with them. If she died first, he would leap into the grave with her, so the answer to that was easy. Hopefully, he would die first. Quite likely he would. Protected as she was from the world, she might live forever.

Lewis felt easier when he knew that he could see her any time he wished, which was assured as long as the two families remained neighbours. For, while Victor was not exactly friendly, he would not turn a McFadden away. Since Mr. Cage's death, the two families did not have much to do with each other, but the fathers had been friends. In the old days, they used to have an ongoing checkerboard tournament which started about November and lasted until March. However, Lewis noted that now there was a certain constraint or awkwardness when he and Victor met. Recalling Emiline's question, he found himself wondering if Victor had resented his parents because of the help they had given him at the time of his father's death and the ordeal with Hester. Or perhaps he resented the help his father had given Mr. Cage during the early years. But it wasn't in Victor's character to be resentful. Rather, he was a person who took what he needed, thinking it was his due. But maybe the problem was that he was 'educated.' Many country people were suspicious of education, or at least felt the difference. Lewis did not know the reason for the uneasiness. He was simply relieved that the two families were still on speaking terms, which was more than could be said of the Cages and some other people in the district, even before Amy Boyce's ordeal. As for that incident, although people generally thought that pregnancy was the responsibility of the female, most of them agreed that Amy did not deserve to be thrown off the place by Victor Cage after he had 'knocked her up,' as the locals expressed it. The Boyces were well-known and well-liked and the Cages kept to themselves. And, while it was true that no one really knew the details of the story, Rob Myles, who picked Amy up on the road, attested to her distraught condition. "Bad shape," reported Rob, "bawling and saying over and over, take me home, take me away from that place, don't let me go back there, ever."

Although people didn't know the truth, that didn't stop them from speculating, and not all of it was unfavourable to Victor. While he was not generally liked in the district, he was respected as a farmer. All Lewis's father would allow himself to say about the Cages was, "It's not good to keep so much to yourself like that. It's not healthy."

Mrs. McFadden sometimes worried the situation, chasing thoughts around in her mind which later emerged through her mouth. She had helped Victor through his last two years of high school. After her bout as a substitute teacher, she had been hired as permanent staff. She had let Victor come whenever he could, staying late with him for extra tutoring, driving him home afterwards since he would have missed the school bus. Lewis would stay, too, and go home with his mother. He remembered Victor's determination to learn, his physical and mental fortitude, for he also had to put long hours daily into farm chores. The two boys never became friends. The three-year difference in age was a large gap in the teenage years but, more than that, their differences of personality were too great. In any case, as Lewis remembered, Victor had no friends. It was not so much that he kept to himself, a trait not unusual among the individualistic personalities reared in the isolation of a pioneering community, or even that he was unpleasant, but that other people had no value for him. Even Lewis's mother was simply a means to his own ends. The hours of help she had given him, getting him through high school, Victor had taken for granted. Lewis had never heard a 'thank you' come out of his mouth. Why should he thank anyone? Other people were put on earth for his benefit, extensions of his will and desires.

When Lewis first left home, he had suffered a great separation anxiety from Hester. But his first stop of study had been Edmonton and he came home most weekends. As he gradually exchanged one life for another, he came less and less often, but by then he had another strategy. He had trained himself to dream of her at will. And the dreams were so real, more real than reality. In some ways, the dreams were better than reality. He could gaze at her face as long as he wished, he could walk with her hand in hand. She was there for him in all her dreamlike reality. As in real life, she did not speak, neither was she more forthcoming with affection and response. Her facial expression was still remote. Yet she seemed to glow, every pore of her skin emanating a glorious light. He always hated to wake from those dreams.

For a long while he thought he should do something about her. As a boy, he thought that she would some day come around, come out of her spell, be with him again. Then he thought he should talk to Victor. But as years passed and he left home and Victor became more of a recluse, the tenuous thread of their acquaintanceship frayed. In the end, he did nothing. He became busy with other things—the war, his studies, from time to time other women. When he got his life sorted out he would do something, he told himself when she surfaced in his thoughts. Sometimes when he woke from a dream of her, he would feel guilty that he had done nothing. It was his duty to do something, he knew that. He was the one who had gotten out, who had seen life, who knew about doctors and psychotherapy. He had a vague and rather uneasy feeling that Hester could be helped, even though it might take years. But he had the feeling, also vague and uneasy, that he might do her more harm than good. Bringing her to life, exposing her to the mundane problems of everyday life, might that not also destroy her? It would certainly destroy the Hester he knew, the perfectly innocent, beautiful creature, cloistered in both mind and body. And was it his business to interfere? After all, he was not God. And to be practical, at Cage Farm she was cared for. She did not seem unhappy or to miss the life other women had. He could not envision her wearing tight skirts and high heels and sitting at a desk typing. It did not seem possible that she could be busy in a whir of mixers and batters in a kitchen, with children tugging at her skirts and a husband coming in the door.

He did not think he might be that husband or even her lover. He might have at one time, he could not be sure now what he had thought before the war. All that seemed to have happened to a different person in another life. He did remember, though, his own innocence, his thoughts, the equivalent of galloping up on a white charger and whisking her away. But that was a boyish romantic dream which did not encompass marriage or any sort of physical union. Hester and his adolescent sexual fantasies had never occupied the same space in his head. It would be morally wrong to ravage Hester, even in his dreams. She did not have a corporeal nature.

Only once had he declared his love. Only once had he held her in his arms. Before he had been shipped overseas, he had come home on leave from Halifax, where he had taken his basic training. It was summer. He walked over to Cage Farm. He knocked on the back screen door. No one answered. The inside door was open. Likely, Mrs. Cage was out in the barn. He would go in and wait a bit. He entered, calling out a 'halloo' just in case. Something was bubbling on the stove. He went into the dining area, stood a moment listening, then poked his head through the door into the parlour. Hester was netted in a gauze of dust motes shimmering golden in a shaft of sunlight raying through the window beside which she was sitting. Seeing him, she smiled her cool smile across the room. He crossed to her and took her hand. Pulling her to her feet, he looked into her face. He wanted to remember every detail of it to carry with him across the sea, into the front lines. He studied the high rounded alabaster brow, the almond-shaped, golden-lidded eyes, the delicately curved eyebrows, the high cheekbones, the slim nose, the full mouth, a face enduring, tranquil, untouched by concerns and emotions that made other faces old. But he did not need to memorize it after all. That had been done long before.

His face must have appeared serious, perhaps stern, for her eyes became wary. Her facial expression threatened retreat. "It's nothing," he said, smiling to reassure her. "Or, at least nothing to cause that furrow in your brow." He ran his fingertips across her forehead to smooth it out once again. "I'm leaving," he said. "I'm going off to fight the war. I'll be back when the war's over. I'll be back. But it may take a while to trounce the old jerry. That's what they say, it may take a while. Oh, I don't know how much of this you'll understand," he said. "But I want to tell you. Before I go I want to tell you, get it off my chest. I've never told you, exactly, although when we were kids together I tried to show it. But I didn't know then, know what love is. Well, actually, I did know, now that I think of it. I did know. Maybe children know about love more than anybody. I loved you then and I love you now and I'll love you forever. No matter what happens, nothing can change that, nothing can change my love for you. You got that?" He looked into her face. She looked so grave. They were still holding hands. He pulled her closer and then, it seemed so natural, he put his arms around her. He thought that he would faint from joy. Her golden head came to just below his chin. He could feel her small bones, they seemed fragile as birds' bones. He could feel her heart beat. It was the heart beat of a wounded baby robin he had once held in his hand. There will never be such a perfect moment for me again, Lewis thought. If I should die now, I have known paradise. He had no idea how long they stood there together until, through the window, across Hester's head, he saw Mrs. Cage come out of the chicken coop carrying a basket of eggs.

He met her in the kitchen. "Hello," he said, "I came over to say good-bye."

"You stay for supper?" Mrs. Cage's face was a storm. Her mouth turned down.

Lewis thanked her profusely, but he was to have this last supper with his folks.

He had had girlfriends from time to time, although nothing serious. Once he wondered if he should get married. After all, most men married. It seemed like the respectable thing to do. But at the time, there was no one around to marry, so it turned out to be a hypothetical question. Anyway, as he told himself, his life had been too unsettled, first because of the war and then because of his education.

As for his love and pain and regret associated with Hester, that had taken on a certain settled form in which he found comfort. He could not even remember when he had started preferring to worship her from afar. Meanwhile, Hester seemed glad to see him, the Cages tolerated him, he was the neighbour, an old childhood friend. No one realized his true feelings for Hester. Oh, they knew of his puppy love but that was a thing of the past, an amusing memory of something between two children.

I will go in, vowed Lewis. Next time. Why shouldn't I go in?

The car was travelling west now, having turned from the Kelsey road onto the Meeting Creek road. Lewis could see ahead of him where the flat surface of the land broke suddenly, as though a quake had silently shuddered the earth, ripping open a jagged tear into which the car might drop and disappear. The Battle River wound its way through the bottom of this valley and a wooden bridge spanned the river. A steep rise the other side levelled out again to the flat road that hurried on to Meeting Creek, Driedmeat Lake and Jumping Pound. This area was crowded with ghosts which, as a child, Lewis had often pursued. They had kept him company, they had been his childhood playmates. Oh, the hours of my life, he thought, spent dreaming along the river's edge, exploring the craggy embankment, scaling the steep cliff, pretending I was an Indian with bow and arrow, pretending I was Natty Bumppo. How Dad and I would escape down to the river for a Sunday afternoon of fishing, how he liked to show me how to tie bait, how to cast.

Just before Lewis would have started the descent into the valley, he turned the car sharply north into the driveway of Thorncliffe Heights.

Why didn't I go in? he asked himself yet again as the car clattered across the wooden cattle guard and under the archway his father had erected more than thirty years before. After building his unlikely mansion in this vast and empty land, Mac McFadden had burned into wood the letters 'Thorncliffe.' He had then mounted the letters on a wooden archway. Thorncliffe had been the name of his family estate in England. At first his neighbours thought it odd. It was unusual to name farms here, perhaps because the majority of settlers in the area, having come from humble peasant stock and never owning so much as an acre in the old country, did not have referrals to family homes in their past lives. But as the years and prosperity progressed, first one, then another and another sign appeared along the country roads.

Lewis raised his eyes to the outjutting of the gable window of his room, above the front verandah, at the corner. The three bedrooms at the front of the house all had similar windows overlooking the river valley. As a boy, he had imagined the gables were lookout posts of a fort.

Why am I putting off seeing her? he worried as he drove under the tall yet bare poplars which lined the driveway. Am I afraid she's changed since I've last been home? What does a tutor mean? They never had a tutor before.

Or was it Cage Farm itself that he did not want to face? For, he had to admit that, with the passing of the years, with his education and his experience of life, he had an increasingly uneasy feeling about Cage Farm. The new girl was right. It was not a happy place. He would go further than that, although he had not indicated as much to her. After all, he did not want to frighten her off. But he sometimes wondered if Cage Farm might be a treacherous place. Increasingly, these last years, when he visited he felt a weight of oppressive gloom. Something dark and uncompromising had settled into the very air they breathed. Like quicksand, there was something about the atmosphere which could draw a person in, some thick gluey dark frame of mind in which a person could become mired, from which there might be no escape.

Should I have warned her? he questioned himself— this girl with her naive ideas of happiness and freedom? Was it fair not to? Should he have told her that no local person would go to Cage Farm after what happened to Amy Boyce? Should he have told her about Victor Cage? How he was a dangerous adversary, how once at school he had beaten another boy into an unconscious pulp and still had not stopped beating. The boy had called Hester a retard, had implied that all of the Cages were tetched in the head. It wasn't the fight that had so appalled Lewis but, rather, the look on Victor's face, a look of cold calculation in the infliction of pain. It was embarrassing to witness something not quite human on a human face. Victor might have committed murder if Lewis's mother had not run out of the schoolhouse to stand between him and the battered boy lying on the ground. Lewis recalled vividly that no one else, himself included, dared interfere.

No, it did not seem right to influence the new girl's approach to the Cages by putting preconceived notions into her head. Perhaps she would fare better if she did not know certain things.

Amazing, though, that they had not told her about the accident or about Hester finding her father. They must not then have told her about the blood. She should know about the blood, so that she could watch, so that she could take precautions. Perhaps he should mention the blood. Just in case. Perhaps not. Perhaps the blood was no longer important.

Here were the dogs, barking, running out from the barn. Stopping the car between the house and the garage, Lewis turned off the ignition and sat with his hand on the key.

A teacher interferes, he thought. That's what a teacher does. That is the duty of a teacher. To interfere and change the course of events, sometimes even the course of history. He saw again the clarity of Emiline Thomas's eyes, eyes that looked at the world with simple vision, eyes that did not see complexities. That young woman would not be afraid to do her duty. He was suddenly afraid.

But there was Al's broad sturdy figure coming from the barn, a pail of foaming milk in each hand. Lewis got out of the car. The solid bodies of the dogs pushed against him. They jumped up to greet him. Slaver from their long tongues wetted his face. There was Millie waiting in the lighted doorway. As he was whisked into the warm bright kitchen, smelling of roast beef and pie, he could forget the quagmire of emotional complexities that was Cage Farm.

chapter 5

Dear Vera: First of all, thank you thank you thank you for your letter. You'll never know how much it meant to me, hearing from the outside, knowing that there is life out there, people, lights, music, dancing, theatre, LIFE. Two months is not that long a time of separation, yet my Toronto life is so far removed from my activities here, both in distance and in daily routine, it seems like it happened in another lifetime, or perhaps not at all.

What's happening in the boonies, you ask. Well, sometimes, I swear I've landed in the middle of Wuthering Heights. Although Victor Cage is no Heathcliffe, no brooding hero full of angst, he's just as fierce and intractable. I can't discover a lost love in his past, a Catherine, although I've dug around a fair bit. There is someone by the name of Amy Boyce. The intriguing thing is that every time I asked about her or even brought up the name, people became uncomfortable and clammed up. Finally, I tackled Millie Hindschmidt, who lives on the next farm and comes for eggs and loves to gossip. Apparently, according to Millie, Amy is a town girl who was employed here and whom Victor Cage spurned after getting her "in the family way, if you know what I mean." "A pretty little thing," Millie said. "She had a lot of fellows after her. You don't have to worry," she added, affixing me with a stern appraisal, while I tried to keep a straight face at her lack of subtlety. Anyway, someone who does that sort of caddish thing can't be a hero, no more than can someone who says, "Them cows ain't gonna milk themselves."

Although, to be fair, Victor does have some heroic qualities, his looks and bearing for starters. And I believe he has some intelligence, and has a strong intuitive sense, perhaps because he's so closely connected to the land and primal things. He may be an empire builder, I'm not sure. It seems to me that he runs the farm in an efficient way, but what do I know of that? Dane argues with him about methods and, especially, about hours of labour. I don't detect any ulterior motive in Victor, such as wanting to rise above being the poor boy of the county. I don't think he would have felt that way after his father's death. There is absolutely no hint of feelings of inferiority in Victor Cage, and I doubt there has ever been. It seems he struts about the world collecting his due for being born into it.

As for Dane, he's much too nice to be the hero. I can see now that his rude and rough manner has mostly to do with an aversion to being ordered about by big brother and perhaps, too, an aversion to manual labour. He's still shy with me but he's not too shy to get all spruced up on a Saturday night and head for town. He's the first one in the bath water and then emerges from his room reeking of after shave, it's enough to keel you over. But he lets me sit and watch for hours while he works on the tractor. I can hear you groan. What's happening to Emmy if her idea of a good time is watching someone put a tractor motor back together? But, actually, the inside of a motor is really quite fascinating....

Emiline was sitting in the parlour. She had opened the window and was braced for a defence of her action if anyone came into the room. Oh, but it's so lovely out, she would say. I was falling asleep. I thought the fresh air might revive me. All of which was true. She had gone to her room after dinner thinking to write some of her recent news to Vera, but the only place to sit was on the bed. Being in bed in the middle of the day made her feel like an invalid. She would end up falling into the deep trap of sleep, a trap that, in spite of her walking regimen, she had to make an effort to avoid.

Until today she had not tackled this part of the house. For all she knew, it was forbidden territory. But she was tired of hiding in her room. Yet, she did not want to intrude into Mrs. Cage's kitchen space and she associated the dining table with lessons. Thus, the parlour it was. Shrouding the window was a heavy drape. It seemed to be made of something like red felt but when she pulled it back, she realized that the dense texture was in actuality a layer of thick grey dust.

Before long the sun threatened to overcome her. Fresh air was called for. She regarded the window, then stood, took the two metal pulls in her hands and lifted. Nothing happened. She tried again, more strenuously. Was the damn thing nailed shut? Ah, a bit of a shift that time, wood against swollen wood. She wiggled the window against its frame, then gave it a great heave. This time it moved, surprising her and throwing her off balance. Then she had to deal with the storm window, but by sacrificing two fingernails she was able to pry open the wooden flap at the bottom, revealing three large air holes. Success! Warm spring mud-smelling air trickled through.

Although Emiline had been passing through the parlour for two months, she had not really seen it before. Because of its low ceiling and draped window, it had been veiled in obscurity. Now she sat back in her chair and looked about. She saw a square box, chopped up by four doors leading to bedrooms, front porch, and dining/kitchen area. The furnishings, various odd pieces, were dark, the fabrics a nondescript greyish brown. Woodwork, china cabinet and tables were of dark wood finish. Curiously, the china cabinet was full of china. When had it last been used? The linoleum was a murky brown and covered with dark mats. Over everything was that layer of velvety grey which made her think of mice. If you dropped something, wondered Emiline, would it shatter the silence? Or would the sound be muffled by years of dust?

It was a fine spring day. The breeze wafting through the three holes was fragrant. The sun's light struggled through two layers of grimed glass to give some cheer to the room. Through the window she could see the barnyard and the distant fields where some green was starting to show. Dane, crossing to the barn, was trailed by cat and dog. He was always followed by some animal or other. When Emiline mentioned this to him once, he replied that all animals like the person who feeds them. But it was more than that. It had to do with his nature which, with animals, was easy and patient. They relaxed in his company, as did she. Victor's presence was so demanding of a response, which, in her case, was extreme agitation and discomfort, that she found encounters with him difficult. On the other hand, Dane demanded nothing. Conversation was unnecessary. She, to whom social chitchat was an constitutional duty, could feel pleasantly comfortable in their mutual silence. And she liked the way his broad, solid, face crinkled like buttermilk when he smiled his shy smile.

The first time she had seen his smile was two weeks before. She had been sitting in her room after dinner reading a novel about a young woman who lived in England and had inherited an ancient castle only to find it secretly inhabited by a dark, handsome, slightly cruel stranger who had been injured in the war and bore a grudge. Hester had retired to her room and Mrs. Cage was banging pots and pans about in the kitchen.

As usual, Emiline had felt herself slipping into the oblivion of an afternoon nap. She forced herself to get up and move for fear she might become incapable of movement. Like Hester. Emiline surprised herself with the thought. Yes, she confirmed her observation. Like Hester.

She swung her legs off the bed, went to the bureau and hid the novel in a drawer beneath her underwear. She picked up her cigarettes, making sure she had matches, she hated manoeuvring around Mrs. Cage who always seemed to be standing on guard duty in the kitchen. She threw a heavy sweater across her shoulders and went through the house, thinking up an excuse on her way. Going out to get a breath of fresh air, she would say, although it did get her back up, having to account for doing something so ordinary. True, Mrs. Cage did not demand an explanation, in fact she showed no interest whatsoever in Emiline's activities and, in any case, seemed to be getting used to her going out on her afternoon jaunts. But Emiline always felt that she *had* to say something. She had been raised in an atmosphere of social intercourse and still marvelled at the ability of these people to go through a whole day without saying one conversational word to each other.

As it turned out, she did not need an excuse. Mrs. Cage had stopped juggling her pots and pans and was nowhere to be seen. Outside, Emiline put her arms into the sleeves of her sweater and stopped to light a cigarette. The match flared brightly, Emiline shook her wrist sharply to extinguish it. She went to toss it on the ground but then remembered to tuck it back inside the cigarette packet along with the unspent matches. When she got matches out of the cupboard, she always took a few extra. That way she didn't have to face Mrs. Cage's disapproving glance more often than necessary. She wasn't sure why she kept the burnt matches, no one had told her to, but she had the feeling that they kept track of spent matches as well as the others.

She headed across the yard, passing the water pump, stopping at the pigpen to watch the pigs. They did not repel her nearly as much as they had a few weeks previous. She saw a movement to her left. It was Mrs. Cage in the garden behind the house. She was raking the garden plot, breaking up clods of earth, crumbling them down, smoothing them over, hurling herself into the task with such energy it made Emiline realize that she need not be that old, she may not be in her sixties after all. She could be in her middle fifties. Many fiftyish women in Toronto watched their figures and were smartly dressed, carefully coiffed and made up, in the prime of their careers. Emiline considered going over to the woman and trying to start up a conversation. But, likely, she would say something rude and unpleasant. She would not want to be interrupted in her work. Emiline turned in the other direction.

The large double doors to the barn were open and in passing Emiline heard a faint crying from within. She stopped and perked up her ears. The sound was more like little squeaks. Tossing aside her cigarette, grinding the butt with the toe of her shoe, she went to the door of the barn and peered in. She had never been inside. It smelled of hay and manure and animals. It smelled of life, of birth and death. This, then, was where Mr. Cage had shot himself.

There it was again, small squeaking noises. She glimpsed a movement in one of the stalls and then saw that it was Dane Cage kneeling in the shadows. He darted her a glance from his startlingly blue eyes, then looked back down at the straw which covered the floor of the stall. Emiline took a step closer and she, too, looked down. There, in a scooped out hollow was a litter of newly born kittens piping high little notes and searching blindly along the length of the mother cat. Stretched long, offering her body, her swollen nipples were like a banquet table.

Emiline could only stare. She felt that she should say something positive but she had never before seen newly born kittens, nor anything else newly born, for that matter. She thought them quite repulsive, wet and squirmy, like large worms. "They seem so helpless," she got out. At least, that was true.

"They are," Dane replied. His voice was soft, so different than the whining defensive tone it took on when he was complaining to Victor or the bullying tone when ordering his mother about or the derisive one when criticizing Maggie.

Looking down at the top of his head and his lowered profile, Emiline noticed for the first time that Dane was a good-looking man. His hair was long and wildly curly. A shaft of sunlight beaming in from the open loft spun it into a golden frame for a ruddy, strong-featured face. His usual surly look was gone now that he was not around his family. Kneeling back on his heels, the material of his jeans pulled tight across his muscled thighs. His hands resting on his thighs, while grimy, were broad and strongly shaped, his forearms thick and muscled, the hair on them golden. And then Emiline did something she had never before in her life done. Afterward, she could not understand why she had done it. Perhaps it was the smells in the barn, the new birth, the cat stretched out offering her body for what it was meant to do. Emiline's eyes shifted to the space between Dane's thighs, to the bulge in that space.

Dane glanced up suddenly. Quickly she moved her eyes to his face. His eyebrows were golden bushes, his eyelashes too were thick, and as curly as his hair. He looked back down. "They're all healthy except for that one there." He pointed to the end of the line, to one which did not have a teat in its mouth, having been edged out by the others. "Runt of the litter. It has something wrong with its leg." She looked where he pointed. One of its back legs was only a stub with a little deformed foot at the end of it. She grimaced. She had a moment of queasiness. "That one won't live," he said matter-of-factly. "But the rest will. Just give 'em a few weeks. And by this time next year, they'll be on their own."

She was surprised at his volubility. He had not said more than a few words to her since her arrival. She decided to take a chance. "Why don't you leave Cage Farm?"

"Whaddaya mean?" he said, keeping his eyes on the kittens.

"Like the kittens. Be on your own. You could get a job in one of the towns. I mean, it seems to me, you'd like that. It seems to me that you don't particularly like it here." I can't help but notice that Victor gets under your skin, she thought but did not add.

"Naw," he said. "I couldn't do that."

"Why not?"

He didn't answer.

"You could leave," she repeated. "There's no real reason why you can't. Victor doesn't own you."

"We have to keep the farm together."

"Victor could hire someone else."

He kept his head down. She could not read his face. Perhaps there was nothing there to read.

"Have you ever been away?"

"Oh, yeah, I've been to Edmonton."

"This country … it seems so awfully … big. Doesn't it bother you?"

"I don't mind it. I guess I'm used to it."

Emiline shivered. To become used to such solitude, to a sort of vacant mindlessness, what must that do to a human mind?

"How about Maggie?" she asked.

"Maggie?" His voice implied that he had never heard of a Maggie.

"Your sister. Wouldn't she like to leave?"

"Maggie? Naw."

"Maybe, at least, she'd like to go to the dance."

"Maggie?" Again, that note of incredulity. "Maggie don't dance."

"Well, she could."

"Naw, she couldn't."

"Maybe she should."

"Naw. She don't want to dance."

"Maybe she'd like it if she tried."

"Naw. She wouldn't fit in at a dance."

"Whatever do you mean by that?"

"She doesn't move right, she moves all jerky. And she's ugly, not like the girls who go to dances."

Emiline could have hit him. "In the first place, she's not ugly, and in the second place, what difference would it make if she was? A woman can't curl up and die just because she's not attractive. Many quite plain women are far more popular than the pretty ones. They learn to develop other traits, their personalities. Besides, beauty is in the eye of the beholder." She stopped, out of breath. She really did feel quite indignant. She must get off her soap box, change topic. "Does Amy Boyce go to dances?" she asked.

Emiline was not sure why she had changed the topic to Amy Boyce, except that from the first mention of 'the other girl' by the station master, she had sensed something forbidden, even menacing, about the subject. Further references to Amy had served to intensify this feeling and raise her curiosity. And now that she had been at Cage Farm a while, she couldn't help but wonder how another young woman in her position had dealt with the Cages.

She was not prepared for Dane's response. His complexion deepened. He shifted uncomfortably and turned his head away from her. He would not say another word.

Since that day in the barn with Dane, Emiline had heard the story from Millie. She now realized that her comment had been tactless. Amy must be a subject that none of the Cages wanted to talk about.

Emiline's chin had fallen forward on her chest. She roused herself out of her reverie and bent over her paper with the lilac sprays at the top left-hand corner and vines trailing a square around the white page. '… quite fascinating,' she read and forced herself to go on.

Getting back to the Lord and Master, like Heathcliffe, he completely dominates everyone on the farm and they're all afraid of him. At table, no one starts until he starts, no one speaks until he speaks, no one gets up until he gets up. Like Wuthering Heights, there's so much brooding animosity here you can fairly cut it with a knife. And the country must be like the moor in its severity of life. Things are often deformed. You see it in the poor stunted trees lacking proper nutrients, punished by the wind and cold. There's nothing to balance the harshness. No one seems to like it here, no one seems to want to be here except Victor, and I sometimes wonder about him. Why they don't just up and leave is beyond me. They're perfectly able to do so. Both Maggie and Dane are of age, they could survive in a town or the city. I've recently learned that Mrs. Cage has a widowed sister in Saskatchewan who wants her to go and live there. Hester could go with her. Although, now that I've put that on paper, it comes to me that Victor would not willingly give up Hester. And even though I don't approve of his dominating her, owning her is the more accurate term, he does seem to be genuinely concerned about her. As for the others, they have a rather peculiar reaction to Hester, mostly avoiding her. They seem embarrassed by her and won't even look at her. Mrs. Cage seems frightened of her. They're all uncomfortable around her. So that, along with being totally cut off from society, she's also cut off from her family. Even Victor doesn't have much interaction with her, except to keep her under his thumb with his presence.

But get this! I was out walking about a week ago when I was attacked by a dog, a very large golden retriever, on the neighbouring farm and had to be saved by the son of the owner of the house! And the house turns out to be called Thorncliffe Heights! Okay, I'll admit the story line is a bit different. Wuthering Heights was the hovel and Thorncliffe Heights is a wonderful old traditional country house, the kind you see in the movies. It rises on the edge of a cliff, a river bluff, but is solidly set into the earth. It was built by a Mr. McFadden more than thirty years ago when he came here from England. The McFaddens, like the Lintons, are very refined by local standards or, indeed, by any standards. They are well-educated. Lewis, the son, is working on a Ph.D., the mother was a school teacher, the father a British Colonel. I haven't met the parents, but from photographs around the place, I can see that they're totally different than the Cages. They listen to music and they read books! They have a library in the house! You can be sure I took advantage of that, having already borrowed half a dozen books with my eye on several others.

Through Lewis I learned that Mr. Cage committed suicide in the barn! And Hester was the one to find him! And that's when she stopped speaking! Still, I suppose the problem could be physical as well as mental, paralyzed vocal chords or something. I'm not really up on such things. What she needs is professional help, assessment by both doctor and psychiatrist, possibly therapy. They took her to a doctor once, but that was twenty years ago. Both she and medical research have changed since then. But when I mentioned this to Mrs. Cage, she gave one of her contemptuous snorts, looked at me slyly from the corners of her eyes and said with a warning in her voice, "Victor won't have talk about doctors around here."

Here at Cage Farm things have settled down into more or less of a routine. Mornings are spent in lessons, using the term loosely as, often, lessons consist of games or grooming. It isn't easy to keep Hester tidy. Although she now has a daily wash and hair combing, she sinks quickly back into the general disarray of herself and her room. I've mentioned how she has strange hands, so narrow, and the bones seem soft. Her fingernails are thin and brittle and break easily. It's a job to keep them trimmed, they grow quickly. One day I did her nails with a clear polish. She stared at them a long time with a curious look on her face, as if someone else's fingernails had gotten attached to her hands.

Afternoons are for naps and walks. The others, except for those stolen naps I told you about, work from the time they get up until the time they go to bed at night, a dull round which on the surface is uneventful. But beneath the surface there is the constant threat of violence which sometimes erupts, although such clashes don't last long because Victor Cage soon puts a stop to them. I wonder that Dane and Maggie still even try to protest. Maybe it's habit, or maybe it's that thing in the human spirit which refuses to give in to tyranny. They seem to know just how far they can rebel before the boot comes down. Usually, at these times I go to my room, or, if I'm already there, stay there until things quiet down and it seems safe to come out. As you know, I've always found violence, even raised voices, upsetting. And what's even worse than the violence here is the lack of mental give and take. There is no discourse, no reasoning and talking about things. It's all action/reaction.

Another problem is that this violence upsets my student. If it goes on too long she becomes quite agitated and starts scratching her arms. This morning there was a ruckus in the kitchen, something about farm work as usual. I was caught at the far side of the kitchen and forced to witness it. Then after Victor put an end to it and went outside, Maggie and Dane set to, yelling and stomping around and slamming things. Even Mrs. Cage joined the fray, shouting her opinions. I was watching Mrs. Cage when she suddenly stopped shouting and her face froze into a horrified expression. She was staring at Hester. We all looked toward Hester. She had scratched her bare arms down to the blood. Well, the others also became horrified, because of Victor. Mrs. Cage bathed Hester's arms and Maggie went to Hester's room and found her a long sleeved shirt. "Victor can't see that," Mrs Cage warned. And for several days she kept an eye on Hester's arms. As it turned out, the scratches were few and superficial and quickly healed over, but since then the others have been careful around her.

I have little to do with the Lord and Master. Sundays after supper, he hands me an envelope rather like he's paying off a damsel in a house of ill repute. In turn, I hide the envelopes beneath my underwear in my drawer, where they remain undisturbed, since I never have an opportunity to spend. He then inquires of me how Hester is coming along. Other than this weekly interview, during which he is always courteous but formal, I might not exist for all the attention he pays me. After I relate her progress, I'm left to my own devices for another week.

The weather has turned into glorious spring sunshine and one day about a week ago I decided that it was positively unhealthy for Hester to spend so much time in her room. So after the men left ('men' also meaning Maggie, since I have trouble differentiating her from the male of the species), after lunch, or as they say 'dinner,' when she turned to go to her room as usual, I caught her by the hand. "Why don't you go for a walk with me?" I suggested. She didn't say no, so I marched her to the back door, found a jacket on the hook, and helped her on with it. She was pliant as an obedient child. Mrs. Cage was the one who was nervous. "Victor won't like, Victor won't like," she kept repeating and flapping around us. I assured her that we would not go off the place. "I'll take full responsibility," I said, whisking Hester out from under her nose, leaving her still fussing. Well, after all, this is the twentieth century! And they may all be prisoners, but I'm not!

We didn't go far, down to the pasture and back, through the grove of spindly poplar to the north of the house, but it was wonderful with the wild grass coming in green and the poplar as well as silver grey willow budding. And you should have seen Hester! She was like a child with the sun on her face. She was like a lamb gambolling amongst the flowers. And when she spotted a patch of fireweed, she grew so excited she trembled. This made me realize that perhaps I should watch her in regard to sensory stimulation, but if she gets out more, she'll get used to it. At present, she's like a prisoner just let out of solitary confinement. What an absolutely feudal situation. We stayed out barely half an hour. But I didn't want to push my luck. After supper, of course, I had to *explain to Victor. But nothing happened. He turned to Dane and started talking about seeding. And I had myself braced for an argument. I was going to say, it's part of her education, we looked at flora and fauna, which was true.*

In spite of what I've said about Victor dominating Hester, when I think about it, she's the only one not dominated by him. He can't own her because she's not here to own, if you know what I mean. Because she doesn't live in his world, she, her mind at least, is outside his jurisdiction, as it were. So, paradoxically, she is the most imprisoned and yet the most free. But the way he seems to view her is interesting too, not as another person but as an extension of himself, I think. I suppose that comes from taking care of her for so many years.

As for my student, I can't decide about her. Is she ill, deranged, brain-damaged, emotionally traumatized? all of the above? Much of the time she does not seem to be of this world but rather off some place in the stratosphere. I don't think she's mentally deficient. She certainly doesn't look it. She is so perfect in appearance, one wants to believe that she is perfect in every way. Most of the time she is remote as a statue but she seems quite normal, even rational. But one day I did see her stick out her lower lip and deliberately drop a glass on the kitchen floor, breaking it. Mrs. Cage's reaction was one of pure terror and a sharp command to hold Hester back until she could sweep up the mess. Then she got down, it seemed with great pain in her stiff old joints, on hands and knees with a damp cloth to make sure she had found every splinter. I tried to think what had happened immediately before she had dropped the glass. Victor had come in for something or other. He had given me his usual look, a combination of arrogance and amusement. Had he looked at Hester? I can't remember. Although she doesn't seem to care about the others, she likes him to notice her. She's like a child that way. Whatever the case, her destructive action suggests to me that there is some frustration hidden within her which occasionally breaks out, frustration rooted in mental torment. And she lives in that silent torment. It's cruel to keep her in there, inside her head, if there's any possibility that she can get out. I must think more about this.

I still have not made it to town. I was all set to go a few weeks ago but at the last minute changed my mind. I couldn't bear the look on Maggie's face at having to stay home. I suppose, now that she has me, a willing victim it seems, she's taking full advantage of it. I feel so sorry for her, she seems so alone, more so than the others. The men are self-sufficient, Mrs. Cage is always preoccupied with work, and Hester is not of this world. Maggie is out in the world but can't find a place in it. Last week, I gave her a two-dollar bill from my hidden hoard and told her to buy something for herself with it. She flashed me that ever-present malevolent expression, looked like she might spit on my offered gift, but then fairly snatched it out of my hand. I heard nothing more about it or what she might have bought. But I did see her one afternoon before the wash basin mirror with a hair comb in her hand, which, upon hearing my footsteps, she stashed quickly into her jeans pocket. When she turned, she flashed me the same deadly look as before.

One good thing—when I'm with Hester, I don't think about Bradley. When I'm with her, I forget about betrayal *and loss. The world again contains hope and promise. While deep inside I will always feel pain and what might be called a sense of desolation, Hester somehow mutes those feelings or helps me to view things differently. It's as though she allows me to split myself into subject and object. When I think about Bradley now, it's as though I'm commiserating with an old friend (me) who was going through a rough patch.*

Please please please keep those letters coming ....

Again, Emiline's head dropped forward. This time the pen fell from her hand into the grey dust. She felt herself being pulled down into her milling thoughts, thoughts of the paths that, for reasons known only to fate, were crossing hers at this particular time of her life, the paths of the people of Cage Farm. And Lewis McFadden, what of him, did he have a place in her life? She saw him occasionally, while walking along the roads, across the pasture land. In the distance, she would discern his rangy lope. Once she met him. He looked different, rougher, wilder. It was a windy raw day and he tossed his hair, longer now, back with his hand. He had not shaved, his eyes were red. He explained that he had been working all morning on his dissertation. Leaving him to go on his way, she had turned back to Cage Farm. She had been gravely thoughtful during the rest of her walk, thinking how people change in this place, how this place changes people.

Through the whirlpool of her thoughts, Emiline knew one thing with certainty. She must pull herself up out of this stupor. She forced herself to her feet and swayed dizzily. Her half-written letter fell from her lap onto the floor. She bent to retrieve it and started to put it down on the lamp table beside the chair on which she had been sitting. Just in time, she remembered that she must not leave anything as intimate as her letter to Vera lying about for others to read. She did not want to be caught gossiping about Cage Farm to outsiders. Somehow, she knew that the punishment for that would be severe. And she did, in fact, feel some disloyalty about the contents of her letters. But she soothed her conscience with the knowledge that she would go quite mad without Vera and this contact with the outside world.

She went to her room and deposited the letter on her bureau, beneath her jar of cold cream. She looked at her watch. It was only three o'clock, time for a walk down to the pasture and back before supper. She must rouse Hester, they must get out of the house for half an hour at least.

Emiline tiptoed to Hester's door. She rapped with a knuckle but did not receive a response. She rapped again. Nothing. Several more raps produced only silence, ominous silence, it seemed to Emiline. She took the doorknob firmly in hand, turned it slowly and pushed open the door. The bed was a mess of sheets and blankets. Emiline despaired of keeping it made up. She had tried but it did not stay neat because of Hester's frequent naps. The cloth on the dresser was askew. Dust motes streamed between grimed window and dresser and were reflected back from the mirror, filling the room with a hazy light. The closet door slanting from a broken hinge revealed a jumble of clothing tossed into a heap on the floor. The secret chamber, Emiline had labelled this room. Lacking order, odoriferous in an earthy way, it suited Hester. Emiline often thought that she should do something about it but so far had been discouraged by the immensity of the project and the general upheaval it likely would cause both with Hester and the others.

Hester was sitting in front of the window, engrossed in what she was seeing. Emiline stepped quickly and lightly across the room, stopped behind Hester's chair and placed her hands on the wooden chair back. The window looked into a front verandah, the rail of which was sagging, as were the floor and steps. Untended vines coming into leaf curtained the space between ceiling and rail. In a corner, a rotting wicker chair was woven with cobwebs. On the other side of the verandah was a width of tall untended grass and, beyond that, some caragana bushes grown wild and high. Emiline peered across the top of Hester's golden curls but could see nothing.

"What are you looking at?" she asked, knowing that she would not get an answer. She rested her chin on top of Hester's hair. "Hmmm? Darling? What is it? Are you looking outside or inside? What do you see? What or who are you waiting for?"

chapter **6**

"There's a new girl at Cage Farm."

"Girl?"

"Woman. By the name of Emiline Thomas. A tutor for Hester."

"Tutor!"

"That's what she calls herself. She answered an ad. Obviously, Victor advertised."

"She must not have heard about Amy Boyce."

"She's from Toronto. She hasn't heard anything. She doesn't know about the blood."

"Oh dear." Mrs. McFadden was making pancakes. She had just gotten some flour from the bin in the cupboard. Turning to the refrigerator to get eggs and milk, she stopped in the middle of the kitchen. Her face showed distress. "They should have told her about the blood."

"Maybe I should have told her."

"Surely, if it was necessary, they would have told her. Maybe it's changed. I don't have much to do with Cage Farm these days. It could be changed. "

"I told her about the accident. She didn't even know about that."

"Why would they tell her? It happened so long ago."

"Well, it is the basis for why her student doesn't speak. And I did mention that they had a fire once."

"Maybe it's better not to tell her these things. Maybe none of it matters anymore. Maybe she can do a better job without knowing all the gossip."

Lewis was sitting at the kitchen table by a window which looked out over the river. It was a Sunday morning. He loved Sunday mornings when his parents were home and his mother made something special for breakfast, pancakes or muffins or French toast. He especially loved it when the weather was stormy, as it was today. A cold spring rain drove at the house, a north wind lashed the leafing tree branches. He felt cozy as a child again in the big farm kitchen, his favourite room of the house. It had been renovated after the war, so was modern by farm standards. Two walls were hung with wooden cupboards. A north window had been changed into a bay with a wide ledge for plants. His mother always said she liked the north light best, that certain plants thrived in it. A new porcelain sink was beneath this window. Thanks to a generator in the yard there was now a refrigerator and electric lights, although the old wood and coal-burning stove was still used for cooking. It was less expensive and, besides, his mother preferred it. You couldn't get pie crusts really brown on the bottom, you couldn't get dark brown thick crusts on bread in these new ovens, she said.

He looked at his mother's broad backside standing before the stove. A smile stretched his lips, emphasizing the creases each side of his mouth. Perhaps she was a little plumper than when he had seen her two years ago. She had always hated her figure, he knew that, had always longed to be slim and svelte, but he loved her short dumpy little body, her jiggly-fleshed arms, her bustly manner. She was an exceptionally clean woman, always starched and coiffed, always washing her hands and cleaning her fingernails, the sort of woman who bleached dishrags daily. He didn't know if this was part of her genetic disposition or whether, confronted by the squalor of homestead living, she had overcompensated and then, over the years, it had become habit.

"You've been over there then?" His mother's voice was unnaturally light. He knew her concerns. "I mean, if you've met her."

"No. The silly girl got herself attacked by Caliban."

"Our Caliban?"

"Mother! What other Caliban is there?"

"Yes, but our Caliban wouldn't hurt a flea."

"She was on the slope just below the house. His territory. Luckily, I was out in the yard."

"No damage done, I hope. Caliban *can* look fierce. And he has no manners."

"I brought her in to calm her down."

Mrs. McFadden started ladling pancake batter onto a hot black iron pan. "So, what is she like?"

"Seems decent enough. I think she's suffering from social and intellectual deprivation."

"Lewis! What does she *look* like?"

Lewis smiled a teasing smile. "Not bad. Brunette, nicely put together. What else can I say?"

"I don't know. You're the one who saw her. Anyway, that's okay dear. What I'd expect from a man. Likely I'll meet her soon enough."

"Why? Do you intend going over there?"

"I suppose I should. We *are* neighbours. I must say, though, I find that place and Mrs. Cage more forbidding with each passing year. But I meant, likely I'll see her in town." She flipped the pancakes and took his plate out of the warming oven.

"They don't let her go to town. She stays home and babysits Hester. But she's taken to dropping in occasionally. I lent her some books."

His mother brought his stack of pancakes to the table, along with butter and maple syrup.

"Mmm, mmm," he said, picking up his knife and fork and digging in.

She returned to the stove and stood, both feet planted firmly on the new low-gloss linoleum, broad hips against the oven door. This was a favourite stance of hers. He didn't know if she was instinctively defending her stove or whether she was drawn to the warmth. A tea towel was draped over her folded arms.

She waited until he had eaten a few mouthfuls. "So you haven't been over there yet?" She fixed her dark eyes to his. Lewis loved his mother's face, the still black lashes and eyebrows, firm lips, short, straight, slender nose, powdered even early in the morning. The shape of the face, the bones, each part was symmetrical, the lines pleasing. Yet it was a face that was more than the sum of its parts. No longer a pretty girl, now she was truly beautiful. Her face reflected her gentle, loving, generous nature, developed and perfected by time.

He knew that what she really was asking was whether or not he had seen Hester.

She knew of his obsession and thoroughly disapproved. He was her only son. She wanted him to be happy. She never stopped prying for evidence that he had gotten over Hester. As if, thought Lewis, such a common term as 'getting over' somebody could possibly apply to his connection with Hester.

"I came here to work, not to socialize."

"Of course, dear."

"You know I want to concentrate on this dissertation."

He had, indeed, been trying not to think about Hester only a few miles distant. He did not want his mind to be distracted from his work. He could not afford emotional upheavals. Emiline's foray into his quiet life had been nuisance enough. It had taken him a couple of days to get his mind back into the appropriate disciplinary mode. And then she had stopped in again. And again. He supposed she needed to talk to someone. Well, it wasn't so bad now, he reasoned, now that he was more or less braced for her, braced so that he could separate her from Hester, from the emotional component.

"Well, I'm glad Hester has someone for company, if nothing else. Such a beautiful creature. Too bad she's not all there."

"Mother! She's not 'not all there.' Her mind is in a prolonged state of siege. Imagine the shock of seeing her father splattered all over the barn. I saw a lot of such trauma during the war."

"Oh yes, it was horrible."

"And perhaps in the way children do, she feels guilty."

"Not only children."

"Yes. I saw a lot of that during the war, too. Guilt actually ate men up."

His mother sighed. "I imagine that sort of thing killed as many as outright battle." He knew that the war had been hard on her, waiting for news of him, the constant worry. She would have found it difficult to put horrible pictures out of her head.

"Yes. Especially if you think of the ones in the psychiatric wards after. Or even the ones trying to get back to ordinary lives, and discovering that it will never be the same. It's possible that Hester thinks she had something to do with her father's death, perhaps even that she killed him. It's not unusual for children, for anyone, to think that they've caused the death of a loved one, either through action or inaction or even merely by being angry with the loved one shortly before the death, or being angry with the dead person for dying, for leaving them, for abandoning them." Lewis became aware that he was lecturing, that he was protesting too much, that he was rationalizing. Was this for his mother's benefit or for his own? "But none of this means that her intelligence has been altered," he finished.

"She may be brilliant. We'll never know since she doesn't speak. But she does seem disturbed."

"Disturbed?"

"Oh, no doubt there's an explanation for such behaviour. But it's still abnormal."

"Lots of normal people do abnormal things."

"Remember that time she got into the chicken coop and broke all those eggs?"

"She got herself lost. She wandered into the henhouse and became frightened. That was years ago."

"But why did she choose to do something destructive?"

"I don't know." Lewis's voice was thoughtful. "Victor must think she has to be watched. That's why he got Amy in. And now this one. But this one is supposed to try to teach her something."

"Well, we'll see if she can learn anything."

"Thousands of traumatized soldiers are now leading normal lives." At least on the outside, thought Lewis. "Through treatment, medication. But she's been that way so long."

"We should've taken her to another doctor."

"How could you have? Victor wouldn't let you."

"I could have insisted that she attend school."

"But if they didn't want to send her."

"I could have contacted the authorities. But one hates to interfere with neighbours. And then one never knows. What if one takes action and only makes things worse?"

"Yes, there's that, too."

"Oh, I'd get all fired up about the situation and then I'd go over there. And they did seem to be coping. Hester appeared to be contented enough. But I fear she's become worse."

"It's amazing that she hasn't come up with some psychosomatic ailment. You read of people losing the use of their limbs."

"Your father has no patience with any of it. He's always thought that something should be done. He'll approve of your new girl."

"She's not my girl."

"Of course not." She stared at his empty plate. "Maybe this new girl is a good thing. She'll see the situation with new eyes. What's most dreadful about dreadful situations is that after a while we accept them. Like some women accept being beaten by their husbands. Sometimes it takes someone from the outside to see a situation with a fresh view."

"But is that view necessarily correct? I don't mean the wife beating, of course. But some situations, for instance, some times it does more harm than good to remove children from their homes, even if those homes are substandard by society's standards."

"I'm not suggesting Hester should be removed. Just that something should be done. This is the twentieth century. We no longer leave people to their own devices. We no longer intern people in snake pit insane asylums where they're left to rot. We try to treat them."

Lewis felt disturbed at the thought of someone interfering with Hester, of someone 'treating' her. She was beyond that, beyond tawdry human manipulation and 'fixing.' But he realized that such thinking did not do Hester any good. Such thinking kept Hester in her present state. Why don't I see the situation more practically, thought Lewis. Why can't I be objective? "The new girl would agree with you," he said.

"I wonder if Hester *could* function on the outside?" said his mother. "She's been confined so long."

"Strange you should use those terms. When I dropped Emiline off that day, I watched her go into the house and it was like watching someone who has been out on parole go back through steel gates. When I was back on the road I felt an immense relief, as though I was leaving a prison compound."

"That place *is* becoming more and more strange." Mrs. McFadden stared at the linoleum as though in its surface design she might find the solution to a conundrum.

"Who're we gossiping about now?" Mr. McFadden appeared in the doorway. "Do I smell pancakes?"

"You sure do." Mrs. McFadden turned to the stove. "I'll ladle you up a batch. There's coffee made."

Mr. McFadden was a tall, broad man, though spare, his flesh used up by time, so that he seemed to be all large knobby bone moving loosely beneath coarse weathered skin. He was completely grey now but ramrod straight and still proud of his flat belly. After pouring himself a cup of coffee, he sat down across the table from Lewis.

"We were just talking about the new girl at Cage Farm," said Lewis.

"New girl?"

"Tutor for Hester."

"Tutor! You must mean babysitter."

"No, this one's a real tutor. With credentials. She's been teaching in a high school in Toronto."

"What's she doing here, then?"

"Maybe she's looking for adventure."

"Maybe she'll get more than she bargained for. Like Amy Boyce."

"Mac! You never believed that gossip," his wife called from the stove.

"You're right. Not of Victor Cage. It's not in the man's personality. If he got someone pregnant, he'd ball and chain both woman and child. But I can't see tutoring doing any good. That situation is beyond fixing in my books."

"You never did have any sympathy for Hester," said Mrs. McFadden.

"It's not a matter of sympathy. I can see how a kid seeing her father with his face blasted off might go into shock. But it doesn't do her any good to mollycoddle her."

Lewis was familiar with his father's views, with his practical approach to life, an approach devoid of subtlety or tact. Certainly, that attitude worked well with farming and was at the basis of his success with the land and the elements.

"I don't dislike the girl," Mr. McFadden continued. "Or like her, for that matter. I don't see her. I can't see what earthly good it does for them to keep her the way they do, like some prize butterfly specimen in a bell jar. She should be working around the farm or helping her mother in the kitchen. She could slop the pigs. Doesn't take brains to slop pigs. And how about speech therapy? Something like that might work."

He's a good farmer. Lewis looked across the table at his father's face, noting how the skin fell in folds, noting the still bright, lucid brown eyes that could and often did become mischievous. It was a face that more often than not wore a pleasant expression. But he's about as sensitive as a rhinoceros, thought Lewis. Still, that doesn't mean he's not a good man. Overly sensitive people don't make good farmers. After a few years of drought or being hailed out, they leave. Some of them become 'bushed,' from the loneliness and the living conditions. Some of them are driven insane. To stay here and stick it out you have to be tough. You have to assume nothing.

His father saw it like it was and called it that way. He did not dream of bumper crops. He never assumed that he would not get hailed out. He waited and watched and took all the right precautions. He made decisions based on facts, not fantasy. On the other hand, his mother was the romantic dreamer. Although living with his father had taught her much in the ways of reality, it could not change her basic nature.

Mrs. McFadden flipped a pancake. "Lewis has met her."

"Who?"

"The new girl."

"What's she like?"

"Not bad looking. Nice."

"Sounds dull."

"I loaned her some books."

"Better be careful. That's how your mother started with me."

"Except, if you recall, I loaned you the books." His mother's voice was amused. She's not worried, thought Lewis. She knew that he would not be attracted to an ordinary, plain, brown-haired girl, that if and when he ever married, he would have to marry a goddess. He had been spoiled by Hester.

Placing a plateful of pancakes in front of her husband, she picked up Lewis's empty plate. "You want some more?" she asked him.

"No thanks. I'm stuffed. They were great."

"I'll get you some coffee."

He let her. He did not remind her that he had essentially been living on his own for fifteen years and could manage to serve himself. He knew that she loved waiting on him.

"She's very high-minded. She wants to help Hester," said Lewis, watching the swirl of thick cream in his coffee.

"That's what any teacher, any good teacher, wants to do." Mrs. McFadden placed the coffee pot back on the stove.

"I think she was making an appeal to me," he said, his voice thoughtful.

"Who? The new girl? What sort of appeal?" His father surfaced from his plate of pancakes to reach for more syrup.

"I think she wants help with Hester."

"You mean with the tutoring?" Mrs. McFadden turned from the stove.

"No. No, more than that."

"What?" Her voice was wary.

"I'm not sure. I think she has some idea of bringing Hester out of the dark into the light."

"You mean the light of knowledge?"

"A greater awareness, perhaps."

"Hmmpf," snorted Mr. McFadden. "She'd better be careful. Likely, she hasn't the faintest notion what's she's dealing with."

"Well," said his wife, "as a former teacher I cannot help but think that knowledge is a good thing."

"Just remember what happened when that other two ate of the tree of knowledge."

Lewis looked across the table to where his father was mopping up the last of his pancakes. "They had to leave," he said, frowning. That would be disastrous for Hester, he thought. At least, for the Hester of his dreams. And, again, Lewis wondered about the selfishness of his love, how he was torn between wanting Hester to remain as she had always been and allowing her to become a real person. "To do anything is to break something," he said, and added. "And perhaps do more harm than good."

His mother was now at her bay window. The rain slashed mercilessly from the north, but it could not touch her where she was standing inside the glass.

"Not much good the way things are now." Mr. McFadden took his plate to the sink, then refilled his coffee cup.

Lewis, who was always attuned to his mother's feelings, noticed how she was studying the landscape. "Soon you'll be out in your garden," he said. "You'll be out among your flowers."

"I do miss it in winter," she said.

He went and stood beside her. "Surely there are gardens in Arizona," he said. "Why don't you start a garden there?"

"It wouldn't be my garden. My garden is here. In winter it sleeps, along with everything else in this country, including the people."

"Is that why you go south in winter? You don't want to sleep?"

"Maybe. I hadn't thought about it but, yes, I don't like to sleep. I used to when I was young but now it reminds me too much of death. In winter here, we're so thrown into ourselves, with nothing to do but think. The older I get, the more I want to live in my body rather than my mind."

Mr. McFadden took his coffee back to the table. He spoke across the space separating him and the other two. "When your mother was young, she'd dream away all winter. Wouldn't you, girl? But there's no good in being so busy dreaming that you miss what the real world has to offer."

Lewis and his mother stood looking out at the rain. Mr. McFadden continued. "Hester is not a princess locked in a tower. She's a real life blood and bones human being. She's not Sleeping Beauty."

"Oh you're right, of course," his wife said. "And I suppose I've always hoped that she would wake up, come out of the trance or whatever she's in, on her own, that the whole business would be accomplished naturally."

"Maybe if she came out of her trance, people would be disappointed," said Mr. McFadden.

"Disappointed?"

"Maybe she won't be what people want her to be. What they've decided in their minds that she is."

Lewis realized that his father was commenting on his and his mother's romantic bent.

"I'm afraid of the pain," said Mrs. McFadden. "For her, I mean. Think of the pain of coming back to life."

"Nonsense," said her husband.

"Think of what it would do to Cage Farm," said Lewis. "It's difficult to imagine Cage Farm with Hester as an ordinary person."

"It certainly would be a different place."

"An ordinary place."

"I'm not sure this new girl is a good thing," said Mrs. McFadden. "It may be best to leave things as they are."

"Yes," said Lewis. "After all, she has chosen this way of escape. Maybe it would be cruel to take it from her."

"Nonsense," said his father again, this time even more briskly. "It's always better to know the truth."

"Truth?" asked Lewis.

"Of what's in her mind."

"It may be something we'd rather not know," said Mrs. McFadden.

"It may be nothing," said Mr. McFadden. "Maybe there's nothing in that head. Or maybe what's there is what's in any young woman's head. Still," he tipped up his cup and drank the last of his coffee, "I'd want to find out. If I was her family. If I was anyone close to the situation. I'd want to find out what's in that head. Nothing to be gained by hiding things."

chapter 7

The last week in May, spring finally came to the prairies. What Emiline would call spring—trees leafing, flowers blooming, a lightness in the air— had held steady for several days now and people were full of hope. Although Victor at the supper table stated that "anything can still happen" and Mrs. Cage recalled the summer of something-or-other when that blizzard hit right in the middle of the July First community picnic and someone-or-other's car went off the road on the way home, racking up the whole family, the prevailing outlook seemed to be optimistic. Seeding was well underway and plans for summer fallowing and haying were discussed. Hopes seemed high for the crop this year and a market for that crop.

Emiline and Hester were down in the pasture. Their short walks had become frequent. Two or three times a week, Emiline would reach for Hester's hand after dinner and smile and ask her if she would like to go for a walk. Sometimes she varied her speech by asking if she would like to get some fresh air. Emiline had no idea how Hester actually felt about this activity, whether or not she appreciated the exercise or the freedom, but like an acquiescent child, she always assented. And once, when Emiline turned to see if Hester was following along a path, she saw her standing stock-still, face raised to a light breeze, eyes closed, her rapturous expression suggesting that she was, that very moment, being transported slowly and exquisitely sweetly heavenward.

They never went far. Road, barn, meadow, trees to the north of the house, these were the boundaries. Emiline especially liked the trees. She wanted to think of the spot as a grove, and yet 'grove' was a word that did not belong here. It was a word for cultivation—a structured, ordered landscape. This landscape was too rude, too rough. Here were forests and scrub, immensity or pitiful tangles. Intriguing paths crisscrossing at various angles, magical mossy spots issuing an invitation to sit and ponder, these were alien.

Then, one day, Emiline, when she was without Hester, ventured further into the trees. To her surprise she discovered a maze of paths and, upon further venturing along one of these, something caught her attention. She narrowed her eyes. She was sure that in a web of overgrown bushes she could detect an underlying structure of interwoven branches that nature itself could not have devised. She got down on her hands and knees. The path was covered with leaves fallen at the end of last summer, left rotting through winter and dried again in the recent warm weather. Crawling further into the bushes, she discovered the partial tree-branch roof and walls of a collapsed structure, destroyed by time and weather. She knelt in flickering shadows, shaded from the summer sun. She breathed in the herby scent of dry leaves and tree bark. Her nostrils filled with a magical dust. She looked about her. Whose secret place had this been?

"Who made those paths?" she asked Mrs. Cage. "In the grove."

"Grove?"

"The trees on the other side of the garden."

"Oh, them."

Emiline regarded the down-turned lips of Mrs. Cage and plunged on. "Yes. Who made those paths and that little hideaway?"

"I never go there." Mrs. Cage clanked another pot down onto the stove.

But Dane said in his usual mumbling manner, "I'm surprised those paths're still there. We used to play in them trees as kids."

Emiline visualized three children, Druids in the woods, Dane, as he would have been then, a golden fawn, or satyr, all bronze and gold, Maggie, a sweet-faced cherub with dark curly tangled ringlets, and Hester, pale hair flying, long robes floating in and out, in and out, a sylph weaving a bright tapestry through the trees.

And what was Victor's role in all this? She could not see him as a Druid. Never. He must have always been serious and stern, always taken care of the farm, taken care of Hester, the duty passed down from his father.

"I haven't been in there for years," Dane was saying, "except to get the odd stray, but they don't make it too far in."

"And how about the little mossy cave made with tree branches?"

"It's still there?" He looked toward the grove.

"Not really. But I found some interwoven branches. Her eyes followed his.

They were standing near the pump. They had to look across Mrs. Cage's bent figure in the garden. She was planting potatoes, moving the bucket of cut seeders along with her as she worked the row.

Dane turned back to pumping water into large buckets.

"Did Victor play in there?" She was curious about her assessment.

"Naw. Victor never played. Even before ..."

"Before what?" Emiline held her breath.

But Dane was bent back to his work. His movements were fluid, without thought or resistance. How easily his body responds, she thought. There seems to be no break, no intervention, between thought and action.

At that moment, Emiline was not unhappy. She took a breath of clean fresh air and looked about her. The sun was shining, the grass was green. From somewhere a cow gave a low bellow, a robin trilled a melodic rift. Water sliced the edge of the tin pail then settled into a quieter rhythm. The pigs in the nearby pen had all lumped themselves off to various corners for liedowns. The clarity of the air, the way it seemed to echo and reverberate, the smells of new growth and mud, indeed, the combination of all these factors gave Emiline the quite wonderful experience of an early evening in late spring in the country.

Maggie crossed from the machine shed to the barn. She was wearing tight pants and a torn man's shirt, likely a hand-me-down from one of her brothers. There was no mistaking that movement, with its contained violence even in the execution of the most ordinary activities. And yet Maggie had been one of the children playing in the woods. For the first time Emiline wondered what it must be like to be the younger, less attractive, sister of Beauty. And not only Beauty but Goodness, although Emiline could not state with impunity that Hester was good. In the first place, she seemed to lack that component of goodness which most philosophers thought necessary, the ability to make choices. But her pleasant manner and disposition made her seem good. There had been a few incidents, such as the scarred page and the dropped glass, which marred the picture of perfection and which might be surface evidence that something, not exactly sinister but disturbing, was hidden in her mind. However, such occurrences indicated to Emiline not a lack of goodness but a need for understanding and medical attention.

Of all the Cages, Maggie was proving to be the least accessible. The only way Emiline knew that she was not as speechless as Hester was in her nasty spitting at her mother and Dane. In spite of the money and the hair comb, she never willingly spoke to Emiline. In fact, she was even more hostile and resentful since the mirror episode. Perhaps, thought Emiline, she had disturbed a thick defensive exterior padding that Maggie did not want penetrated. Perhaps Maggie construed Emiline's action as pity or charity, neither of which Maggie wanted. Yet, she had taken the money. She had bought the comb. Emiline kept trying. When she encountered Maggie in the house, she made pleasant remarks, even asked direct questions. Maggie would pretend that she had not heard or would answer with a baleful scathing regard which implied that the question was so stupid as not to deserve acknowledgement, let alone response. One day, Emiline cornered her in the barnyard. After a few desultory attempts at conversation, out of desperation in an attempt to get a reaction, she burst out, "Why don't you go to the Saturday night dance with Dane?"

"Dane?" Maggie's eyes slid off to the side.

"Your brother. Get him to take you to the dance."

"Are you kidding? I wouldn't go to a dance with Dane."

"Well, someone else then."

Maggie abruptly turned to walk away.

"You could go with other girls. Amy Boyce."

The remark was an attempt to keep Maggie talking. She wasn't prepared for Maggie's snort of contempt. "Are you kidding? That hussy."

"Who says she's a hussy?"

Maggie gave her a look of disgust, then turned and walked away. This Amy was starting to sound like quite a character, thought Emiline. In her mind's eye, she conjured up a voluptuous country maiden lolling in the hayloft with a come-hither look in her dark eyes and a straw protruding from pouty lips.

Of the two, Dane seemed less unhappy than Maggie. He was more in his element as far as work was concerned. If he left Cage Farm, likely he would merely change places, ending up in the same or similar occupation, farm hand on someone else's farm, or perhaps a truck driver or grease monkey in a garage. If Maggie left, what would she do? Where would she go? Housework, waitressing, mother's helper? Emiline could not envision her in these jobs and was struck by the sad fact that Maggie seemed to have no real identity, not even as female. She had no social life, whereas Dane did. Maybe he had a girl. From what she knew of country dances, it was not unusual for young couples to end the evening in parked cars.

Now, standing at the pump, filling water pails, Dane kept his eyes down, not letting himself, it seemed to Emiline, lift them up toward the trees. He seemed so much the small boy trying to be brave. "They could be built again," she said. "Those secret places and the paths leading to them are not totally destroyed, although all grown over and difficult to find."

"That's just for kids," he answered.

Thinking about that day a week ago and watching Hester today, the way she sat, face up toward the sky, eyes closed, enjoying the freedom of being outdoors, Emiline began to understand why Victor was wary about taking her out for walks. It *is* dangerous, she thought. Rediscovering those woods, opening up those secret places. No wonder Dane doesn't want to have anything to do with it. To think, to desire, those activities of the human mind and heart can lead to discontent, even pain.

Hester always wore long flowing garments, skirts and loose tunics and large sweaters, rather than the modern garb of short skirts and sweater-girl tops or, what would be more practical for farm life, the slacks that most women nowadays were wearing. Emiline wondered who had chosen her clothes. It must have been Victor, or Mrs. Cage directed by Victor. The result of this choice was that Hester's body was invisible. Perhaps it was this seeming lack of body that caused Emiline, when bathing Hester, out of courtesy and a sense of delicacy, to not really look at her, to keep her mind distanced from what was before her eyes. In separating her intellect and her senses, she did not think of Hester as a woman.

Emiline looked around her at the blue sky and green meadow, brightly spotted with flowers and clover. Still nervous of the livestock, she took careful note of where the three milk cows were situated, contentedly munching away, their calves by their sides. Her eyes circled back to Hester, her golden hair shining in the sun. On impulse, she stood up from the log on which she was sitting and noiselessly stepped close to the rock, wanting to enjoy Hester's face when the other woman was unaware of her gaze. But Hester's eyes popped open suddenly and caught Emiline in the act of adoration. The eyes of the two women met. Hester held out her hand. Emiline took it in her own. "Time to go," she said. But for a full half minute, the beautiful golden-eyed face, something startled out of its depths, had blazed at Emiline, causing her heart to leap wildly.

Hester was communicating with her, communicating directly, blatantly. Emiline was sure of it. What could it mean? It didn't matter. Whatever it meant, Emiline responded. "Just tell me what to do!" she cried. "Tell me what you want!" And then, suddenly, she knew what it was. Love. Love me, Hester's eyes had said, the whole expression of her face had said. She might just as well have spoken the words out loud. Emiline could scarcely contain herself. Hester was sending a message to the outside world!

She squeezed Hester's hand and held it a moment longer. She tried to smile her most reassuring smile. "You must know that I love you," she said. She was surprised at the words coming out of her mouth. Since leaving her childhood, she had seldom said those words, and never to another woman. But once she said them she realized that they were true. She did love Hester. Not in the way she loved Vera, which was the affectionate love for a friend, but in another way. She loved Hester with a spiritual and, therefore, deeper love. It was the sort of love you might feel for a sister, Emiline surmised, although she could not be sure, not ever having a sister. But she thought that love for a sister would embody spirit and emotion, perhaps even some physicality. She felt quite confident that such a love was acceptable. Whatever the case, her affection for the other woman had grown and developed over the weeks into love. Love, thought Emiline. Yes.

She must be real, thought Emiline. There must be something there. You can't love something that isn't there.

She pulled Hester gently off the rock into a standing position. Hand in hand, the two young women wound their way through the pasture and up the slight slope to the house. Emiline was trying to think what it all meant. She was happy for this breakthrough, what seemed to be a real step forward. She was moved and excited, but she was not sure what she should do. It's going to be some job, getting her away from Victor. The thought sprang fully formed and unpremeditated into Emiline's brain. She was shocked. What do I mean? What a thing to think! It's not my job to take Hester away from Cage Farm. Yet, why did she have a sudden burst of optimism when she thought of Hester away from this place. Free!

She was excited about telling the others that Hester had so clearly 'spoken' with her eyes and expression. But when at the supper table she opened her mouth to triumph the progress made, somehow she could not do it. She knew that they would say nothing, would look at her as if she were spouting nonsensical gibberish. Her endeavours would be trivialized by their attitude. Their indifference would erase her in much the same way as the landscape did. Look at me! See me! Make me visible! is the cry of everyone, thought Emiline, which was the same as asking for love, for love made people visible to each other. She closed her mouth, suddenly fearful of divulging information, feeling that it might be used against her. What had happened today would be a secret between her and Hester. She looked up from her plate, toward Hester, to find that, in return, Hester was looking at her, looking at her and smiling that enigmatic smile, shy and winsome and yet with its hint of knowledge, secret knowledge. I don't know what you require of me, Emiline tried to say with her eyes, but I'll try and do it, try and be it. At that moment she felt that, if need be, she could die for Hester.

Dear Vera: Just a note to let you know I'm still alive. You must be wondering what's happened to me but I've been so busy lately with Hester. Morning lessons as usual and then most afternoons we go for walks. I still try to talk with Dane and Maggie and Mrs. Cage. Not much luck with Maggie, I'm afraid. But at the supper table the other night, I was looking at her face and, honestly, it's not that bad. If she'd do something with herself, comb her hair and brush her teeth, pluck her eyebrows (which go straight across her forehead), and take that scowl off her face, she could be quite attractive. And she has a good figure, slim and erect, she could wear clothes beautifully. She doesn't need to be a clumping country bumpkin.

Anyway, to get on to more exciting information, I believe more and more firmly that Hester has a great deal of potential. The other day, it was raining and we could not walk, so out of sheer boredom for something to do after dinner I turned on the radio in the parlour. Along with a cloud of dust and a lone moth that fluttered out from the back where it had been happily munching away, came some sound. By some miracle the batteries in the old thing still worked, the green light went on and a scratchy voice came out of it, wouldn't you know, announcing weather conditions. But I turned the dial until I got something resembling music.

I was totally engrossed in amusing myself, trying to find different stations, when I felt a presence at my shoulder. I had seduced Hester out of her room! not with the pipes of Pan but with an old radio so full of static we could scarcely make out the sound. I don't believe she had ever heard music before! or perhaps so long ago it was out of her memory. I took her hand and we twirled around. She loved that. The Tennessee Waltz came on and I placed her hand on my waist and showed her some waltz steps, then we foxtrotted to Your Cheating Heart. She took to the steps immediately. We were having a great time when Mrs. Cage showed up at the door. I must confess, I had thought the old dragon was out in the garden, that's where she is most of her noncooking hours these days. "We don't play that radio," she said. It was on the tip of my tongue to ask why not, but I decided to let it go and ask Victor for permission later.

Although, right now, I'm afraid I'm in Victor's bad books. I believe I told you in my last letter the strange phenomenon of Hester always stopping stock-still at the municipal road. Time and again, we walk along the lane or driveway, past the ditch which is like a cornucopia of wild grass and grain and weeds and wild rose bushes this time of year, to the end of the lane and the beginning of the road, at which point Hester will not go one step further. It's as though she's under some magic spell of the place and if she steps across the line she'll turn into a pumpkin.

Well, on Monday last—I believe it was Monday, I lose all track of time here, one day is so much like another— Hester and I had come to the edge of the drive. As usual, she wouldn't go any further. Our long afternoon shadows were cast out into the road and I wondered if it were the shadows that frightened her.

"Come on." I smiled into her face and tugged gently at her sleeve. "It's only our shadows."

But Hester's feet seemed frozen to the earth. She was like a statue that cannot move. Or like someone programmed—we used to read about those prisoners of war being brainwashed. I must show her that there's nothing magical about this boundary, thought I, stepping boldly into the road. I must show her that a shadow is only a shadow, that it has no power. I made a game of trying to get ahead of my shadow, of trying to step on it, jump on it, dance on it, only to have it keep bouncing away from me. We laughed. I tugged at her hand. She stepped across the invisible line! I was wild with success and exhilaration, and also fear, for it did seem to me that perhaps I had truly overstepped a boundary, that there was a mystery here of which I was unaware and the violation of which could have serious repercussions. Well, we got only a short distance when I spotted a vehicle coming at us from the north. As it clattered closer, I could see it was the Cage Farm truck. Please, please, don't let it be Victor, I prayed, but of course it was.

I was not going to stand at the side of the road waiting like a child who knows punishment is in store, so I kept Hester walking, slowly, toward the oncoming truck. It stopped beside us and Victor Cage rolled down the driver's window. He said nothing, only looked at us with a thunderous scowl on his face. Of course, I started blabbering like an idiot, explaining that we intended going only a few yards along the road but he said, "I think you've gone far enough," and so we turned around and went back, like two chastised children. I have to say, it infuriates me to be treated that way.

Hester wouldn't look at me the whole way back and when we entered into the gloom and doom of the house she went straight to her room. I knew that I would have to face Victor sooner or later, so I went and sat at the dining table. He kept me waiting a good long time, too, as I became increasingly nervous, but of course he does this on purpose to gain even more control, as if he needs it. Eventually, I saw him through the window sauntering across from the garage where he had parked the truck. I heard the back screen door slam. I heard him get a drink at the water bucket. I heard his boots clump across the kitchen. And then he was standing at the dining room door. His face never looked so hawk-like. He's already quite brown, even though it's only late spring, but he works out of doors so much and he has a dark complexion to start with. His hooked nose had a smear of grease to one side, his lips curled disdainfully. I know that sounds dramatic, but it's the only word for his attitude. He leaned against the door jamb, arms crossed, one leg crossed over the other. Standing there with his hat pushed back on his head, in his greasy work clothes, he stared at me until I was a complete wreck. Inside, that is, for I was determined to show nothing on the outside. Finally, he said, in a quiet voice, "Don't let that happen again." But it was the way he said it, the tone of his voice—absolute command. Who does he think he is? I thought, speaking to me that way, and I was all set to give him a run for his money. But then he said, "If it does happen again, I'm afraid I'll have to ask you to leave." And when he said those words, I realized that I could not leave Hester, I could not leave her here in the clutches of these people who do not see her.

"You may think you know what's best for Hester," Victor went on. "But you've only just arrived here. I've been taking care of her for twenty years. Now who would you say knows better? You don't understand things here.

You don't understand our ways. You think you know the answers. You don't. So you must promise me, no more taking her off the property. I'll take your word. If you can promise me that, I'll let you stay."

Can you imagine? The pompous ass! But I must give in. I must stay and try and help Hester. I must not lose the advantage of taking Hester out of the house for walks. I must submit. For the time being, at least.

That's all for now. I'll write a longer letter later, but I want to give this to Dane tomorrow to post in town. I believe tomorrow is Saturday. I've given up ever getting to town. Anyway, I don't care any more. There would be nothing there for me. I'd rather stay with Hester. Strange to think that going to town seemed like an adventure at first. Now I know that the adventure is right here, under my nose. The adventure is Hester.

Emiline stopped writing and lay back on her pillow. With one eye open, she looked at her alarm clock on the night stand. Eleven. The others had been in bed for some time now. Apart from the occasional creak of bedsprings as a body heaved itself over in sleep and the low rumble of someone snoring, the house was quiet. The only light was from the beam provided by her propped-up flashlight, still the borrowed one. When she had burned out the original batteries with her nocturnal activities, Dane had, quite willingly and without question, provided her with more.

She could not tell from which rooms at the back of the house the sounds came. No sound ever came from Hester's room. She must sleep as though drugged, thought Emiline. Ah, there was the moan of someone either in physical or mental distress, an aching muscle, a bad dream. Emiline suddenly found herself wondering if Victor Cage wore pyjamas. She thought not. She saw him lying on his back, his bare shoulders and arms heavy and relaxed. What would that hawk face look like in sleep? Was he asleep? Likely. Likely he had nerves of steel and fell asleep as soon as his head hit the pillow. And he would be physically tired. Certainly, he would not be lying in his bed thinking thoughts of her.

She must finish off this letter and join the rest of the house in sleep. 'I'm dead tired,' she wrote and stopped again.

She could think of nothing else to say. She could not tell Vera of the submission in her voice as she had whispered, "No, no, don't do that. Don't ask me to leave. I promise this won't happen again." She was too ashamed that she had given in to Victor Cage's power. She felt herself sinking into a still pool of black thoughts. Struck with an overwhelming need to get out of the house, she swung her feet to the floor.

She found her bathrobe in the closet and, clutching cigarettes and flashlight, made her way through the kitchen and out the back door. But she didn't need the flashlight. The moon was full, or nearly so. Crossing the yard to the water pump platform, she lit a cigarette and inhaled deeply. There, that was better. Anyone might find themselves thinking weird thoughts in this place. No wonder the whole Cage tribe was strange. The important thing was to apply reason and morality to impulses. That was what made mankind different than animals.

She became conscious of the warm night air. The moon hung suspended like a huge bright balloon against black velvet dotted with stars and planets. Around her was a cacophony of crickets, behind her a soft snuffling from the pigpen. As she smoked her cigarette at a leisurely pace, she vowed to guard herself carefully during her remaining time here. She must not let her own anarchy gain control.

But what was that? Who was there? Someone was emerging from the bushes back of the house. There was no mistaking that tall powerful figure. It was clad only in briefs. Her first thought was, he doesn't wear pyjamas. Her second thought was, a man with any decency would slink into the house and pretend she had not seen him. But Victor Cage was not a man of either decorum or pretence. He sauntered across the yard. She took a deep pull of her cigarette. He stood before her. "Can't sleep?" was all he said.

Smoke slowly escaped through her slightly open mouth. "No," she said.

"It's the full moon," he said.

She dared not look up. She thought he might be looking at the night sky, the moon. Would he say more? She found herself wondering what Victor Cage might say to a woman he was interested in. What had he said to Amy Boyce?

"Well goodnight then." He turned and went back into the house. At first she did not look. Then she did. As he sauntered across the compound, she gazed at the powerful thighs, the muscled shoulders. Her gaze was impersonal, she might have thus studied a panther at the zoo. No matter how repulsed she might be at this animal in human form, she could not help but be struck by the grace of a creature that seemed so attuned to its own nature. She could not help but be in awe of the savagery of its power.

chapter 8

"What are we going to do about Hester?"

"What do you mean?"

"You know what I mean."

"I don't know what you mean."

"So that's the stand you're going to take. Head in the sand. I might have known. After all, you're an academic."

"Perhaps you're the one who refuses to see the truth," Lewis said. "I see a person who had a bad experience as a child and has not spoken since. I see a brother who takes care of her, who has done all he can for her, had her to doctors …"

"Twenty years ago," Emiline interrupted, drawing her sweater close around her. Although it was June, the sky looked cold. The sun could not penetrate the thick cloud layer, neither could a brisk wind dissipate it.

"Who has hired companions, a tutor …"

"You know as well as I do that there's something wrong with Cage Farm. We talked about it before. It's an unhealthy place."

Lewis turned and continued walking along the river bank. He was mildly annoyed that his plan for a solitary walk had been interrupted by this energetic young woman with such outlandish ideas. She had marched over after dinner with the excuse of returning a book but with the obvious desire to talk. He wanted to think about his thesis, about whether or not he should develop a particular thread. But that would mean adding another chapter, when what he wanted was to get the damned thing done.

Emiline had taken to visiting Thorncliffe Heights when, as she put it, she "felt the need for human communication." Lewis knew that if encouraged she would come more often than she did, but he was reluctant to do this. He was here to work. Besides, he did not want the intrusion of Cage Farm into his life. He disapproved of his mother's urging her to visit whenever she liked. Mrs. McFadden was delighted at having another teacher with whom to share interests. Much to Lewis's dismay, she had taken to making what he considered arch comments, she considered them to be subtle, regarding the young lady's possible future. Mr. McFadden was somewhat more reserved in his opinion. While he liked the young lady well enough, he snorted at the idea that she knew anything about the ways of country life or the people out here. He thought that she was treading on dangerous ground, the way she'd barged in, made judgements, decisions, took action, in a situation of which she was totally ignorant. Still, he liked her brightness and her spunk.

As for Lewis, he enjoyed Emiline's company. The more he saw of her, the better looking she seemed to become. He felt comfortable with her and found her to be an interesting conversationalist. They had in common books and music, the Toronto crowd, an awareness of what was going on in the world. But he did not want company this afternoon. And he did not want to think about Cage Farm and Hester, a subject which distracted his mind and interfered with his work. When Emiline had knocked at the door and he had answered because he was the only one home, he had tried to put her off by saying that he was going for a walk. "Good, I'll go with you," she had answered.

They were down in the river valley, one of Lewis's favourite musing spots, only he was not allowed to muse because of this earnest female at his side who seemed determined to disrupt the universe.

"The country is different place," he said. "You may as well accept the fact. They do things differently here. People are isolated and mostly uneducated. They aren't sophisticated. That doesn't make them evil."

"You, yourself, said that Cage Farm is a prison," said Emiline, lengthening her stride to fit his. They were walking with the flow of the river. The wild grass and the scrub growth were dullish green because of the overcast day. McFadden cattle grazed in the flat between river and hill.

"A lot of homes are prisons for the people who live there. Responsibilities, familiarity, even love can make people prisoners. And maybe Hester, given her temperament and sensibility, her affliction, needs a sanctuary. Maybe she needs stability and security. Just like a child."

"But I tell you, Hester is intelligent. I know she is. She prints. She draws. She understands what I read to her. And in other ways, too. When we go for walks, she notices things. In any case, she's a worthwhile human being. And she is being wasted, absolutely wasted, in that dreadful place."

"How wasted? What would you have her do? Get some job at the five and dime? Then she wouldn't be wasted?"

"Every person has the right to their potential. To a life of their own. She has the right to make her own decisions about her life."

"Maybe she doesn't want to."

"Maybe she should be encouraged to do so."

"Maybe she has made her decision. Maybe she has decided to stay at Cage Farm."

"If that's the case, that means she can make a decision. And I agree that that might be the case. But think of it! Think what she's doing to herself! Hiding in her mind, in her refusal to speak. Well, I refuse to put up with it. I won't let her stunt herself that way. I've got to get her to someone who will rescue her from her silence."

"What if she doesn't want to be rescued?"

"She should be rescued whether or not she wants to be. Don't you see, if what you say is true, she's destroying herself. You wouldn't stand by and watch someone commit suicide."

"Well, we don't know that she's capable of making decisions. I'm just trying to get you to look at various possibilities. And have you thought that perhaps by forcing her to speak you might violate who she is, destroy her integrity...."

"Nonsense. Learning to speak is part of human life. Children who refuse to do this are considered abnormal or ill."

They were crossing the bridge now, their footsteps echoing on the wood. Lewis stopped and put his elbows on the railing. Emiline stopped beside him. Together they looked down into the Battle River, swift flowing that time of year.

"She has a mind," said Emiline softly. "I know she has a mind inside that perfect skull. It's cruel to keep it locked up."

"But nobody is keeping it locked up. I don't see why we must do something. She seems happy, or at least contented, where she is."

"A prisoner cannot be happy," said Emiline.

Lewis sighed. "Perhaps we're all prisoners of one sort or another."

"That sort of defeatist attitude makes me want to scream!" Emiline faced him squarely. "That's just the sort of romantic nonsense which I personally find appalling. We aren't all prisoners. We don't have to be prisoners."

"Hold on." Lewis straightened and held up both palms toward Emiline's furrowed face. "What I'm saying is Cage Farm is her home. The Cages are her family. Perhaps, if she can feel affection, she feels it for them."

"There's no affection at Cage Farm. Love requires a free atmosphere in which to grow."

"I disagree. Love can be found in strange places." Lewis turned back to the river.

"Twisted love. Love based on fear or duty." Emiline put up her hand and raked back the hair that the wind was lashing across her face.

"Anyway, perhaps she likes her life."

"She can't like it. And if she does, she shouldn't like it. It's masochistic. To be submissive to that brother of hers."

"Has she ever indicated to you that she might want any other life?"

"Anyone would rather be free."

"Most people aren't free."

"Don't be thick! You know what I mean. Hester may as well be in jail. Under lock and key. A person who loves her chains ... well, that's sick."

"Maybe so, but maybe she wants to be left alone in her sickness. Have you considered what she wants?"

"At least she should know the alternative so that she can make a choice."

"Be careful. You don't want to destroy what she has and have nothing to offer in its place."

"You don't know the atmosphere around Cage Farm. You don't know the cloud that hangs over that place. The cloud of Victor Cage. It's like a black ... no, not a thundercloud. A thundercloud is mild compared to the feeling in the house when he's there. I once experienced a tornado, the edge of it. I was a child but I'll never forget that greenish brownish colour in the sky rolling inevitably toward us. I remember the look on my parents' faces. Before that, I thought they weren't afraid of anything. Well, Victor Cage is that sky. Everyone's afraid of him, afraid to speak, afraid to think. Maggie and Mrs. Cage and Dane, too. Fear keeps them from being able to think. Sometimes Dane talks back and then there's a terrible row. Victor wins, of course. He's so much bigger and stronger. And even if he weren't, he has the authority. I haven't actually seen Victor hit Dane but once Dane had bruises on the side of his face. I'm sure he's hit Maggie too, in the past. But he doesn't have to any more. He established fear in her at an early age and now all he has to do is give her a look and Maggie jumps to it."

Lewis regarded the river's banks where the flow of water had made deep undercuts in the soil beneath the grassy overhanging ledges on either side. His eyes lifted to the wolf willow, pussy willow, wild caragana and thornberry which covered the rise up to the house. He loved this view of Thorncliffe Heights, the way it magnificently crowned the cliff edge. The wrap-around verandah assured him that there was still a life where graciousness persisted. Slow visits of a Sunday afternoon, sitting with a glass of cold lemonade on a hot day, the low murmur of Millie and his mother gossiping as they shelled peas and peas dropping with a tender thud into the pan, all that was still here in a world gone crazy with greed and killing. "Violence is not unusual in farm life," he said. "Men beating up wives, parents thrashing children. It's common to use physical means to discipline children."

"Oh yes, people hit and punch their children in the city, too. Men beat up their wives. But that doesn't make it right."

"It was up to Victor to keep that farm together after his father died. And have you considered what it must have been like for him to have his father commit suicide? Suicide is always so …" Lewis searched for the right word. "… defeating. After all, we take our views of life from our parents. A parent who simply gives up, or seems to in the eyes of a child, Victor would have had to rise above that. And at fifteen, to have to suddenly become a man. As unfair as it may seem, it's not unreasonable that Victor would want Dane to stay on the farm and help out."

"He could get a hired man."

"You don't understand the economics of farming. Most farmers don't have a lot of ready cash."

"And Maggie, she works like a slave. She is a slave."

"There again, he needs her help. Many women work in the fields alongside their husbands during harvest. Not so long ago, women would actually pull the plough, homesteaders couldn't always afford horses. What people in the district see when they look at Cage Farm is a young man trying to hold the family place together, and they would condone whatever it takes to do that."

"Well, it's bestial."

"Maybe. But that's the way a lot of people, maybe the majority of people, in the world live."

"People can work hard and still have a happy home."

"Maybe farms are not happy places, maybe it's only in children's story books that they are. Farmer Jones and so on. Maybe they are mostly bestial labour and crude passions and uneducated minds."

"I don't care about the relative virtues and faults of farm life, or about what's normal behaviour on farms. I don't care about farms, period. I'm concerned about Hester. I can't tolerate the idea of a mind being destroyed by its environment. I refuse to let her remain a victim of that environment. Something must be done about her. And if you won't help me, well, then, I'll just have to do it myself."

Lewis felt alarm. He must try to keep this headstrong woman from doing anything foolish. He straightened and turned and Emiline followed suit. They continued across the bridge and along the bank just below Thorncliffe Heights. Caliban, who had been worrying a gopher, pranced joyfully beside them. Emiline had become used to his exuberance, and he no longer considered her to be a stranger.

"The best thing we can do for Hester," Lewis said, "is, by our concern and affection, leave the way open for her to communicate with us."

"Bullshit, if you'll pardon the expression. I can't believe I said that. You see, Cage Farm is rubbing off on me. But what good would that do when we're dealing with a person who does not know how to communicate. What's needed is action."

Lewis's alarm escalated. "You can't just interfere in someone else's life," he warned. "It could do more harm than good."

"Human growth always involves upheaval," stated Emiline firmly. "For Hester's sake, we must not back down because of that."

Now Lewis felt a descent into dismay. He had a sense of impending disaster unless Emiline was reined in. Quite suddenly, he felt weary. He did not want this problem in his life. He did not want to become involved. He wanted to be left alone with his thoughts about Wordsworth westering the Greek muse in the English countryside. Now he would have to keep his eye on the situation and find out what her plans were. "What do you propose to do?" he asked.

"Get her away from Cage Farm."

Disbelief was Lewis's immediate response. That's impossible, he just about said, but thought better of it. Being contentious was not the way to get information. "And how do you propose to do that?" he said instead.

"Oh, I know it will take time," Emiline said, scuffing the toes of her walking shoes on the path and spraying small stones. "I'll have to wean her from Cage Farm slowly."

"And what do you propose to do about Victor while this weaning process is going on? And the others? You can hardly expect them to stand around sucking their thumbs while you're busy scheming to abduct their child."

"Maggie and Dane won't care. They don't have anything to do with her anyway. As for Mrs. Cage, her attitude implies that bearing that child was a curse." Emiline paused. "Victor will be a bit of a problem."

Lewis felt both incredulity and admiration. This girl was plucky, no doubt of that, but her sheer lack of knowledge was astounding. Victor Cage, a bit of a problem, indeed. He had deliberately soft-pedalled, even misrepresented, the person of Victor Cage to Emiline. He had not wanted to contribute information that would make it difficult for her to work at the Farm. But Lewis knew that Victor Cage was capable of great retaliation against someone who did him a bad turn or got in his way. He was capable of great cruelty. He was capable of murder. Emiline might be lucky if all she got was, like Amy Boyce, to be tossed bag and baggage out into the road, having to make her own way back to civilization.

They had been climbing the hill up to the house, an exertion which interfered with their capacity for conversation. At the top, they stopped, both panting slightly. "More than a bit," Lewis said. "And even if you succeeded in getting her away, Victor would find her. He wouldn't rest until he did. He simply won't let her go."

"Don't you see!" Emiline cried. "In your very words, the grotesque possessiveness of the man, the terrible lack of freedom in Hester's position. Won't let her go! She's a grown woman. She can go if she wishes."

Lewis's mind was busy trying to decide how he should respond. He might say, as far as I know, she does not wish to go, or, she is not really a grown woman, or, Victor is no more possessive than many protective parents. But he had said all of this before to little effect.

While he was thinking, Emiline spoke again. "I'll simply have to try and get around him. For Hester's sake."

She was silent a moment. "I wondered if you have any suggestions."

"I'm afraid not. You see, I think she's best left as she is."

"You can't mean that. Not if you really think about it. Not if you realize that through neglect, or even misplaced duty, I'm willing to grant the Cages that, a perfectly normal young woman has become somewhat retarded."

Since Emiline seemed determined to proceed, Lewis decided that he had better find out just what was in that wilful head. "What do you have in mind?" he asked. "Specifically, I mean."

"I've thought about this a lot," Emiline started. "At first, I considered talking to her and persuading her that she should leave. I do believe she understands every word I say. I'd tell her that we'll go away together, that I'll stay with her after she leaves. We could go to Edmonton. I could get a job there and look after her until I can get her professional help. Hopefully, some day she would be able to take care of herself."

"Did you say any of this to her?"

"No, no I haven't, yet."

"That's a relief. In my opinion, if you spoke to her of this she wouldn't know, I mean really know, what you were talking about."

"You're right," stated Emiline. "And it might frighten her and likely would confuse her. It would be too big a step, to go from Cage Farm directly to the city. No, the whole process will take some time. First, I must somehow persuade Victor to let me take her to town occasionally, little shopping expeditions, that kind of thing. And before that to take her on walks outside Cage Farm. I thought I might work on getting permission to bring her over here to see your folks."

"Bring her to Thorncliffe Heights! You can't be serious."

Emiline started walking again, across the lawn, around the end of the house. "I'll have to get Victor to agree. Call it socialization skills or something. But he knows your family. Your fathers were friends. We could walk over. There's nothing wrong with Hester physically. Gradually, we could come more often. She would get used to another place. She would see that another world exists. She might even remember that she's been here before, even though it was a long time ago. Thorncliffe Heights might trigger some memories, get her brain going."

As Emiline chattered on, Lewis was silent. He could not see Hester anywhere but at Cage Farm. That was where she belonged. Just as Keats' figures belonged on the Grecian urn for eternity, unchanging in their dance, so Hester must remain at Cage Farm. Just as it was inconceivable that those figures would climb down from the urn and enter human existence, so it was inconceivable that Hester would become a mere mortal, that she would drop in for afternoon tea, that she would buy groceries in the general store. By God, this girl would have her joining the women's league and whomping up goodies for the bake table.

"Oh, I would certainly rather just take her away, get her into a vehicle, that's the way it would have to be done, and drive away from here, irrevocably and forever," Emiline was saying. "But I can see that that wouldn't do. It would cause too much of a disruption for Hester. And you're right about Victor. He'd track us to the ends of the earth, I'm sure. No, I do agree that I must somehow work with Victor, hateful as that is to me."

Lewis jumped at the chance to turn the conversation in a slightly different direction, to give him time to think. "You really don't like Victor, do you?" he said.

"I don't think I've ever known anyone with such a total disregard of other people's wishes. He always acts in his own interests to satisfy his own desires. He insists on having power over other people and, what's worse, he enjoys that power."

"And yet you propose to pit yourself against him," pointed out Lewis. He did not want to say ... you, with civilized sensibilities, against Victor's savage instinct ... or, you, with a respect for rules, against a man with a no-holds-barred attitude. He especially did not want to say ... you, a frail female, against a strong forceful male.

"That's where you come in," Emiline was saying.

"Me?" Not bloody likely, he thought. For what did he have to do any longer with Cage Farm, with its uncomfortable teetering on the brink of some violent action, with its lack of mind? And was not this a description of the country itself? Had he not freed himself of this? He had gone through the struggle, he had gone through a war. The outcome of life as passion rather than reason had been revealed to him in the spurting blood and eruption of human entrails on the beaches of Normandy. His future lay in the quiet sanctity of the ivory tower, he was just about there. He did not want to return to a cesspool of emotional entanglements. He did not want to become involved in feelings, either his own or other people's. Things seemed under control at Cage Farm. And if Emiline was right, if underneath the surface something strange was going on, he did not care. He did not wish to disturb the way things were, nor did he wish to enter Victor Cage's arena.

But what was this astonishing woman saying now? "Victor might be more agreeable to letting me bring Hester here to visit if the relationship between the two families was renewed."

"I've had very little to do with them for a number of years," protested Lewis.

"Maybe it's time you re-entered the life of Cage Farm. You could drop in, or whatever you used to do in the old days. Stay for supper."

"I'm not sure bringing me or my family into it would convince Victor Cage of anything."

"Hester would get used to you again. So that when I do bring her over here, she'll feel more comfortable."

Perhaps it will delay things, thought Lewis. Perhaps this is all a tempest in a teapot, perhaps Emiline Thomas will become bored and go back east. But if not, it will take a few weeks for me to visit, and then some time to convince Victor of the walks. Maybe by then I'll be back in Toronto.

And so by the time they were back at the house, he had agreed. "You won't regret it," Emiline turned to him. "Something must be done to break the spell. For it is a spell, a bad, unhealthy spell. Oh, I very nearly succumbed too. I found myself longing for sleep, being overwhelmed by sleep, sinking into it. I found myself walking around in a constant doze. Until I decided I had to wrench myself out of it. But by keeping quiet and doing nothing we're collaborating in the killing of something precious. I'm not sure what it is exactly—something essential to the human spirit. At the very least, we're ignoring an unhealthy situation."

Lewis watched Emiline walk briskly across the yard, past his mother's flowerbeds of scarlet geraniums, purple lithium, fragile pink and white poppies. He watched her pass through the air fragrant with damp lilac, cross the scythed grass and the wild grass dotted with small bluebells, then climb through the barbed wire fence and head across the field. She was so dismayingly ignorant of the situation. She did not know about the way things were and always had been. But perhaps this very lack of a preconceived position would allow her to be successful. Lewis shuddered. He found himself speaking out loud. "Hester in Edmonton. It's unthinkable."

chapter 9

Hi kiddo! How are things going? You owe me a letter, you naughty girl, but since I've never been one to stand on ceremony about such matters, I decided to wait no longer. Frankly, I'm a little concerned. Are you all right? The way you describe Cage Farm and the creatures that inhabit it makes me wonder if you've been taken prisoner and allowed no communication with the outside world. Ha, ha, just kidding.

As for my life these days, all I can say is it's been one damn thing after another. I finally got to the dentist (remember how I was having that pain last winter) after two years of procrastination and the news is both good and bad, but mostly bad. The good is, the pain can be easily rectified with a plastic mouthpiece which I must wear at night. Apparently, unbeknownst to me, that's when I'm busy grinding away due to stress, which is not surprising given the function I must perform five days a week in the bedlam which is Sprucewood High. The bad news is, the dentist managed to find a whole lot of other disease and decay. So now I'm booked into a series of weekly and biweekly visits involving such horrible sounding things as root canals. And to look at my teeth, they all seem quite lovely and straight and fairly white ... but what evil was lurking behind and underneath them! I hope and trust that this experience doesn't herald *a similar breakdown in my body, which to all intents and purposes seems just fine.*

Plans for the summer are working out nicely. I've been looking at books and maps, The Hosteller's Guide has become my bible. Can't believe I leave in two weeks! Boy, do I need the break! From the kids but, even more, from the school politics. Bill is up to his usual antics, calling staff meetings so that everyone has an opportunity to voice an opinion, thus demonstrating his democratic sensibility, then going ahead and doing what he damn well pleases anyway. It's so infuriating, especially this time of year when we're so busy. Why doesn't he send out a memo telling us what's he's decided instead of wasting our time with these stupid meetings? By the way, Bradley got the promotion to vice-principal starting in September, but less said on that topic the better, I'm sure ... except you might want to know that she, as of September, will also be employed at the school.

It's that time of year again. You wouldn't believe the pile of exercises I must wade through. The little darlings, why do they have to be so prolific? And then there's awards night, the annual picnic, various field trips and convocation. Besides which most of our friends appear to be having crises—mental, physical and financial— necessitating my involvement. God, I'm tired. I even occasionally find myself envying you out there in the looney boonies, if you can believe it, with only the weather and nature to deal with and, of course, those awful Cage people. Just keep telling yourself it could be worse. You could be back at Sprucewood High.

Your Hester does sound like a bit of a riddle. She could be half mad or retarded or simply afraid of the outside world. I wouldn't pretend to have the faintest notion of what may be in her head. A case for the experts, I'd say. Are you sure you're not being taken in by her and crediting her with more smarts and personality than she might have? I only mention this because you do tend to get carried away at times. Remember Bradley. Be careful about believing just because you want to believe. In my humble opinion, this Hester must be assessed by a doctor. There's no way you or I or anybody else without training in these matters can really know her abilities. There is nothing you can do except suggest this to that cretin, Victor Cage. You're only the visiting nanny. And you have only a couple months to go. Apropos of that subject ... you don't have to stay until September. I have to say that your last letter bothered me. That Victor Cage sounds like an all around bad egg. Leave them all to their own devices is my suggestion. Believe it or not, Hester will survive without you. You can come home any time. If you want an excuse, I can send you a wire saying someone's died. But, personally, I see nothing wrong with simply admitting you've had enough. There's a time when cutting one's losses and getting out is the sensible solution.

I must stop now. I want to spend an hour on those exercises and then out for dinner with Ralph Dowd. Do you remember him? He was the one I went to that party with last New Year's eve and we ended up getting stuck in that snowbank and he was so sozzled I had to dig us out. Remember how he phoned during Jan. and Feb. and I kept hanging up the phone? Well, a couple weeks ago, I ran into him on the boardwalk, of all places, one Sunday afternoon. To make a long story short, he took me for

*coffee and we've been seeing each other ever since. He
really is quite a sweetie, although he does require a sense
of humour on my part. He still apologizes for New Year's.
Says it wasn't typical of him at all. We'll see. Meanwhile,
he takes me to the quaintest little restaurants, red-
checked tablecloths and sputtering candles and flickering
fireplaces.*

*I won't ask you about your love life, or even your
social life, which subject I'm sure is totally depressing.
I well recall those prairie towns where women aren't
allowed in the beer parlour, or any place else for that
matter, except the kitchen and the birthing room.*

*Do write soon. Your last letter was so short. Are you
running out of material? I suppose nothing much happens
there. It does sound deadly dull and uninspiring. I don't
know how you stand it. Just remember your room is
waiting here for your return.*

Love as usual from your old pal Vera.

*P.S. Be careful. You can be quite ruthless when you
decide that someone needs your help.*

Now why did she say that? wondered Emiline. And
who's Bradley? When she read the name, the thought
flashed a moment in her mind. Although she remembered
immediately, it was like recollecting a character in a
novel she had finished reading some time ago, a novel
that was not particularly memorable. She pushed Vera's
letter into a drawer.

When had she last written Vera? Why could she
no longer write to her? They lived in two such different
worlds, of course, they no longer had anything in
common but, more than that, she could not write to Vera

because she could not say what was in her heart. Her last few letters had been stilted notes about the weather and the farming operations. When she sat down to write, secrets which she did not wish to disclose choked off her voice. This was partly because she did not want Vera's practical advice: "Your job is to be a teacher, do your job, be a professional, don't become involved in the personal lives of your students." This advice might work when you saw your students for a few hours each day and then went home to your own flat and friends. But when you were confined with your student for twenty-four hours a day, it became quite a different matter. The other thing was, Vera would not take her concerns seriously when she had no real evidence of something more sinister going on. When she wrote to Vera about a secretive, unsettling element shadowing her every day existence, Vera's cheerful reply was, "sounds like all the farms I used to know."

It was a late Saturday afternoon in July. After dinner, Maggie had taken Mrs. Cage to town for supplies and to pick up the mail. This time of year there was too much farm work for everyone to go to town and those who went did not stay long. Maggie had returned with Vera's letter and, after thrusting it angrily into Emiline's hand, had taken a long drink from the dipper, dropped it back into the water bucket and, presumably, gone out to pick up her work where she had left it off. Hester was in her room. Mrs. Cage, after changing out of her town clothes, had gone out to the garden to glean vegetables for supper.

Emiline walked through the quiet house, ending up at the dining room window just as Victor Cage drove the tractor into the yard. He parked it alongside the machine shed, climbed down from the high seat and, with his characteristic strut, disappeared into the shed.

She should tackle him now. The thought did not formulate itself in Emiline's brain so much as present itself as a vague fuzzy notion that caused her heart to trip and her breath to shorten. She must tackle him sooner or later. Her plan depended on it. And now another person was privy to her intentions. Lewis McFadden would think her one of those people who did not carry out what they said they were going to do. She had already had a couple of good chances to approach Victor but had excused herself with an 'I'll do it tomorrow,' or 'this isn't an appropriate occasion.' If she did not act soon, the impetus to act at all would fizzle out.

Turning on her heel, she marched resolutely back to her room.

She stood before the mirror. She must have full confidence in her artillery for this encounter. Off came her slacks and shirt. She shuffled through the few clothes hanging in the small closet and chose a red-checked dirndl skirt with a flounce along the bottom edge and a white blouse with elastic around the top. Women in Toronto, where this outfit had been the latest thing for casual wear last summer, often wore the blouse down on their shoulders, exposing more or less cleavage as desired. It was the Jane Russell look. Emiline had no idea what women here wore to produce the same effect. For this occasion, she intended keeping the neckline firmly up as close to her throat as possible. She rummaged around in the bottom of the closet for her one and only pair of white sandals and slipped her bare feet into them.

She looked at her body in the mirror. Did she appear too obvious? She recalled the movie where the hero had seduced Jane Russell in the hayloft, or had it been the other way around? But seduction was not her intention. Her intention was to look appealing so that he would give her what she wanted. Wasn't that what women had to do in a world where men wielded the power?

She looked at her face in the mirror and caught her breath. Why, she was quite attractive! Not so scrawny as when she had arrived, better colour. Just for the fun of it, she pulled the blouse down on her arms. She regarded her shoulders and the top of her bosom. Her breasts were fuller, firmer, and she had curves rather than angles. Had it been that long since she had looked in a mirror? She had been so involved with Hester, she had scarcely given a thought to anything else.

She pulled the elastic back up and leaned closer to the mirror. She decided that she had an honest, straightforward face. Her eyes were a complex combination of brown flecked with green and dark blue. They were not seductive eyes; they were friendly, frank eyes. They did not flinch from themselves. No, she did not want anything to happen between her and Victor Cage. She did not like the man. She did not want to give herself up to his control. Such a scene between them was unimaginable. Oh, she might feel a physical excitement in his presence, she would admit that much, but she could never let herself be swept away by another person's power over her. Even if she might wish that she could, she knew that she could not.

She picked up her hairbrush and brushed out her hair. She had to admit it did look nice, long and thick and shiny, likely due to all the cream that she had been ingesting. Her complexion, too, had improved. And because her skin had a lovely smooth tan, she no longer needed makeup. It's amazing what clean air and nine-hour sleeps can do, she concluded, to say nothing of being away from the dirt and grime of Toronto.

These days, Emiline lived two different lives. On the one hand, there was daily life at Cage Farm, a life which had Hester at its centre and, because Hester was like a child, a life that was child-oriented. Apart from lessons and walks, Emiline was constantly thinking up little activities the two of them could do together. One day they made finger puppets, another day they created designs with glue and sawdust. They played Snakes and Ladders and Parcheesi; they made collages of bits of stick, leaves, string and grass. Emiline was so enchanted with Hester, so mesmerized by her grace and charm, that she did not think to wonder at the narrowness of such an existence for the person she used to be, a career-focused individual. Her present life contained her love for Hester. That was all she required to be content, even at times happy. But in addition, she had a bonus, not of Hester's affection, for Hester did not seem to have the ability for affection, but of Hester's apparent gladness of her presence. Hester smiled when she saw her and readily took her hand. Emiline told herself that she could not or should not expect more.

The part of Emiline which had gotten into the habit of Cage Farm found itself enjoying some of the aspects of country life, such as watching the chickens peck about in the farmyard in the sunshine or the cows sway back from the meadow for milking, their bells resonating the evening air. She stood awed before the big sky and the incredible sunsets. Her heart lifted at the cacophony of bird sounds. She was amused by the frisky squirrels leaping from tree to tree.

But another part of her mind was operating on a more complicated level. She had to free Hester. Since revealing her intentions to Lewis over a week ago, her mind roiled with creative schemes, especially in the soft shadows of the middle of the night, most of which in the cold hard light of morning she discarded as impractical. It had been a good thing to speak to Lewis, she decided. It had made her realize how she had been missing the presence of another mind operating on this other level. She needed a cohort, a partner who thought the way she did. And sharing the plan with him forced her to look at it in a sensible way, which raised the venture into the possible rather than the fantastic.

Today, she would carry out the first part of her project.

Her feet in white sandals picked their way steadily and resolutely toward the machine shed, sidestepping dusty troughs where tire tracks had dried into deep ruts and then been eroded by wind and weather. Even though she tried to stay on matted and worn patches of weeds and grass, by the time she arrived a powder of greyish brown filmed her bare toes and the white leather.

At the open door, she was faced with darkness. She took a step forward. To her left was a movement. She turned her head and narrowed her eyes. The black interior seemed to swirl a moment, then out of its centre emerged the figure of a man. "Oh," she said, jumping slightly. "There you are. I couldn't see, coming out of the bright sun like that."

"Yes?" Victor Cage, with imperial authority, moved out of the shadows into the rectangle of light from the open double garage doors.

"I was looking for you."

"Is something wrong?"

Why would something necessarily be wrong? she thought. "No," she said. "Or, rather, yes. Well, not wrong exactly. I just wanted to talk to you about Hester."

"What about Hester?"

"Her future."

Victor said nothing. He simply stood there, waiting for her to go on. Why did he not help her out, make small talk, at least be pleasant, which would give her an opportunity to gradually introduce the topic? She had planned to create a relaxed conversational atmosphere and then bring up the subject of Hester, how well she was doing, how much she, Emiline, enjoyed working with her, how rewarding it was to have such an apt pupil. Then she could drop the bombshell question about taking her for walks. Instead, in his intimidating silence, she found herself blurting out, "I'd like to take her for walks."

Victor strutted into the centre of the slab of light. He took an easy stance against a greasy-looking motor which was sitting on a work bench a few feet inside the doorway where she was standing. His jeans and shirt were streaked with grease. He smelled of machine oil and machines. The black hair on his lower arms took on fiery glints in the sun. In a sudden swift movement, he lifted his right hand to his left shirt front. She took a quick step back.

Slowly, he took makings out of his shirt pocket and started to roll a cigarette. His eyes were steady on her face. "You take her for walks," he said.

"I mean out of the yard, off the farm."

"Now why would you want to do that?" His black eyes flashed across the cigarette paper which he licked with a quick flick of his tongue. His tongue was wet and like a flash of silver.

Why would I want to do that? thought Emiline. "It's easier to walk on a road," she said and, then, suddenly inspired, "There aren't as many mosquitoes this time of year. I don't see that it could in any way prove hazardous. There's hardly any traffic."

Victor put the cigarette in his mouth, dug around in his shirt pocket for a match which he lit with his thumbnail, then held to the tip of the cigarette. All this time he regarded her with that strange gaze she had noted before. There was something uncanny in it, something that was almost inhuman. Emiline recalled how she had watched him the night of the full moon, how she had thought of a panther.

He took a long drag of smoke into his lungs and exhaled. Still he looked at her. She began to feel uncomfortable. She felt herself grow warm. She hoped she was not turning red.

"Okay," he finally said. Turning his head slightly but not his eyes, he spit a bit of tobacco out of his mouth with the tip of his tongue. "I don't see a problem with that." He crossed his ankles, leaning his weight more heavily on one foot. He crossed his arms.

Emiline was stunned. She had braced herself for an argument. She had her forces marshalled, her points in logical order. She felt unbalanced, almost disappointed. Was it going to be this easy? "Well, all right," she said. "Thank you." She could have bitten her lip then. Why was she thanking this person for giving her permission? Why did she need permission? Both she and Hester were adults.

"As long as you don't go far," he added. "A mile or two down the road. Don't get her lost."

Oh, how she longed to be rude, to put him down with a scathing remark. But she knew that to get her way she must be agreeable. "No, of course not." She could think of nothing more to say. She started to leave.

"Just remember," his low drawl coiled around her turning figure, "Hester is ours. Not yours."

Emiline stopped. She turned back. "What on earth do you mean?"

"You forget that sometimes." He spoke through one side of his mouth, the cigarette clamped between his lips at the other side. His voice came out of a haze of smoke.

"I have no idea …"

"You come here from the big city thinking you know everything when, in fact, you know nothing. You don't know anything about Hester and yet you want to make her yours."

Emiline forgot to be cautious. "I know that human beings should not be owned by other people. One should not have to come from a big city to know that. Hester is not anybody's. She is her own."

One eye winking through spiralling smoke, his look now was a long, hard, steady evaluation. His eyes took in her blouse, her skirt, her bare legs. He raised them to her face. "You're young," he said.

"I doubt I'm much younger than you."

"Young in experience."

"I should think my experience wider than yours. As you say, I come from a big city."

He raised one arm and took the cigarette from his mouth. "People in cities get confused. They don't know why they're alive. They forget simple truths. The simple truth is, people belong to a place and to the people in that place. Hester belongs to Cage Farm. All the Cages do. We're all part of the story of Cage Farm. We all belong to each other."

Emiline was amazed. She had never before heard him expound on what might be termed a philosophical subject. Several replies dashed through her thoughts. The one that surfaced was, "Stories change."

"They only seem to change. You think you've got out of the story and into a different one. You think you've escaped the inevitable. You look over your shoulder some day and there it is, waiting, ready to pounce."

"I don't believe that. I believe people are freely born, that they have a right to freely live."

"You're never free of the place where you're born. Or of your own nature. It takes some people a long time to learn that, some of them a lifetime. Seems to me it's a waste of time not to admit it in the first place."

"I don't agree with you. I believe people come before a place, that they can get away from where they're born. That they can change."

"But then they become someone else. Take Hester. If she lived somewhere else she would be someone else."

"Would that be a bad thing?"

"It would take away from her. Here, she is somebody. In her own way, she knows who she is … On the outside, she would be nobody. It would bring her nothing but grief. You try and change the story, you bring on nothing but grief."

"I believe that we can change our lives, that we don't have to submit to a stupid destiny."

"That's why you're like a hen on hot bricks most of the time." Again, his eyes flicked her down and up.

Indignation flared up like a torch inside Emiline. She felt insulted, physically violated. She was so incensed, she dared not speak. Again, she turned to go.

Again she was stopped by his voice, a throaty growl at her back. "Another thing. Don't talk to Hester about freedom. You'll only confuse her."

"I have done no such thing …." She started to defend herself.

"Maybe not. But you want to. It wouldn't make any difference to her. She wouldn't have any idea what you were talking about."

Yes, she would, Emiline thought, but said nothing.

"But then, I'm sure you won't. You wouldn't want to upset her."

"But why have I come here?" Emiline burst out. "If not to free her from ignorance? Why did you send for me if you don't want her to grow? Surely, you knew that a teacher might change her."

"I've nothing against her learning to read and write and draw pictures. What I'm telling you is, I know what she's capable of. And it will never be enough for her to be able to leave here. If you put such ideas into her head, you'll upset her. She becomes agitated when she's upset. You wouldn't want to upset her would you?"

"Of course not. I'm only thinking of Hester. I'm here for her."

"As we all are."

Emiline stood silent, wondering what in the world he meant by that remark.

"Well, then," he added, "do as I say."

Emiline thought of his words that had so alarmed her before. 'I'm afraid I'll have to ask you to leave.' The innuendo of those words was present again. 'Do as I say, or else,' hung unspoken in the tense silence. Emiline longed to respond—you don't have to ask me to leave, I quit. But that would mean leaving Hester to the mercy of these people and, what was worse, in the hands of this man. She was more determined than ever to somehow get Hester away from Cage Farm.

But she had to show him that she was not intimidated by him. "I'm surprised you haven't asked me to leave," she retorted.

"Hester likes you," he said. "You're doing a good job with her."

Since Emiline didn't know what to say to that, certainly not 'thank-you,' she turned once more from the darkness toward the blazing doorway. Blinded by the light, she stumbled and almost fell before righting herself with one hand against the door frame. All she could think was, 'He's wrong, he's totally totally wrong. What a horrid man.' As she walked, half ran, back to the house, she felt what was becoming a familiar anger with herself for submitting to another's control, for letting herself be manipulated in such a fashion. And as she stood in the dim light of her room and tore off her blouse, her skirt, kicked off her shoes, kicked the mess into a corner of the closet, vowing that she would never wear those clothes again, she felt the muscles of her face twisting. Throwing herself face down on the lumpy mattress, she felt her throat swell. She felt a sob rising up. But then a thought took hold. Hester could not help but be better off away from this place. The conversation that she had just had with Victor Cage reinforced her in this belief. She must rescue Hester. And soon. She would not be able to withstand the power of Victor Cage much longer.

chapter 10

"How am I going to tell her?" thought Lewis looking around the table at the faces lowered over their food. Victor, at the end closest to the window, his back to the wall, was leaner than Lewis remembered. His nose was more aquiline, the bridge of it thinner. Was it this that made him appear predatory? Victor's face had always had a hard edge. Even as a boy, even before the death of his father, he had not had a soft boy's face. The wide high cheekbones, the unyielding mouth, had given him a mature appearance even then, as if he had been born with experience.

Maggie, along with Victor, seemed lifted out of some mysterious gypsy camp. She was sitting directly across from Lewis, looking more than ever like a raven, her black hair shiny with its own oil, her black brows winging in one continuous undulation across her forehead, her eyes shining like black beads. When she had come into the house and seen him there, talking to her mother in the kitchen, her eyes had flashed like one lightning stroke across his face, but she had not spoken to him then or since.

Lewis was shocked that the younger generation of Cages looked so old. Not old, of course, but older. In his mind, they remained the kids he had grown up with, had seen every morning on the school bus, had sat with in rows at crude desks in that school room with a blizzard raging at the windows, all of them wondering how they were going to get home. Or, conversely, with a sun blazing through the glass, frying them like ants as they tried to memorize the multiplication tables or comprehend the Magna Carta. By the time Maggie started school he was nearly finished. What he remembered of her was a skinny, snotty-nosed urchin, haggard-faced even then. She always seemed to have a patch of impetigo on one cheek. Dane, he remembered better. He had taught Dane to read. Still, he had never gotten to know him. For one thing, there had been too great a difference in ages. But when he thought of it now, he regretted that in all the years, he had never cracked Maggie's defensive veneer, or inspired in Dane a confidence to surrender his shyness. And he had to admit, he had never tried. He had not cared.

Lewis shook himself out of his reveries of the past and back to the supper table. The thing was, the Cage kids were his contemporaries, give or take a few years. How could they be looking so weary, so resigned? And, yet, why should he be shocked and saddened? People did change. They grew up. Had he expected they would not change because they had stayed here where nothing ever changed, at least in his mind. But why shouldn't they change? He had changed. He wondered what they saw when they looked at him. The war had changed his face, but he always felt that, inside, he was the same person. Perhaps because of the strong values of his parents in that direction, he still believed in the fundamental goodness of people and that tolerance and understanding between human beings was the ultimate solution to peace. If people kept trying they might find these qualities still alive in the world. He believed in love. He acknowledged that he was an incurable romantic. Always was and always would be. It came to him now, though, that the war had changed him, that it had separated him even more firmly from reality. He wanted nothing to do with a world of confrontation, competition, strife, the world of commerce, custom or traffic. And while he had always had this predisposition, the war had intensified his feelings. Since the war, he had retreated even further into himself, into his books and intellect. Perhaps that was it, then. People did not change much on the inside. They only settled more firmly into who they always were. Perhaps the outside, too, was not so much a real change as a development into what was always there, waiting.

Well, one thing was obvious, the house had not changed. The windows were still small, the ceilings low, the furnishings dark. Whenever he had come here as a child with his father and, later, by himself, he had had the sensation of entering darkness.

This room had not changed. Along one wall was the same heavy sideboard with its dusty doilies and ornaments bought at Ladies' Aid rummage sales or the five and dime in town, before the death of Mr. Cage, Lewis supposed, a more normal, if not happier, time. The same wireless sat on the same shelf, the same pot-bellied stove to warm the room in winter stood in the corner. The same linoleum, nailed down where it had split, and along the edges so it would not curl, covered the rough plank floor. The old remembered wallpaper was still yellowed and curling back at the seams and along the baseboards. On the walls, the same cows grazed in the same pasture, the same three kittens played with the same ball of wool. He wondered at a Mrs. Cage who must have chosen these pictures thirty years ago. Where had she gotten them? Were they calendar pictures she had cut out and framed? He could scarcely envision her taking that action, sitting at a table in the dim light of a lantern earnestly cutting and fitting and pasting, taking the time out from work or sleep to try and add some beauty to a rough farm house. Looking at her now, it hardly seemed likely that she had ever had a sense of beauty or a sense of home other than as a shelter from weather and a roof under which to prepare food for men and children. And yet she had produced Hester. To Lewis it seemed a miracle, it spoke of something fundamental in the purpose of life—that this lovely creature sitting across from him had been issue of this old woman, that beauty had come out of this place.

"Do we call y' Doc yet?" Mrs. Cage spoke.

"Not yet."

"When'll that be then?"

"Be a while yet."

"Seems like it takes a long time to become a Doc."

"It does. Especially when a war gets in the middle."

"That war slowed a lotta people down."

Hester was seated between Maggie and Emiline. Lewis glanced in her direction as often as he dared. When he looked toward either Victor or Mrs. Cage, he managed to sweep his eyes up and across Hester's face. On the road here, he had felt as nervous as a boy calling on his first girl. There had been a tightness in his chest, coupled with an exhilaration of the spirit. And when he had first seen her, when he had gotten out of his truck and she and Emiline had been returning from their walk, and he had seen her face framed by her unbelievable golden hair, for one instant he had been transported beyond this world into a place where all existence was confirmed. Yes, the old feeling was still there. Irrational and hopeless as he knew his love to be, he supposed it would always be there, always part of him, no matter what other women he might meet, no matter whom he might end up with.

Hester, like the house, had remained unchanged. Her face might have been sculpted from white marble. Surely, if she suffered, as Emiline suggested she did, she would not bear such an unmarked countenance. It struck him that this was what Emiline wanted to destroy. If she was successful, Hester would, like other people, change and grow old.

"How am I going to tell Emiline that I can't be part of such a plan?" thought Lewis.

"I can't remember when you were here last." Mrs. Cage handed him a large bowl of potatoes to go a second round.

"That's what I'm trying to remember." Lewis passed the bowl on to Dane, who sat next to him, elbows on table, sleeves rolled up, thick lower arms darkly tanned. Dane spooned most of the potatoes onto his plate before passing it, in turn, on to Victor. "It's nearly two years since I was home."

"But you never come over that time." Mrs. Cage accused. She frowned with the effort of remembering. "I'm pretty sure of that. Have some more meat."

"No, I think you're right." As he lifted his arm to take the platter, his eyes brushed Emiline, who was sitting on Mrs. Cage's right. She kept her eyes down toward her plate, but he detected a controlled excitement in the rigid posture of her shoulders and her bent head. She would think that he was here to start her plan rolling when, conversely, the reason he had come was to tell her that he had reconsidered. He felt a significant burden of guilt.

After taking a small slice which he did not want, he passed the meat platter on to Dane. He had to take something, otherwise it would appear that he did not like their food. His eating habits had changed since he left home and he found it difficult, even sometimes in his parents' home, to eat in the manner which was expected of him. He also felt uncomfortable helping himself before the ladies, but this was the custom of the place. It would be thought odd to do otherwise, it would be futile to protest. "I can't remember when I was last here for a meal."

On his last few visits home, Lewis had tried to avoid mealtimes at Cage Farm. As the years had passed after the father's death, the Cages had become more of an island unto themselves. Since the war, they seemed to be uncomfortable with him, although he did not think the war had anything directly to do with it. Perhaps he had become more sensitive to the situation because he was more removed from it. Today, he sensed that he was interrupting something between family members, perhaps a disagreement, something unpleasant at any rate. Maybe they did not like having visitors. Perhaps visitors interfered with them in some way and did not allow them to be themselves. He had the distinct feeling that he had unwittingly stumbled into the middle of a situation, into a place where he was not supposed to be.

He considered that he might be the problem. The Cages might be uncomfortable with his city ways, with his educated ideas and language. The awkwardness, the constraint in the conversation, might be because they did not have subjects of discourse in common. Even farmers who wanted education for their own children sometimes felt odd and uncomfortable around educated people. It was sad and yet brave, that they encouraged their children to do the very thing that would drive a wedge between them.

Mrs. Cage's voice again rose above the taciturn silence of the others. "And how's your ma these days?"

She takes it a little easier than she used to, he almost said. Then he looked at Mrs. Cage. He had noticed earlier that she was more bent than he remembered her. When she brought the bowls of food to the table, she swayed more slowly on her bowed legs. Now he saw her stained and calloused hands, the fingernails jagged and dirty. He raised his eyes to her face, to her dark greying hair falling out of its pins. Her face had cuts so deep they looked like knife slashes, cuts around the eyes from holding it against the sun and the wind, around the mouth from holding it against disappointment and disaster. The mouth itself was like a short straight cut, so tight and grim was it set. As a child, he had been a little frightened of her. She was always so grumpy, he had felt that he'd done something wrong. But when he was older, he learned that she never smiled at anybody.

He would not mention that his mother got her hair done in Camrose once a week and went shopping in Edmonton once a month. Or that she and his father, when in Edmonton, always went to the Dairy Lunch for supper because his mother loved the strawberry shortcake they served there.

"Busy in her garden as usual," he answered.

"A garden does keep y' busy."

"We don't have as big a one as we used to. Not like yours. And Millie does most of it now with the vegetables. But Mom likes to take care of the flowers." Damn, he thought, I shouldn't've said that about Millie.

"I remember that, how she always loved the flowers. Even in with her vegetables, she always had flowers."

"She still likes trying different ones. She can hardly wait for the seed catalogues to arrive in the spring. Dad keeps telling her she may as well throw her money down the well. She orders plants that don't have a chance in this climate." There I go again, he thought. Mrs. Cage could never squander money like that.

"She always was that way."

"One year she tried to grow hydrangea outside. She got it to grow all right, but a poor stunted thing it was. She was so disappointed when it didn't look like the picture in the catalogue."

"They fool you with them pictures, all right." And, after a pause, "There might be some place on earth where it grows like that."

Lewis did not expect the men to do much talking. It was the busy season. They ate quickly and heartily. When they were full, if they had a few minutes to spare, they would push back their chairs and talk about the weather, the crops, or the latest machine to break down and need expensive parts. But why the devil didn't Emiline pitch in and do her share? There she sat, silent, almost demure, as she kept her eyes down and flicked about bits of food on her plate with an indifferent fork. It was her fault that he was in this deplorable situation of being two-faced with people he had known all his life. Lewis was torn between guilt that he must disappoint her and annoyance that she had dragged him into this dismal morass. He felt a great sense of relief that he had come to his senses in time, nothing irrevocable had yet been done, but he was dismayed that he had let himself come so close to being used by her to further her scheme. Every time he thought of Hester being anywhere but Cage Farm, and in particular being at Thorncliffe Heights, entering his space there, disturbing his routine and requirements, he felt a shock of disbelief.

In the interval since Emiline had told him of her plan, his thoughts had been swinging first one way, then the other. At times he thought, what harm can it do? Other times, he thought, flatly—no. No. It would be too upsetting for Hester. It would be too startling for all concerned. What would his parents think? do? say? His mother would feel that some fine point of etiquette was being breached, that thirty years of neighbourly relations with the Cages was in jeopardy. His father would think it odd. It was the oddness of the proposal that struck him. Hester had not set foot off Cage Farm for twenty years. Would not the heavens open, the thunder roar, the lightning flash? Then his rational mind would take over once again and he would think, what, after all, can possibly happen? If Hester became disoriented or in any way confused, he would simply take her back to Cage Farm immediately in the car. Things would progress slowly. Nothing would happen quickly. Hester and Emiline were to walk over. If, on the walk, Hester became disturbed, Emiline would simply turn around and take her back. If things went well, they would have a cup of tea, he would run them home. What could be more simple than that?

What more world-shattering?

He had grown so tired of thinking about the situation that he had determinedly put it out of his mind and forced himself to spend more hours every day on his dissertation. When he could sit no longer, he went outside and helped his mother in the garden, his father in the barn and fields. Still, he couldn't sleep. He would wake at three in the morning and wonder if, in years to come, he would regret not trying to do what he could to help Hester? On the other hand, would he be sorry for his part in disrupting people's lives? Maybe things were better left as they were. But what if Emiline was right? What if Hester was a person of normal intelligence whose intelligence was being retarded and distorted because of the life she was leading, forced or otherwise, on Cage Farm?

He would get up and start working on his added chapter, forcing himself to focus on the material before his eyes.

When he did sleep, his subconscious was still busy with the problem. He woke tired and with another slant on the situation, another determined decision which would become vague by breakfast and by noon would have disappeared into an opposite resolution.

This vacillation went on for two weeks. The first part of the plan, bringing Hester over to Thorncliffe Heights for a visit, was absurd enough, but the long-range plan was totally outside the realm of reason. You can't just snatch a child away from the only home she has ever known and plop her down some place in a large city, he would tell himself. That Emiline refused to believe that Hester was like a child was immaterial. The fact was, no one knew what she was like or what was in her mind.

And so, before coming over today, he had decided once and for all that he would not be a part of Emiline's folly. He must somehow contrive to be alone with her after supper so that he could tell her this. Leave things alone, he meant to tell her. Leave things as they should be. Things may not be perfect at Cage Farm, but then what is perfect? People cope somehow. Somehow people put up with their lives.

While thinking these thoughts, unaware of what he was doing, unmindful of the others, Lewis stared across the table at Hester. Her face was quiet, remote, removed. She doesn't belong to time, he thought. She is like a work of art. No—he told himself sternly, I must try and see her with less imagination. I must try and see the truth.

Hester did not seem to be part of the prickly atmosphere, but although she was outside of it, she absorbed the ugliness and unhappiness of her family, their despair and all that was mean and unpleasant in their lives. She was a vessel for it and yet remained innocent and good. It struck Lewis how, even if it was being done unconsciously, her life was being sacrificed so that the others could exist as a unit. He understood then what Emiline had been talking about. But Emiline was concerned about Hester's mental health, her potential for growth and development, for living an independent fulfilling existence, what might be called the practical aspect of the situation. While Lewis also appreciated that aspect, his eyes now were opened more fully and he saw that a sort of evil was at work here. Hester was being used in a quite horrendous way. Of course, people who live together, people in close relationships, did use each other. Perhaps because of the interaction in such connections some degree of symbiosis was inevitable. But there should be limits. There should be limits to what was acceptable to transfer onto a child, or a childlike person. Lewis had a revelation. Or seemed to. What was happening here was not acceptable. Hester was the centre of Cage Farm. She held it together. But in order to do this she must remain forever in the role in which she had been cast, accidentally or otherwise, the role of the child who must be cared for and provided for. She must remain forever a sleeping beauty. If she woke up, if she grew up, if she left, Cage Farm would be destroyed. But if Hester was the vessel into which all the issues and frustrations of the other family members were deposited so that the family could remain intact, then it should not remain intact. If Hester was the sacrifice necessary to hold the family together then it was not right that it be held together.

Thus Lewis understood that Emiline was right after all. They must take Hester away from here. They must take her into a different life. He must agree with Emiline's plan.

Lewis felt his left arm jostled. Dane had come up for air. He had wiped his mouth on the sleeve of his shirt and had pushed back his chair. Victor, too, had finished eating. He was leaning forward, elbows on the table, chewing on a toothpick. He was saying something about the weather, asking about the McFadden haying operations. "Your dad was telling me the other day that he's just about finished farming," he said.

"He does seem to be leaving more and more of it to Al."

"Said he's thinking of retiring permanent to Arizona."

Lewis was shocked. While his father had been talking this way for years, Lewis had never taken his remarks seriously. But if he was making public statements—where? in the beer parlour? at the Co-op? It struck him. What if he could no longer come home? What if Thorncliffe Heights no longer existed for him? He was shocked to think that people other than McFaddens might live in the house that his father had built. What if the place where nothing ever changed, changed, completely and forever?

"He *is* seventy-five this year," Lewis said, his voice sounding hollow to his ears.

"I told him if he's interested in selling off some of his land to let me know. After last year's crop I might be able to swing something." Victor stood up. "Gotta take advantage of these long evenings," he said with a nod. Dane and Maggie followed.

Mrs. Cage started to clean up the kitchen. "Tell your ma to come over and visit me," she said, her words friendly but her tone hostile.

Why don't you come over and visit her? he started to say. He looked at her standing amongst piles of pots and pans littering the stove, towers of dishes leaning haphazardly on counter and table, limp clothing hanging on racks and lines above the stove. Soon the men would return with pails of milk to be dealt with. The words stuck in his throat.

"I will," he said. "I certainly will."

Lewis stepped out into the air of a balmy July evening. He breathed in deeply, as though trying to clear his lungs. Things will change, he thought. Whether I want them to or not. He looked about. The road was there and beyond it wheat fields shimmering in a low sun. Above, an airplane glinted silver in a sky the colour of a robin's egg. Beyond this farm, he thought, beyond this place was a town, beyond that a city, beyond that the world. There is life out there, he thought. I must get back to it. I'll do this thing, and then I'll get the hell out of here. I can finish my dissertation in Toronto.

Hopping up into the truck, he circled round until he was out on the road. He drove slowly, waiting a respectful interval, before gearing up and raising the dust in his haste to get away. From what, he was not sure.

chapter 11

For two weeks, Emiline had despaired of Lewis. After their talk she had waited, expecting him daily. Every evening, her hope defeated, her expectation crushed, she brushed out her hair, rubbed cold cream on her face, visited the outhouse one last time and washed her hands in a scoop of cold water at the basin, all the time wondering whatever could be the matter. "What is he doing?!" she screeched frantically to herself. I'll walk over to Thorncliffe Heights tomorrow, she vowed more than once. But, then, in the morning she would think, one more day, I'll give him one more day. For what could she say to him? She supposed she could niggle and nag him but she could not force him to help her. If he did not show up soon she would have to think of another way of easing Hester away from Cage Farm.

And then he had appeared. He had stayed for supper. Was it only yesterday? But there was something about the way he chatted with Mrs. Cage, the way he was at ease, that she found worrisome. He seemed to be on their side! Of course, he was on their side. He had known them all his life, he had known her for three months. The meal was not unpleasant, as meals at Cage Farm went. He would go away confirmed in his belief that the best place for Hester was with her family. From the dining room window, she had watched his truck round the corner at the end of the lane and disappear in a dust cloud.

But he had returned. Was it only this morning? She and Hester were sitting over lessons at the table when the McFadden station wagon drove into the yard. It was a fine day and the crew was off haying. It turned out that Lewis knew they would be, he had passed them in the fields. In his hands were several empty flats for eggs. He came into the house, called out a greeting, spoke to Mrs. Cage in the kitchen. She trundled off, out the back door and across the barn yard, flats in hand. After a moment, he stuck his head through the doorway.

He looked at her, then at Hester, then back to her, his dark eyes piercing, the fine lines either side his mouth creasing as his lips lengthened into a grim line. "I think we should do this quickly," he said. "I'll expect you this afternoon."

He went back outside and followed Mrs. Cage's path to the henhouse. Emiline sat very still, watching the henhouse door. After some minutes, Mrs. Cage emerged from the slant-roofed shack, followed by Lewis holding up in his hands full flats. They came back across the yard, stopped at the wagon, spoke a moment. Lewis set the eggs down carefully on the passenger seat, rounded the front of the car to the driver's side, got in, and with a wave to Mrs. Cage was off. Emiline breathed out.

For the next four hours she worried and fretted. She scolded herself—this is what you wanted, don't be feeble-minded, what's wrong with you? For two weeks, since discussing her plan with Lewis and seeking permission from Victor for the first step, she had been preparing Hester to make the leap into another world. Gradually, day by day, she had been leading Hester farther from Cage Farm. Along the roadway, across the open fields, daily their walks covered new territory, expanding the potential for further exploration. Emiline paid particular attention to the pasture between Cage Farm and Thorncliffe Heights. Leaving the road, she would step through the tall grass and weeds of the ditch, bend through the barbed wire, then turn to help Hester, who followed her without persuasion. They would amble, skirting herds of dairy cattle, stopping to pick flowers or to pet cows. Hester especially loved the square hard heads of the calves, grown quite large now in midsummer. Scratching the curly hair between their ears, she let them eat the bluebells and daisies in her hand. She smiled at the touch of their soft muzzles. Turning herself in circles, arms outstretched, she danced across the rough terrain, floated to a stop and bent to scoop up another handful of flowers.

Is this what freedom does? wondered Emiline.

She knew that Hester would change when she was in her new life. Of course, she hoped that she would learn or relearn how to speak. But even if she did not, Emiline was sure that she would somehow take her place in the regular world. She would have opinions, make choices, and in time become a healthy person. Oh, it would require much hard work before she could function as a normal human being, but Emiline looked forward to that effort. She envisioned the future, she and Hester in some cozy little apartment somewhere, she with a job teaching at a school, Hester possibly finding some employment. But it did not matter whether or not she did, Emiline would earn enough to keep both of them in simple accommodations. She envisioned the scene, Hester's golden head bent in the evening lamplight over some handwork, embroidery perhaps, while she sat in the other large soft chair, reading or marking papers. The main thing was, they would be in a bright cheerful place, out of the bog, out of the darkness. Together. She and Hester would be together.

Today's plan should work, thought Emiline, slipping her legs into a pair of slacks. She had gone to her room directly from the dinner table, which was not an unusual procedure, she assured herself. She knew that she must not do anything different. She must not show her excitement or otherwise arouse suspicion. She must not upset Hester. The only difference between today and other days would be that today they would end up at Thorncliffe Heights. Emiline would plead thirst. She would explain to Hester that she was going to knock on the door of this house and ask for a drink of water. She would tell her that this was where Lewis lived. Hester had remembered Lewis when he had come for supper. He would greet them at the door. He would ask them in. Nothing must appear out of the ordinary to Hester. Nothing must happen unexpectedly or too quickly. No sudden change must cause apprehension, fear, stubbornness. If everything was accomplished gradually, if everything was kept calm and serene, then success should follow.

What could possibly happen? thought Emiline. Nothing could go wrong. Unless Hester would not go into a strange house. She'll follow me in, decided Emiline as she buttoned her shirt. Hester trusts me implicitly. She was surprised to find that her hands were trembling and that she had trouble with the buttons.

She had not had to face Victor over the noon meal because Maggie had taken a lunch out to the field for the men. This seemed like a good omen for the project, for how she would have sat through a dinner with Victor Cage without revealing something, she did not know. The night that Lewis had come for supper had been ordeal enough. Though she had been careful not to look at him, she had found it exceedingly difficult to act in a typical manner, and Victor was very sharp-eyed. But, she assured herself, so far she had done nothing that could be construed as wrong. So far, all she had done was take Hester for walks along the road and into a neighbouring pasture, for which she had been given permission. Today, at supper, she would report to Victor that they had been close to Thorncliffe Heights, had gone into the house for a moment, had been asked to stay to tea. Would he wonder at the coincidence of this happening so soon after Lewis was at Cage Farm?

Tucking the tails of her shirt inside her slacks, she zippered them up and glanced quickly into the dresser mirror. Her eyes were glowing with excitement. If Victor had come in for dinner, he would have known that something was up. Anyone looking at her would know. I must get a grip on myself, she instructed those bright eyes. Hester was so sensitive to other people's moods, to the very atmosphere around her. But, something *is* up! she silently exulted. Today she was going to lead Hester to liberty. This is only the first of several steps, she reminded herself. Still, it was always the first step which seemed the most monumental. If things worked out satisfactorily today, then the rest of the plan might become a reality. Today would be the beginning of the end. The beginning of the end of darkness, the beginning of the struggle out of the shadows into the light, the beginning of the reassuring appearance of the normal right world.

They stepped out, closing the door softly behind them. Emiline took Hester's hand, although there was no longer any need to do so. Hester scarcely hesitated now at the boundary. Emiline thought how far she had come, how the obstacles between Cage Farm and the outside world were gradually falling away. All it took was patience and understanding, Emiline assured herself. There was hope for the future.

They walked along the dirt road a piece, then Emiline tugged at Hester's hand and led her off through the pasture. The somnolent cows, grazing peacefully on a warm, lazy July afternoon, looked up with only mild interest as they passed. Hester wanted to stop to touch them but Emiline pulled her onward. When Hester held back, Emiline had to resort to playing a game of tag in which she ran forward, calling to Hester to catch her. Hester easily fell into this ruse and, in this way, they reached the barbed wire fence that separated the pasture from the road. They climbed through more barbed wire

into the McFadden field, which they then had to cross
to get to the house. It was in the middle of this field that
Hester started to lag. She seemed to plod rather than
float, and when she bent to go through the final fence
she did not lower her head sufficiently. A long loop of her
hair became entangled in the wire. Emiline knelt in the
rough grass beside her, attempting to unknot the strand
of hair. Hester's nose turned pink at the edges and she
blinked rapidly as though her eyes were smarting. Emiline
worried that maybe this had been too big a leap for one
day. She undid the last of the tangle, pulled Hester gently
to her feet, squeezed her arm. "We're nearly there," she
smiled, hoping that Hester would not sense her anxiety.

They followed a path through the stand of aspen
poplar just north of the house and stepped into the
clearing. Emiline drew in her breath. She had not been
at Thorncliffe Heights for a while and was not prepared
for the effusion of colour which exploded in her face. The
grass was emerald green, the rail fences looked as though
they had been newly whitewashed. Flowerbeds near the
house and along the edges of a red cinder path sprang
out of the soft black soil. Sweet peas climbed the fences,
purple and yellow irises stood tall and majestic, orange
and yellow and red poppies waved in bright patches,
trollius bobbed its butterball head, grape hyacinth
clustered. Across from the house were barn and sheds,
newly painted a brilliant red with white trim. In a fenced
area near the barn two horses were grazing, their long
necks bent gracefully to the lush grass. And the smells!
flowers, freshly turned earth, new-mown hay, and from

somewhere, a scent like honey. And the sounds! robins, meadowlarks, bees droning.

Is this paradise? wondered Emiline. Or is it just that it's so different from Cage Farm as to appear so?

Emiline turned to catch Hester's reaction, but she was busy combing her hair with her fingers, rummaging through the strands that had caught in the wire. They climbed the step up to the back door. Emiline knocked. Through the screen, they could hear the sound echo inside the house. They could see Lewis, a dark shape coming toward them.

Then came the moment of entering a strange house. Would she or wouldn't she?

Emiline went first. Inside, she turned. She looked across the threshold at Hester. She smiled. She held out her hand. Hester, like a trusting child, took the hand. She took a step forward. And another. Thus, it was accomplished. Hester had a roof over her head other than that of Cage Farm for the first time in twenty years.

Lewis led the way through the back entrance, a large mud room where the men could shed their dirty greasy clothing and boots before entering the house proper. Its walls were lined with shelves and cupboards filled with a variety of items such as canned goods and discarded clothing to be used as rags. Hester moved slowly through this room and into the kitchen. Emiline directed her toward a chair. She sat down. She put her hands in her lap. Then she saw the little postman.

"Do you think it's wise to let her play with that ornament?"

Both Lewis and Emiline were leaning forward as though ready to leap into action.

"I suppose not."

"It's your mother's pride and joy."

"I don't like to take it away from her."

"She does seem to be holding it carefully."

From a shelf beside her chair, Hester had picked up a small porcelain figurine—a boy postman carrying a bag of letters, holding up a special one stamped with a red heart. It was a Hummel. Mrs. McFadden had shown Emiline her collection during a past visit. The figurine was expensive but, even more importantly, it was precious to Lewis's mother.

Emiline realized that they were both watching Hester too closely, as though she was an experimental specimen. She turned to Lewis. "How's the dissertation coming?" she asked before thinking. She knew he did not like that topic. "Don't answer," she followed quickly. "But let's talk about something. Let's try and be natural."

"Yes," he said, lowering himself onto the edge of a chair. But he didn't seem able to think of anything else to talk about, either. "Fine," he said. "It's coming along fine. Actually," he said, "a few more weeks and I'll be going back to Toronto."

Emiline felt a sharp drop in her spirit. She turned her head quickly toward him. His eyes were still on Hester. "Wonderful," she said. "Wonderful."

What would the country be like without Lewis? She could not even imagine it. I couldn't stay here without him, she thought. She suddenly knew the truth of her thought. This place would be too entirely oppressive without Lewis. She must work quickly. She must have herself and Hester away from Cage Farm before Lewis was gone.

Hester was holding the boy in both hands, running the fleshy part of her thumb across the letter bag, her index and middle finger across the top of the boy's hat. She seemed to find delight in the smooth texture of the porcelain.

"How about a drink of something?" The question seemed a sudden inspiration. Lewis turned to the refrigerator. "We seem to have some punch here, coloured water at any rate."

Hester ignored the proffered cup. She seemed to have lapsed into a reverie concerning the figurine. Looking down at the little boy postman in her lap, her face reflected an inner drama which she alone could see, she alone could hear. Then, quite suddenly, she laid it aside.

"Isn't this lovely," Emiline said, breathing out, looking around the bright room. "Isn't this lovely," she repeated. She could scarcely believe they had made it this far.

They heard someone at the back door. Emiline and Lewis looked at each other. It was Mr. McFadden. Lewis had told his mother the plan, or at least the part of it that involved the social education of Hester by having the two young women drop in for a short visit. He had suggested to her that for this first time Hester might feel more comfortable if no one but himself was around. He had not thought to warn his father of the visitor and of the special conditions as, usually, Mr. McFadden did not come into the house this time of day in the summer. But today he did. He stuck his head around the door frame to say hello. "Hello," said Emiline. She turned to Hester to see her reaction to this newcomer. But Hester had stood up and moved to the cupboards. She picked up a small jar of something. She set it down. By turns, she picked up a biscuit tin, a wooden spoon, a salt shaker. She looked at each briefly and set it down. She walked, a sideways dancing movement, to the windows at the far end of the room. Again, she combed her hair with her fingers. She looked up at the ceiling and around at the walls.

Other than that, the visit went well.

"It went well," she said to Lewis when they were in the station wagon returning to Cage Farm. "All things considered."

"Yes," replied Lewis.

"Except maybe for that bit when your father came in. I've never seen her act quite that way before, I mean so sort of out of it. But what can you expect? when you consider this is the first time she's been anywhere different, almost the first time she's seen anyone different, in all these years. At least it wasn't a disaster."

"No," said Lewis.

"Did you have a good time?" Emiline turned to Hester who was in the back seat, looking out the side window. A little frown creased her brow. Emiline thought how it was like puckers in satin.

Emiline continued to be in an excellent mood for the remainder of the afternoon. Hester went to her room, presumably to rest. Emiline helped Mrs. Cage in the kitchen, the older woman having evolved to the point of letting the younger woman set the table and put food into bowls. The men came in for supper and she related the adventures of the day. "We were parched and we were so close to Thorncliffe Heights we thought to stop in for a drink of water and got invited for tea," remembering only as she spoke that they had not had tea.

Victor said nothing, only watched her face. She was careful to modulate her expression and be as nonchalant as possible. She thought she had brought it off and felt the satisfaction of successful achievement. Hester had not appeared to feel uncomfortable in a different house. She had become a little restless toward the end but, overall, had passed the test with flying colours. Yes, Hester would do just fine. There was nothing 'wrong' with Hester.

Across the road, across the fields, the McFaddens were also dining. They sat in a closed-in porch off the kitchen at the north end of the verandah. It was a lovely light and airy space. Mrs. McFadden had filled it with green plants and white wicker furnishings. A bright cloth covered the table. Supper was cold roast beef and potato salad. For several minutes the three ate in silence, looking out to a splendid view of the river valley.

"There's something strange about that girl," said Mr. McFadden, taking a piece of Millie's freshly baked bread and applying to it a thick slab of home-churned cold butter.

"Well, of course, she is odd. She doesn't speak," said Mrs. McFadden.

"Odd?" Lewis felt a sudden chill in spite of the warmth of the evening. "In what way, odd?"

"It's her clothes," said Mrs. McFadden. "I wish they'd find her something to wear besides those drapey curtainy things. Why don't they get her some modern clothes?"

"Not Hester. The other one. Emiline."

"Emiline?" Lewis was startled.

Mrs. McFadden, two little lines in her forehead, looked at her husband.

"She's changed. Since she came here. I always thought she was ignorant of the way things are done here, but I gave her credit for being sensible. I thought she had her head pretty squarely on her shoulders, but now I'm beginning to wonder. What's she doing traipsing around the country with that crazy girl?"

"Mac!"

"All right, all right. What do we call people like that now? Handicapped or some damn thing? Anyway, she should be at home where she belongs. It's only going to upset her, dragging her over here. What kind of a fool thing is that? Where everything's strange for her. It's too much for her to cope with. There," he turned to his wife. "Do you like that word? Cope. Part of the new psychological jargon."

Lewis was silent. We haven't done anything definite yet, he thought.

"I really must try and grow camellias next year," said Mrs. McFadden in a light voice. She was looking out the window. "In that bed by the fence. You'll have to bring in some manure, but that soil is good, it's been well worked. As long as they can stand the wind. I must ask Millie what she thinks."

When Emiline was undressing for bed, she found a folded paper in the pocket of her slacks. She brought it out and unfolded it. 'Dear Emmy,' it read. 'Italy was absolutely totally unqualifiably marvellous. You'll never guess what happened …' Emiline remembered then that she had stuffed Vera's latest letter into her pocket. When? When had she last worn these slacks? She could not remember.

chapter 12

Emmy: Are you out there? Where are you? Please answer this letter, if only a line to say you're all right ...

Emiline took Vera's letter firmly in two hands and tore it directly across. She then placed the two pieces one on top the other and tore again. She took these four pieces, turned them at a right angle, and tore again. Then she dropped all eight pieces into the stove where they immediately flared up. She clanked the stove lid back into place. She was very angry with Vera. She could not ever remember being angry with Vera before but Vera was interfering with her life, trying to tell her what to do. Vera's letters were altogether inappropriate. She, Emiline, was a grown-up woman capable of making her own decisions. She was sick and tired of these letters from Vera trying to get her to return to Toronto, trying to separate her from Hester. Never, never would she leave Hester and that was all there was to it. With Hester she could forget about Toronto. She had forgotten about Bradley, except when Vera's letters came and she was reminded all over again. And Vera had written more frequently these last few weeks, since she had returned from her trip, writing more frequently and demanding responses. There was something about a Ralph, something about a ring. Well, she, Emiline, had more important things to think about than answering gossipy letters to Vera.

It was the end of August, the fields were brown, and Emiline was pleased with herself. Hester had now been to Thorncliffe Heights on several occasions and seemed able to tolerate the new surroundings and to enjoy the visits. While Emiline could never be sure what was going through that estranged enclosed mind, the last time they had been there, Hester seemed to know the way. She kept her head low when she ducked through the fence, as though remembering the first time when she had caught her hair. She was able to tolerate a fourth person in the group. Mrs. McFadden usually joined them at some point during the afternoon.

They assembled in the living room. Hester sat in a corner of the sofa, having been directed there by Emiline, looking down at her hands in her lap, smiling occasionally, on the whole agreeable and well-mannered. The lapses in decorum which arose were simply due to ignorance in such matters, not surprising, Emiline and Lewis assured each other, when you considered that Hester had never been exposed to social occasions.

On the second visit, Hester accepted the cup of tea brought in by Mrs. McFadden. Emiline sat on the edge of a nearby chair, afraid that Hester might spill the tea on the sprightly upholstery fabric. Finally, unable to endure the suspense any longer, she took the tea from Hester's hands and set it on the end table near her elbow. When Mrs. McFadden passed the cream and sugar, Hester poured in a great dollop of cream and then, to Emiline's horror, picked up the handle of the sugar bowl and poured sugar into her tea in a like manner. She then, rather primly, set the sugar bowl back into the serving tray and proceeded to drink down her tea at one gulp, holding the cup in both hands as she did so. On the third visit they discovered that she very much liked canned apple juice, a luxury unknown at Cage Farm.

Another time, Mrs. McFadden served jello, thinking Hester might like the sweet treat, much like the apple juice. They watched to see her reaction. Did she sense that she was the centre of attention? Her face took on a look of childish mischief, then quick as a wink her hand darted forth into the jello which she squished through her fingers.

Lewis stretched out his hands as though to stop her, but they did not reach far enough. Emiline jumped up and Mrs. McFadden rushed to get a towel. Emiline heard Lewis behind her laugh a false nervous laugh.

"That's all right dear. It's all right," Emiline repeated senselessly as she mopped up Hester's hands and removed the bowl of jello.

"It could happen to anybody," said Mrs. McFadden, hovering. "Anybody who's never had jello before. After all, how is she supposed to know what to do with it? It looks solid enough."

"She does have ... not strange ... but *different* reactions to many things," Emiline admitted to Lewis when they had a chance to discuss the matter in private.

"But how could it be otherwise," agreed Lewis. "She hasn't had experience with these things."

"Like one of those children lost in the jungle and raised by apes. She'll learn," Emiline was emphatic on this point. "With education and socialization, she'll learn."

One matter which did concern Emiline was that Hester did not seem to notice that Thorncliffe Heights was a nicer place than Cage Farm. Education, she decided, when she mulled over the problem, depended upon discernment of difference. Without such discrimination, no matter where she might take her, Hester would still mentally be at Cage Farm. Without such discrimination, Hester would always remain a prisoner. Perhaps she does notice the difference, ruminated Emiline. Just because she doesn't react or show anything doesn't mean she doesn't notice. What did she expect Hester to do? Jump up and down with glee? Clap her hands? No, but perhaps she had thought that Hester would be impressed, would show delight, would want to stay in the nice place.

She also found it disturbing when Hester became restless, the signal to return her to Cage Farm. An hour or two into each visit, Hester would get up from her chair and wander through the room. She fluttered from window to window, batting herself softly against the glass like an imprisoned moth. At times her actions seemed stirred simply by an aimless restlessness, but other times her discomfort built into an intense agitation. Her slight body would seem suddenly heavy with the force of its own concentrated intensity, so that the very air in the room became strained.

Was it something in the surroundings? in the people? in the situation? This was a mystery that must be solved. If she was going to take Hester away from Cage Farm, it would be necessary to have a place in which she was comfortable for more than an hour. Perhaps Thorncliffe Heights was too orderly, too bright and attractive. The ceilings were high, the windows sparkled with Millie's elbow grease, the curtains were light and airy, the hardwood gleamed. The house smelled of flowers picked from the beds so faithfully nurtured. Was it possible that Hester was so used to Cage Farm that anything on a higher scale caused her discomfort? Could even a dark pit such as Cage Farm become a comfort zone if reinforced by habit? Well, she, Emiline, would just have to get Hester into the habit of a better existence, for how could she know what she had not experienced? How could she know about taking tea in china cups with little spoons in the saucers? Or that when people served dainty cookies on a silver tray, you were supposed to take only one? How could she know not to shrink from good manners, or squirm beneath graciousness, or be confused by kindness?

In time, Emiline assured herself, Hester would respond to love and kindness. Once she experienced love, rather than exploitative, dictatorial possession, she would prefer love. Once away from relationships that confine and smother, that consider not the person but only the significance of that person in the lives of others, she would blossom and grow. Meanwhile, things were proceeding as planned.

Another worry was that Victor was not protesting. Was he becoming more tolerant? Or was he simply too busy right now with the field work? Maybe he did not consider the situation to be threatening. After all, Hester was merely visiting the neighbours. Perhaps there was no reason she had not done so before, except that the occasion and opportunity had not presented itself. Or they may have thought she wouldn't be able to handle it, just as they thought she would not like going to town. The Cages were not the sort of people who believed in stimulation of the mind as an aid in learning. To them, education was about memorizing multiplication tables. It was not about innovative thoughts or excitement over an idea.

But there were times when Emiline intercepted a look from Victor. One afternoon when she and Hester were leaving the house, he was walking across the yard from the barn. The expression on his face seemed one of indulgent disdain. He might have been saying, I know what you're up to but it doesn't matter, go ahead and have your fun, I'll put a stop to it when I think necessary. Perhaps he was curious to see how far she would go. Perhaps he was giving her the rope to hang herself.

But, as with Hester, she could not be sure what he was thinking. For all she knew, he may not have a thought in his head about the visits to Thorncliffe Heights. Perhaps he was occupied with thoughts of harvesting, broken-down machinery, or that subject dear to the hearts of all farmers, the weather. Her curiosity as to what was in his mind teased her to such a degree that for several days she had been in a state of constant agitation.

Her nerves were on edge, her muscles poised to act, her tongue ready to leap. So that after she watched Vera's latest letter flare, after she settled back the stove lid, when she heard the back door open and close and turned to see Victor's shape filling the doorway, words sprang from her mouth without any preconceived intention on the part of her brain.

"What do you think of Hester's visits to Thorncliffe Heights? She seems to like socializing." Her voice sounded high and hollow and false in the still room.

He looked at her across the water dipper. She detected amusement, a sardonic glint in his eye. She could smell him, she could have reached out her hand and touched him. Suddenly, the shadowy kitchen seemed intensely warm.

"Is that your fancy expression for visiting the neighbours?" he said.

"Well, she *is* learning something." Careful, Emiline instructed herself. Don't sound defensive. At least she had managed to bring her voice under control, lowering it, steadying it.

"Is it a necessary thing for her to learn?" Victor dropped the dipper into the bucket and wiped his mouth on the back of his hand. His lips looked red, fresh from the cold water. His black hair was longer than usual, his face was brown from the sun and black where he had not shaved, his skin glistened with perspiration. He stood

large, square to her, his hands in loose fists on his hip
bones.

"People are social beings."

"Some are, some aren't."

"It gives her some stimulation. I believe that's what
she needs, more stimulation. They've done studies which
prove that infants who receive little stimulation don't
develop normally."

"Are you sure you're thinking of her?" She thought
his eyes flicked down and up.

"What do you mean?"

"Maybe you're thinking of yourself."

"Why would you say that?"

"Maybe she's not the only one getting stimulated."
He grinned.

She wanted to strike him, to beat her fists against
him. It took a supreme effort of control for her to say, in a
calm level voice, "I suppose that's the sort of remark one
might expect coming from ..." Oh, how she wanted to
say, uneducated country bumpkin. "... one who doesn't
understand the educational process."

"Oh, one understands all right." His voice was light,
but his words were spoken not as one stating an opinion
but as one stating the truth. "One understands that
education is control. You like having control of people.
Teachers are like that. That's why they become teachers.
They like to have control of other people's minds."

Emiline was aghast. The man suffered from delusions.
He was transferring his own obsession with control and
power to her.

Suddenly his large black shape came at her. It seemed it would crush her with its weight and density. She jumped and moved to one side. But he sauntered past her and went to a kitchen cupboard where he took down a thermos. "You don't have to apologize for it. That's simply the way teachers are."

She was revealing too much, her fear, her discomfort. She forced herself to be sensible. "Perhaps a teacher does have some influence on a student, but I'm not exploiting that. I haven't tried to change Hester, that is, her basic self, who she is. Just the opposite. I encourage her to be herself, to develop her potential. Why would I want to change her? She's a wonderful magical person the way she is."

"Maybe you're trying to make her more like you." He went to the side of the stove and lifted the blue enamel coffee pot which was sitting on the reservoir.

"I wouldn't want her to be like me. And, even if I did, given the circumstances, I don't see how that could be accomplished."

"It could be accomplished," Victor emphasized the word, "by trying to take her out of her life and put her into yours."

"That's nonsense." I'm trying to take her out of this hellhole, if that's what you mean, she thought but pressed her lips tightly together.

"Anyway, it won't work. These visits to Thorncliffe Heights, they won't change her."

That's why he agrees to them, thought Emiline. He thinks they don't matter. She wanted to tell him that they did matter, that Hester was already changing. Be careful, she instructed herself. That's not what he wants to hear. "She's coming out of herself a bit," she said, "she's responding to other people. You must agree, that's a good thing."

"Maybe. But she won't really change. She's who she is."

"She wasn't born this way."

"She always kept pretty much inside herself. The old man killing himself brought it out, that's all, made her more the way she had a bent to go in the first place."

Emiline did not have an answer to that. She had not been present those many years ago to know whether or not Victor was right. What if he *was* right?

"That's why she belongs here. I told you that before. She's part of Cage Farm." Victor's voice had lowered. It was very quiet. It sounded serious. It sounded dangerous. He was pouring coffee into the thermos, seeming to be concentrating on the stream of brown liquid.

To Emiline his voice implied, 'she's part of me.' Was it his confidence in his ownership that so incensed her? Still, she was able to keep her voice low and measured. "That's insane."

"So anyone who thinks different from you is insane."

"No one belongs to a place or to another person. At least they shouldn't. And you accuse *me* of being controlling."

Victor set down the coffee pot. He screwed the lid onto the thermos. "It's circumstance," he said. "Circumstance controls things."

"Only to a certain extent. People do move, in case you haven't noticed. They change their circumstances. Often they thrive in another place, under different conditions. It's not unreasonable for people to try and better themselves in this life. Most people do. How about the immigrants who came to this country? Your folks? Didn't they try and make a new life in moving from one place to another? Change their circumstance?"

"That's different."

"I don't see how."

"People who immigrated came because of the way they were, their natures. They were only developing their story, not changing it."

"You and your stories. How do you know so much about stories?"

"Oh, even I went to school. We had quite a good little school. It all depends on the teacher. Mrs. McFadden tried to drum some literature into my thick skull. She got me through matriculation. She was pretty good. Days I could get away she gave me extra time. It was like having a private tutor."

"Well, then, you should know, life is not a story."

"That's where you're wrong. There's always a story. The way I see it, it's our job to recognize our story and then develop it the way it needs to go. It's not our job to interfere with it and twist it into the shape we want it to be."

I think you're quite mad, Emiline just about said. "I think you're quite mistaken," she said instead. "We are free to choose whatever story we wish."

"Put it this way. I'm a person who recognizes necessity. You're a person who would change Othello into a happy ending."

Emiline was surprised. Then she remembered that a Shakespeare play was always on the high school curriculum. "Did Mrs. McFadden teach you Othello?"

"She was a stern taskmaster when it came to Shakespeare. We had to memorize long passages. She put on a play every year. The last year I was there, it was Othello. I always liked that play."

"The story of a man who kills the thing he loves through his own stupidity," she murmured as though to herself.

"The story of a man who doesn't know who he is, which leaves the way open for someone else to manipulate him." Victor, thermos in hand, passed in front of her again on his way to the door. This time, she was ready. She drew herself in, her whole body, drew it in and back against the stove. He paused at the door and half turned. "I know who I am."

Why, he thinks of himself as the hero in his own story, she thought. The man's ego was truly awe-inspiring. It was also frightening. For Victor Cage was a man who would see to it that his story was played out as he deemed it should be, and in the drive of his own ego, he would disregard other people's stories. An ego so enormous and relentless must be satisfied, even if it meant the destruction of everything and everyone around it.

Against her better nature, Emiline gave in to a wilful parting shot. "Why don't you fire me?" she said. "If I'm so unsatisfactory." She was aghast. What had she said? What if the man took her up on it? Oh, foolish, foolish.

But all he said was, "I didn't say you were unsatisfactory. Just immature."

She pulled up her chest and prepared to be outraged but she couldn't think of an appropriate scathing retort.

Victor continued. "I told you before, Hester likes you. So far, I see no real harm being done. When I do, you'll be the first to know. And to go." He smiled his mocking, supercilious smile. "Actually, I'm going to miss you. You're quite a source of entertainment."

Emiline could not sleep. The thoughts were tumbling too swiftly, too erratically, around in her brain. Her encounter that afternoon with Victor had left her shaky for the remainder of the day. His presence was so overpowering, a session with him always left her feeling battered. Today's had been worse than usual. His accusations as to her character, his questioning her integrity as a teacher, his stupid fatal philosophy of life, what could she say against such ignorance? Superstition and susceptibility to an ignorant way of thinking, rather than an intellectual process, led him to his conclusions. Intelligent debate would have no effect on his wrongheadedness.

And there had been his words, "I'll miss you." Alarming words. For what could they mean except that one of these days she would be getting the sack? One of these days he would decide that she had gone too far. He would decide that she was interfering with his story. His plot. Yes, he too had a plan, a scheme. She was not the only one with schemes. What happened when schemes crossed? Well, in this case, she would be turfed out bag and baggage. Next train out of town. The most she could hope for was that Dane would be allowed to drive her to the station, that she would not be set out on the road like Amy What's-Her-Name.

Then Victor's words of today mingled with those of Lewis. "A few more weeks and I'll be packing it in, here." When Lewis packed it in, her time, too, would be up. She was counting on his support, both physical and moral, to lend her and Hester transport and to shore up her motivation and faith. She must get Hester away from Cage Farm before he left. In any case, in a few weeks, summer would be over. Nearly six months had passed since she had stepped off the train into this appalling blank landscape. She had accomplished much in these six months. Now she must finish the task. There was nothing to be gained by dragging it on. She could not simply hope that things would work themselves out. People wasted whole lifetimes with that kind of sloppy thinking. She could not let things go on much longer without a resolution. If she did not act quickly, her chance to rescue Hester would be gone forever.

So what? part of her mind asked. You don't have to rescue Hester. It's not your job. Why don't you simply leave? There's a life out there, other places, other people, real life. That's what Vera is saying in her letters.

But, no, she must not even think it. Thinking that way weakened her resolve. And the truth was, if she failed to rescue Hester, she would have failed to end the suppression of a human soul. Ignorance and darkness and death would rule at Cage Farm forever. If she failed to rescue Hester, life would not be worth living. Victor Cage thought of life as a story. Well, thanks to him, she was in the Cage Farm story. She must see it through, for better or for worse. If she left now, she would never know what might have been. She would always wonder about the ending.

I'm starting to think like him—Emiline shuddered, for it seemed such a cold-blooded view of life. In that kind of thinking, people did not matter much. People were slotted into the big picture without thought to sensitivities, weaknesses or strengths, without thought to human complexities and differences. Why, that sounded like what you read about communist countries! Or what you used to read about fascism!

Flat on her back with her toes holding up the sheet, Emiline heard something. What was it? A shuffle, a light shuffle or ruffle, so light she wondered if she had, in fact, heard anything. She pricked up her ears. There it was again, a sound like a sigh passing. The country was quiet tonight, a hot windless night. Someone was up, perhaps going outside. The sound seemed to be on the other side of her door, in the living room. Was it Hester? But Hester never got up. In the six months that Emiline had been at Cage Farm she had never once heard Hester up in the night.

Quietly, Emiline pushed back the sheet. Her door was partly open. Silently, she slipped through the narrow opening and into the parlour, staying close to the wall. Although the room was dark, light from the stars and the moon shafted through the window, through the gap in the drapes which she had opened on that spring day that now seemed a century ago, and which, since, had remained open.

The sound was coming from across the room. It was hardly a sound at all, more an aura of a presence. Emiline narrowed her eyes. Against Hester's door was the figure of a man. Man or statue? He made her think of the sculpture of the discus thrower, the way he was bent, legs crouched slightly, powerful shoulders lowered in a curve, thighs and buttocks hard and muscled, the way he was proportionate and graceful. But this figure was not a statue. This figure was real, black head bent, face fierce and fixed as a carved demon in white light. The figure was Victor Cage. The force of his body, of his male nakedness, struck her a blow from across the room. His hand was on the doorknob. As Emiline watched in disbelief and horror, the figure disappeared into Hester's sacred chamber.

chapter 13

Lewis was lost in a dream.

"Lewis." Someone was calling.

He did not want to wake up. He wanted to stay with his dream. He wanted to find out how it ended. He settled back into its warm fuzzy fog. It was about Hester. Hester was coming for him. She was going to take him some place where they could live happily ever after. Hester was better now. She could speak. Although she did not speak in the dream he had that knowledge—she could speak. He was sitting on a bench at a bus stop and when the bus came she got off the bus and came over to him and took his hand and he knew complete bliss. They started walking, but then she must have let go of his hand because she was walking in front of him, leading him. For some reason, not clear in the dream, he had slowed down. Maybe he had stopped to look at something. Something happened, he couldn't be sure what, but he was left behind several paces and when he looked up she was gone. He had lost her. He must hurry, he must find her, she must not get too far head of him. He tried to quicken his pace but something was interfering. Something was threatening to wake him. Threatening the dream. If he woke up now, he would lose Hester forever. And that would be the end of any happiness he might ever have on this earth. He must not lose her. He must not wake up. He must sink back into unconsciousness. He must get back the dream. It was the only way he could find her.

"Lewis. Lewis." The voice again, closer now. It was not a loud voice, more of a whisper. Still, it came between him and Hester.

He would not wake up. Let them call all they wanted to. He would stay asleep. He would get back the dream.

Someone was shaking him gently by the shoulder. "Lewis, Lewis." He half opened his eyes. This other place, where everything was peaceful and floating, was so much more pleasant. No wonder it was stronger. No wonder it held him.

But the person would not let up. The hand on his shoulder was firmer now.

"Lewis."

The hand was so insistent. Perhaps he should wake up. Perhaps it was something important.

"Lewis, wake up!"

"What is it?" He struggled to the surface. He looked down at his arm lying diagonally across his thighs, to his hand pointing downwards to the striped awning of the porch swing cushion.

But why was he lolling on the verandah in the swing? Why had he been sleeping?

"Are you awake?"

He remembered. He had scarcely slept last night, his old insomnia acting up. Finally, at three in the morning, he had gotten up and slung on some clothes and set himself to work on his thesis. He had worked all morning in a frenzy of energy. It seemed as though the more fatigued he became, the more adrenaline pumped through his veins. He did not go down for dinner. He heard the threshing crew come in, but he would have found their camaraderie, their jokes and good cheer, intolerable in the mood he was in. Besides, he did not want to lose his focus, his train of thought. After they left, after the trucks returned to the field, he crept down to the kitchen, made himself a pot of coffee, brought it out here onto the verandah. And, now, here was his mother shaking him awake, her flowered house dress bending close so that he could smell its starchy cleanness.

He raised himself up. At the same time, he had a terrible wrenching feeling of separation from his dream. He had come so close to finding Hester again. He felt unutterably sad. It was no use. She had disappeared into some region where he could not follow. Now he would never find her. "What's up?" he said.

It was turning out to be a strange day. What had started out as a beautiful cool sunny morning was now a stifling afternoon. He must have been in a very deep sleep, otherwise he would not have this sense of being torn, jagged edged, up from his roots, away from himself. A hot breeze whispering through the poplars matched his agitated nerves and increased his discomfort. He knew that his mother was going to tell him something he did not want to hear.

"What is it?" He sat up another notch straighter.

"I thought you'd never wake up. You were sleeping like a drugged person." Why was her voice alarmed? Why was her face concerned?

"It's so hot. There's no air."

"I know. Dog days. I feel all done in myself. But Lewis ...," and here his mother lowered her voice to a stage whisper.

He spoke loudly to compensate. "Yes. What is it?"

"It's Emiline." The lines of her face deepened in her anxiety.

"Emiline?"

"And Hester. They're here."

Lewis frowned. There was nothing unusual about that. Except that they were here only a couple of days ago. "I wasn't expecting them," he said.

"They're not supposed to be here."

"Why not?"

"Or, at least, no one knows they're here."

"I don't see ...," Lewis raised his voice.

"Shhh. What it seems like ... I know this sounds crazy, but it seems like they've run away."

"What?" Lewis sat up straighter still. He had a vision of two women fleeing across a field, stumbling, rising, tripping, hair streaming, looking back across their shoulders with terrified eyes, an apparition like Simon Legree at their heels.

"Or something like that. To tell the truth, I can't make it out. Emiline is very upset. Almost distraught. And I'm afraid she's transferring some of it to Hester. You know how Hester is so sensitive to what goes on around her. I really don't know what to do with them."

Lewis stood up so quickly he felt dizzy. He held his head. "Where are they?"

"In the office. Well, I couldn't very well take them into the kitchen, could I? Millie's doing up the lunches. They're elbow deep in potato salad. I asked the girls if they wanted tea. I thought that might calm them down a bit. But Emiline just gave me a blank stare."

Lewis followed his mother through the living room and across the front hall to his father's office. He still felt peculiar—disembodied, lightheaded. He supposed it had something to do with the heat. From the kitchen came sounds of women working—pots clanking, fridge door shutting, voices raised. Millie laughed her deep hearty laugh. They would be preparing food to take out to the men for the evening meal. With weather like this, the crew would work until midnight. The noise and gossip and something to do with the way these tasks went on year after year reassured him of the regular world with its straightforward perspective. He felt better now, more whole, more solid.

Eyes lowered to the backs of his mother's heels—she had to wear sturdy footwear for arch support—he found himself thinking again of his dream. Certainly not a subtle dream, in fact obvious, a lifetime spent trying to capture Hester. No, not entirely true, he had known for several years that it was hopeless. He had given up thinking that the dream would ever become reality. He had not had those dreams since shortly after the war. Had he, these last few weeks, begun to hope again? Had Emiline brought that hope back into his life? Perhaps. And if he had not been awakened would he have captured his lifelong desire or would something in the dream have intervened so that once again it would slip from his grasp? Or he might have awakened himself. That was the way dreams were. You always woke up before the end. Dreams contained flashes of revelation, insights, but never a resolution. Perhaps we don't really want a resolution, he thought. Perhaps we couldn't stand it if our dream came true. For what would there be then to desire? If our dream came true, we'd destroy it, he decided. What else would there be to do with it? We're not strong enough to live with our dream and not destroy it. Likely, the best plan would be to have your dream come true and your life end simultaneously. Anyway, it was only a dream, he told himself. It didn't mean anything. It was only a dream.

In the office he found Hester pacing. Her footsteps were unusually firm and determined. It was as if her specific density had increased. She seemed to be concentrated energy, heavy with something. What? Perhaps with what he had sensed that evening at the Cage supper table, a residue of troubles, of the others and of the place itself, a residue of sorrow and suffering that contained not only a crude, wretched existence but, what must be even more terrifying, violence and blood.

Emiline was following Hester, flitting about her, trying to get her to sit down in one of the leather-bound armchairs. When she heard Lewis and his mother at the door, she hurried over and grabbed Lewis by the arm, then pulled him back into the living room. She spoke in a whisper. "I shouldn't have let her see how upset I was. I'm afraid I've upset her. I've got a grip on myself now. But it's been a dreadful day."

Lewis looked down into Emiline's upturned face. It was haggard with strain. Her hair was in disarray. She looked beaten down, older. He could see the schoolmarm in her, the thin-lipped, resolute spinster she might become. What does she see in me? he wondered fleetingly. For he must also look exhausted and perturbed. At least she did not have a beard stubble.

"What is it?"

"It's a nightmare."

Lewis felt a flicker of irritation. What was she going to tell him? Obviously, something he did not want to hear. Why, oh why, would people not let him sleep? If he had gotten a good sleep, he could have worked far into the evening on his dissertation. Oh, how he wanted to finish the miserable thing and get back on that train, the train that would take him out of this confusion and back to clarity.

"What's happened?"

"I don't know if I can tell you. It's too awful."

Why had the idiotic girl come here and disturbed his sleep if she had no intention of explaining to him the problem? "Come now," he said in as sympathetic a voice as he could manage. "It can't be that bad."

"It is. It's terrible. Something terrible has happened." Emiline's voice started to rise hysterically. She put her hand to her lips. She put her hands over her face. "I didn't know what to do."

Lewis felt himself in no condition to deal with a crisis. But he was going to have to hear what she had to say. He may as well get it over with. He reached up with both his hands and took hers away from her face, then brought them down to her sides and held them. He looked into her eyes. He saw pain. "Is anyone dead?" he asked.

"No, but ..."

"Well, then ..."

"It's worse." Again, her voice started to rise. She made a visible effort to calm herself. "We can't talk where others can hear."

"We'll go outside."

"Hester ..." Emiline made a movement back into the office.

"Mother will watch her."

"You're right. I'm not good for her now anyway in the state I'm in."

Holding her hand, Lewis led her outside through the front door and around the corner of the verandah to where he had been sleeping. He sat her down in the swing and sat beside her. "Now," he said, "tell me. What is it?"

"You must take us in."

"Take you in?"

"Let us stay here. We can't go back there. Ever."

"Why not."

"Something's happened."

"What, for God's sake."

"I'm not sure."

Lewis kept silent. He thought if he opened his mouth he would shout at her.

Perhaps Emiline saw the exasperation on his face. She sat up straighter. "I'll try and tell you ... as best I can. I'll say it quickly. Yes, I think that's the better way." Pausing, she took a deep breath. She let it out all in a rush, along with the words, "Victor's been interfering with Hester."

It took Lewis a few seconds to comprehend what Emiline was trying to say. He lifted his face. He stared out into the trees, across the valley, into the limitless sky. "You must be mistaken," he said.

"I should know what I saw."

"You mean, you saw ..."

"Last night, about midnight. I couldn't sleep. I heard a noise. I thought it might be Hester going out. I got up to help her. I went to my door. I can see Hester's door across the parlour from mine. And that's when I saw ..."

"Yes?"

"Them."

Lewis did not want to hear more. As it was, he had heard too much. He could not think about this. His mind would not accept this information. This could not be true. Emiline must be mistaken. And yet, and yet, another part of him knew how possible it was. Isolated farms, people living strange, unnatural, lonely lives. Evidence abounded. His brain reeled off a list—madness, disease, deformities, inbreeding, incest.

But, no, he didn't believe it. Not of Victor Cage. Not of Hester. If it were true, Hester would not be Hester, the person he had known all his life, the person he had loved all his life. She would be someone other than who she was. It was not possible. If it were true, everything would be over. His life would be over. If it were true, a great shattering would take place inside of him, as though joints were being wrenched from their sockets, muscles torn from skin.

"You must be mistaken." His lips felt numb.

"No, I'm sure." This was said slowly and calmly enough. But then the flow of words came, quickly in a stream, as though she had memorized events in a linear, orderly fashion so that she could make sense of them. "I didn't sleep at all last night. I couldn't breathe. The air seemed contaminated and it seemed that if I breathed that air, I would catch some terrible disease. He was in her room all night. I kept thinking I should do something, but I didn't. I'll never forgive myself. I don't know what I could have done but I should have done something. But I did formulate a plan. I knew that I would have to get Hester away from that place today. I could no longer even think of easing her out of the situation. I would have to act immediately. And I lay awake wondering how to do that without upsetting her. I decided to try and get through the morning with our usual routine. Hester's so used to that. Breakfast, lessons, dinner, our walk. There was Mrs. Cage to consider, too. If we left in the morning, if we didn't come home for dinner, she would alert Victor.

Oh Lewis," she turned to him, she clutched at him. "We have to think of a plan."

"What kind of plan?"

"This is too big a thing for us to deal with alone. This is serious. We'll have to contact the authorities. There must be authorities, even here. The police ..."

Lewis thought of Bill Stanton. Bill stopped speeders on the highway and patrolled the parking lot for hidden mickeys at the Saturday night dance. What would Bill do in a case like this? In the first place, he wouldn't believe it, no matter what Emiline said. He would think Emiline, to use his vernacular, was off her nut.

Emiline was talking again. It seemed that she had to talk. "I don't know how I got through the morning ... I stayed in my room until the men left ... until he left. And then I tried to give Hester the regular lesson. But my voice ... it sounded hysterical, even to myself, and of course Hester is so sensitive. When I was reading to her, I looked up and caught her look. She knew, she knows that something is up. She feels ... Oh, I know for her sake I must try and stay calm." Emiline paused, then spoke in a lower voice. "The men didn't come in for dinner. They sent Maggie to fetch it. Mrs. Cage went out to the garden. That's when Hester and I made a run for it."

"I should have taken it more slowly, in the usual way. I fairly grabbed Hester away from her dinner and pushed her out the door and started running. That was the wrong thing to do, I can see that now. But how can I explain it? I felt spooked by that place, by that house, even by the air around it. I was stricken with panic. I'm a bit ashamed of myself now. But at the time it seemed like the only way to get out of there. The only way to break the bond was to do it quickly." Her grip on his hands tightened. He could feel her fingernails dig into the soft places between his bones. "We cannot go back to that place. Hester must never go back."

The front screen door opened and banged softly shut. Emiline jumped and stiffened. Lewis looked up across her shoulder. It was his father. Deep drooping furrows draped his face. "Your mother said to ask you," he said to Lewis. "What's up?"

Lewis wondered if he had to tell the old man the truth. But, yes, his parents must know. It would not be fair to have them harbouring Hester without knowing. And Victor was not going to sit still. Sooner or later he would come to get her. Briefly, Lewis outlined the story as told to him by Emiline, while she sat silent, evidently willing to let him do the talking.

His father's immediate response was, "This is impossible."

"That was my first thought, too …"

"I should know what I saw," Emiline defended herself.

"… but I wonder if we can ignore the charge," Lewis finished.

Mr. McFadden had come around the swing and now stood facing both of them squarely. He looked hard at Emiline. "This is a very serious charge, young lady. You can't go around accusing people of this sort of thing."

"Not unless it's true. I know that."

"I'm going to have to ask you, and the law will do no less, what exactly did you see?"

"I saw Victor Cage go into Hester's room. That was about midnight. He didn't leave until early morning. I kept watch. I kept my door open."

"That's not hard evidence."

Emiline's voice rose. "What do you need for evidence? I know, I tell you. I know what I saw. There was something in his movements, the way he was sneaking around. He didn't have any clothes on. Why would he go into her room in the middle of the night without any clothes on? Do I have to draw you a picture?" Her voice had risen still further. She brought it down. "We must protect her," she said. "That's our first duty. We have a responsibility. We must call in the authorities."

"Around here people don't take kindly to interference by the neighbours or by the authorities."

"People should interfere when they see wrong being done. You can't just stand aside and let these things happen."

Lewis interrupted what he could see might be a confrontation. "I agree that we must call in the authorities if it seems warranted. But we must first of all face Victor Cage with the charge."

"He'll deny it, of course. What would you expect him to do?"

"I sure as hell have no intention of asking Victor Cage about this," said Mr. McFadden. "It'd be a gross insult to the man."

"I suppose we can let the authorities deal with it," said Lewis. He had no desire to face Victor Cage with the charge, either. "But not much will be done today. We can get it sorted out tomorrow."

"We can't send her back there. Not even for a day. He might kill her to hide the truth."

"Aren't you being hysterical?".

"Hysterical? What do you think he will do? Just wait for the axe to come down on his own neck?"

"We don't need to tell him anything at this point … if you go back now, he need not know until the law knocks on his door."

"I, for one, have no intention of staying another night under that roof, and I'll let Hester return over my dead body." Her voice became scathing. "I can't believe you're resigned to letting her return to a man who has her in some sort of horrible bondage."

Lewis was stung by her tone. He was not resigned, but he had the feeling that things were not being thought out. He had the uncomfortable feeling that if they were not careful, something ill-considered, even violent, could take place.

Mr. McFadden spoke. "First thing we have to do is get everybody calmed down. Then we can think straight. Mother's having a time of it in there with Hester." He looked pointedly at Emiline.

"Yes," said Emiline. "You're right." She stood up. "I'd better go in and see to Hester. She's not used to other people."

"And," Emiline was stopped in her departure by Mr. McFadden's voice. "Mother doesn't need to know about this, I mean the business with Victor."

"You're right," said Lewis. "She'll know soon enough, if it's true."

When Emiline had gone back into the house, father and son turned to each other.

"She's put us in an awkward situation." Mr. McFadden sat back on the verandah rail and crossed his ankles. "Damn me if she hasn't."

"Yes," said Lewis. "We can't ignore what she's told us. And yet to accuse Victor Cage of such a thing, well it seems ludicrous."

"We must do nothing underhanded as far as the Cages are concerned." Mr. McFadden was emphatic on this point. "We've been neighbours for thirty years. Everything must be handled above-board. We must phone over and let them know that Hester is here. They'll be worried."

"Victor will be out combining like everybody else. He won't know until midnight that Hester isn't at home."

"Mrs. Cage'll go out and tell him."

"He'll insist they return. Hester, anyway. He'll come and get her." Lewis hesitated. "It might be just as well if they stay the night. Then we can get things sorted out tomorrow. Try and determine just exactly what Emiline saw."

"Stay the night! You're talking about a crazy woman who's hardly been out of her yard for twenty years, let alone sleeping in another bed."

"I know, but under the circumstances ... They're both pretty upset."

"The way to get Hester calmed down is to take her home."

"Emiline won't hear of it. She'll insist on calling the law first. And what if, just if, it is true? And we let Hester go back into that situation."

"I don't like the idea of the law getting into it. Once they're in on it, it's out of our hands, out of private business and into public gossip. And these things snowball something fierce. Whether it's true or not, Victor Cage's name will be mud forevermore." Mr. McFadden paced to the edge of the verandah steps. "Damn me," he exclaimed, "but I don't like to have to face a man with a charge like that."

"We don't have to face him with a charge. We're not accusing him of anything. We simply tell him the truth. That Emiline has come to us and told us this story. We're not saying that we believe it." Both men were silent a moment. "Of course, Emiline will never be able to return to Cage Farm," mused Lewis. "I hope she's thought of that. Even if this all comes to nothing, she's finished at Cage Farm. She's finished with Hester."

chapter 14

"Oh, Lewis, don't you see? We've lost her."
Emiline's voice threatened to break.

"You must pull yourself together."

"Yes, I must get a grip on myself."

She was half-lying on the sofa in the living
room. He was sitting beside her with one arm
around her shoulders. It was ten o'clock, eight
hours since Lewis had been rudely awakened
from his dream, seven since the decision to
harbour herself and Hester until this messy
business could be straightened out. The woman
who had been helping Millie in the kitchen had
gone home to a neighbouring farm. Her cheery
good-bye, the clatter of her rust bucket half-ton
down the driveway, had been heard about half
past seven. After a final swipe at the cleaning
up and arranging things for an early start in the
morning, Millie had retired to her own house.
Hester, after much coaxing and manipulating,
had been put to bed in the spare room. Mr. and
Mrs. McFadden had been sent upstairs by Lewis
after his mother nodded off over her knitting and
his father fell asleep reading the paper, mouth
open, snoring "fit to wake the dead," as his
mother put it. Lewis had shaken him gently by
the shoulder. "We'll wait for Victor," he had said.
"Don't worry. Everything will be all right."

That had been a half hour ago. Since being alone with Lewis, Emiline had gotten the shakes. She had held up fine during the telephone calls to Cage Farm. The first had taken place shortly after five o'clock. Mr. McFadden had wanted to phone earlier, but she had put it off with excuses—Mrs. Cage will be out in the garden, she'll be busy preparing food. At the same time, Emiline knew that if Mrs. Cage did not hear from her by supper she would sound the alarm, even if she had to trek a mile out to the field on her bandy legs to do it. Emiline's thought was to wait until Maggie had come in and gone back out with the evening meal. That way there was a chance that Victor would not know of any unusual happenings until he returned late that night, hopefully too late to do anything until tomorrow. And tomorrow at the earliest opportunity, they, she, must contact someone with authority, someone who would know what to do.

Emiline didn't know what she would do if Victor answered the telephone. Not that she expected he would. He should not be there. Still, there was an off-chance that he might be in the house for something or other. She held the receiver to her ear and dialled the number. As she listened to the ringing at the other end, she could see the black grease-covered instrument on the wall back of the stove along with a yellowed fly-specked calendar and a fly swatter hanging on a nail. She imagined its shrill ringing, startling the shadows of the slumbering kitchen where such a sound was scarcely ever heard, so rare Mrs. Cage might not at first recognize what it was. And, indeed, it did take several rings before there was an answer. Emiline was about to hang up when the receiver was lifted and the old woman's voice shouted across what seemed like a long empty distance.

"Yes ..." Suspicion and wariness were written into the tone.

"This is Emiline," Emiline said, feeling immense relief at hearing the harsh familiar voice.

"Oh, Emiline. Why are you not home for supper? Where is Hester?"

"We're at the McFadden's. We're fine. Everything's all right. We've been asked to stay here for supper. I thought I should let you know. So you won't worry."

A silence at the other end of the line conveyed Mrs. Cage's digesting of this information. Emiline could envision the scowl on her face.

"Victor won't like it," she finally shouted. "You better come."

"But we want to stay here for supper. Lewis will bring us home later. Don't worry."

What a coward you are, she told herself. Why don't you say it now and get it over with? We won't be home tonight. But if she said that, all hell would break loose. If things could be managed by stages, by getting people used to each stage, one at a time, the situation might be defused. Later, she would have to phone again and make some excuse for staying the night. She had no idea what that excuse would be. First things first, she surmised.

"You should come," emphatically stated.

"And we will, later. Are the men still out in the field?"

That seemed to remind Mrs. Cage. "I have to tell Victor."

The voice that came across the wire was so full of consternation, Emiline had a twinge of conscience. She was causing the old woman distress. "Never mind Victor." What useless advice, thought she, but it was worth a try. "By the time he comes in, we'll be back at Cage Farm and fast asleep in our beds."

"He won't like it. This will be very bad."

Emiline hung up the phone and returned to the living room. She paused in the doorway. Hester, wearing a longish summer dress made of a light gauzy material, was pacing from one window to another, then to the sofa, to a chair, back to the window. It seemed that she might start tearing at her hair. Emiline, coming upon the scene suddenly, saw it as an impartial observer. She was reminded of all the madwomen, in attics, in closed rooms, on lonely farms, who had populated the books she had read. Standing outside the picture, for one brief instant, she wondered if, perhaps, there *was* something wrong with Hester, something more than behaviour or habit, something more basic, something askew from the normal. But, no, she decided, Hester's actions were appropriate to the world in which she existed, a folk tale peopled by gypsies, crones, sorcerers, odd creatures of all sorts, a world of dungeons and wicked witches and magic spells and potions, a world of superstition and ignorance, a world of danger and violence. Because it was not the world in which the McFaddens lived, her actions seemed bizarre at Thorncliffe Heights. The scene that was taking place should not be happening in this house. It was the wrong venue, the wrong stage set. Here, studious thought, rational life, quiet contemplation, reigned. The extravagant behaviour, the brooding passions that Emiline felt underlying life at Cage Farm, which seemed appropriate to that place, were inappropriate here.

Here, it was difficult to believe that Cage Farm existed. In the light of day, amongst ordinary people, Emiline wondered for an instant if last night had really happened. Immediately, she dismissed her doubt. She had seen what she had seen. If she wavered, all would be lost. That was the trouble with the normal world. It did not recognize evil.

Emiline paused in her thoughts. She was shocked at herself. The word 'evil' was not in her vocabulary. She was not accustomed to thinking the word. She had been brought up with a vague idea that evil, a sort of neutered form of it, could be described as lack of good. Before today, she had not believed that it existed as something real, she had not considered it as a force in itself. That sort of thinking, she considered medieval. In the modern enlightened world, evil was like the bogeyman under the bed, nonexistent to a mind of reason. But she had learned at Cage Farm that evil did exist, that evil was people having power over other people and manipulating their minds so they could not think straight, so they did not even realize that their thinking was distorted. Evil was something that got into people's brains and ate away at them like a dark, coiling worm and made them think, finally, that evil was right.

Emiline, poised those few moments in the doorway, saw how the McFaddens were caught up in somebody else's evil, and they did not have the faintest notion of what they were dealing with or how to deal with it. Their way was conciliation, an attempt to smooth things over, when, as she could see now, the only way to deal with evil was to rout it out and destroy it. She felt a great responsibility. She must bring the evil of Cage Farm into the light of day. That was the only way it could be dealt with. That was the only hope for all of them. She must see that justice was done.

Most of the afternoon, Mrs. McFadden had ministered to the distraught Hester, trying to calm her down, patting her and murmuring "now, dear," without any effect whatsoever. Mr. McFadden had sat in his chair and appeared extremely uncomfortable at witnessing such an excess of emotional display. Finally, expressing his disapproval with a grunt and a frown, he went outside, climbed into his truck and bounced himself off to where the threshing crew were working in a nearby field. Emiline didn't blame him. She thought how her own unusual behaviour must be confusing for these people. Mrs. McFadden, especially, must be bewildered, since she had not been told the details of why the women from Cage Farm were here. "What's wrong?" she had asked. No one had answered. At some point she had turned to Lewis. "Perhaps it would be better to take her home."

"Oh, I don't know," Lewis had said, not meeting his mother's eyes.

Millie and the neighbour woman, who were in the kitchen taking care of food for the threshing crew, discreetly remained uninvolved. About six o'clock, Millie called through the kitchen door. "You folks in there want a bite to eat?"

Mrs. McFadden looked up from where she was hovering over the sofa where Hester had flung herself and was clawing at her bare lower arms with her fingernails. "Oh dear," she said, "you must all be starving."

"I couldn't eat a thing," said Emiline.

"It would be something to do," said Lewis. "Maybe Hester is hungry. It might do her good to eat."

"I'll go and see about it," said Mrs. McFadden, seeming relieved that duty called her outside the room.

Hester refused to sit at the table with the others. Emiline tried to persuade her, took her limp hand and tried to pull her up out of the low sofa. Hester held fast and would not budge. Her face wore a stricken childlike expression. But, thought Emiline, sitting again beside her, trying to coax a few choice morsels between her set lips, she is not a little girl. She is a twenty-eight-year-old woman. When Emiline studied the lowered face, she saw that the fresh clear look was gone. Fine blemishes could be seen in the sallow skin. The features were set in a certain pattern. Why did I not see this before? wondered Emiline. This did not happen in one day.

Emiline knew then that whatever the outcome of today's events, she had lost her innocent love. They could no longer be girls together, skipping in the meadow, playing hide and seek in the woods of Arcadie, telling fairy tales around the dining room table. The spell had been broken. We're both twenty-eight, thought Emiline. We're not childhood friends. But they could not be woman friends, either. Smashed was the picture of the cozy apartment, of her coming home from her employment and Hester being there waiting. Vanished were the evenings of a loop of Hester's hair catching and holding the lamplight as she bent over her embroidery and walks in a park and quiet holding of hands. For no matter how this day ended, no matter what happened tomorrow, Hester was not intact. She had been broken, fragmented, by experience. Even if by some miracle she found her voice, even if she tested out as being of normal intelligence, even if she agreed to years of analytic digging around in her trauma, there was no 'cure.' Emiline could not know, could not imagine, with what bizarre and warped rules and beliefs and images Hester's mind teemed. It had been corrupted by years of submitting to the imposition of another's will, by collaborating with that dark force.

Looking at that unhappy contorted face, Emiline felt pity and also guilt. Hester was her charge and she had not taken proper care of her. She had found at Cage Farm a contented prisoner, asleep perhaps, misused certainly, but at least accepting of her fate. She had disrupted her life, turned her into this distraught creature. But, no, she must not think like that. Hester was the product of years of neglect and abuse. The fact that she accepted her life did nothing to recommend it. She, Emiline, was not the cause of those years. But she was the cause of her disruption. Had she done Hester a favour? Had she done the right thing?

The lowering sun filled the window. It lit Hester's tired tear-stained face. She had picked a spot raw on the skin of her arm with fingernails that were long and jagged. I haven't cut her fingernails lately, was Emiline's first thought. I've had my mind on other things. Hester continued to pick in a distracted manner, drawing blood. She stared at the blood but it seemed she could not stop her hands. It seemed she was fascinated with drawing more blood. Emiline was horrified. She looked toward the dining room door. For some reason, she didn't want the others to know that Hester had scraped her arms raw. The action seemed too bizarre. She tried to stop the movement of those strange narrow hands, but Hester pulled away. Then she saw a sweater on the back of a chair. She succeeded in stuffing Hester's arms into the sleeves. Although Hester's plucking movements continued, her skin was protected from further damage. Through all of this, she would not look at Emiline. She had not looked at her all afternoon. All afternoon there had been something hateful, almost violent, in the way she kept her head turned away. But now she was quiet. She seemed to have lost interest.

It took some time to get Hester settled down for the night. Emiline succeeded in bathing her face but she did not want to tackle anything further. She had not thought to pack belongings for either of them, an oversight she now saw as unbelievable and unforgivable, for she doubted that she would ever see her things again. She was like a spy who could never return to the country which she has betrayed. If personal effects of either woman were ever retrieved, it would have to be by neutral authorities who could go into enemy territory.

Mrs. McFadden had offered the use of night clothes but Hester would not have them. She would not allow her own clothes or even the sweater to be removed. Every time Emiline's hands lighted on her, she tore them away. Finally, Emiline persuaded her to lie down on the bed as she was, minus her shoes.

There was then the second phone call to Cage Farm, answered this time by Maggie, who accepted the message, 'Hester exhausted, vehicles all away,' without opinion but with the announcement, "Victor will come for her." Useless to debate the subject, thought Emiline wearily, replacing the receiver in its cradle. All there was to do now was wait.

After sending his parents off to bed, Lewis had gotten out the whisky bottle and two tumblers from the kitchen with the comment, "I don't know about you, but I could use a stiff drink."

"Yes," said Emiline.

The room was dim, lit only by a single table lamp. A veil of amber dust hung in the air, mellowing everything to smoky topaz. It was the end of growing things. What remained in fields and gardens would only ripen further. All that was left was to reap and store before another winter arrived with its cold clarity.

Here, all is tranquility, thought Emiline, moving her head in a semi-circle from the stone fireplace to the large windows overlooking the ravine. The wood floor, the richly textured rugs, the upholstery, the books and paintings, gave the room a warm congenial atmosphere. This afternoon that atmosphere had been shattered. Hester had brought chaos into this house. And she was the one who had brought Hester here. She eased her conscience—one night. Only one night. Then these people could get back to normal.

And how about me? she wondered. Will I ever get back to normal?

Emiline could have wept for her loss. Surely, she had never known such moments of unqualified joy as those she had spent with Hester. She would never have such perfect moments again, not if she lived to be a very old woman. She knew that with certainty.

"Oh, Lewis," she said, "her life is finished. What chance does she have to ever lead a normal existence?"

"Shhh. Shhh." He patted her shoulder and sipped from the tumbler of whiskey in his other hand.

"What will become of her now?"

Lewis hesitated. "Maybe she should go back to Cage Farm. I mean," he added hurriedly, "if it isn't true."

"Of course it's true!"

"But you didn't actually see … anyway, it will have to be proven. Victor will admit nothing. I imagine they do physical examinations in such cases."

Emiline inwardly squirmed. She had not thought of that. She did not want Hester to have to go through that. But she must stick to her story. She must not let other people confuse her thoughts and twist her mind into thinking that she had been mistaken. She must not let this evil be neutralized by other people. Cage Farm was not merely a bad dream from which she had awakened. "We must carry on as planned," she said. "Sending her back to Cage Farm is unthinkable. Imagine her suffering!"

"Perhaps she wasn't suffering."

"Of course she was suffering."

"Perhaps Cage Farm is where she feels comfortable. After all, that's what she knows."

"That's beside the point. Even if she wants that kind of life, it isn't right." Emiline sat up, out of Lewis's arm, away from his shoulder. She looked at his face. "What's wrong with you? You seem to have given up on her. You're starting to sound like your father. Hester is not simply a girl on the neighbouring farm who's not quite right in the head, the crazy girl of Cage Farm."

"I don't know," said Lewis. "I mean ... aside from this business with Victor, which of course we'll have to find out about, perhaps she's best left with her family. Perhaps they're the best ones to take care of her. Oh, the evening I was there for supper, I got some notion into my head about her being a scapegoat, about her bearing the brunt of the family's troubles and holding Cage Farm together, making it possible for the others to survive. I decided that she should not be destroyed for the benefit of the others, that even if she was capable of making choices and wanted to sacrifice herself like that, she mustn't be allowed to. But now I wonder ..." He paused. "She's formed the way she is, deformed perhaps, but she's grown and set that way and it's too late to change it." His next words were said quietly, almost sadly. "I wonder, too, if I was seeing more than there really was that day, if I was making up a story for myself."

"Well, that's all irrelevant now, now that this other thing has happened. Surely you can't be suggesting that we send her back to that?"

"No ..." Lewis looked straight ahead. "Have you given any thought to Victor? To what he will do? He's not going to simply give in."

"I don't care what he does. I'm only sorry I didn't do something last night. Oh, I should have done something. I should not have been such a coward!"

"What could you have done? Against Victor Cage?"

"I don't know. Something. I should have done something. I could have screamed, banged on the door. I could have called Dane."

"Dane is no match for Victor."

"Oh, and who knows? Maybe Dane knows what's going on. Maybe they all know. I believe that's typical in these cases. The family collaborates. That would explain the strangeness in that house. And the cloud that hangs over it. Evil does have a certain atmosphere. I know that now. I should have known before." Emiline heard herself raving like a fanatic. Before today, she doubted that she had ever said the word 'evil' out loud. Today it had passed into her vocabulary and, like a child with a new word, she seemed to be repeating it over and over as if to reinforce its existence and thus the existence of what it signified.

"Stop it." Lewis reached out and jiggled her shoulder slightly. "At this point we don't know what happened last night."

"I know. Oh this waiting seems to go on forever. It's almost as bad as last night. Lying there, waiting for that door to open, for the night to be over. But then it wasn't over. Day came but the night wasn't over. And now it's night again."

"You've got to stop this. You're working yourself up into a fit." Lewis stood up abruptly.

"Where are you going?"

"I'm only going to check on the temperature." Lewis walked over to a window.

"Yes. Usually the day cools down. What's wrong with the weather?"

"Still seventy degrees. And it's eleven o'clock."

"Eleven o'clock? Maybe he won't come."

"He'll come." Lewis walked back to the sofa.

"Why doesn't he come then? So we can get this over with?"

"They'll work all night if it stays like this."

"They mustn't work all night. He must come. He must come and we must have it out. Otherwise, it will be a terrible night."

Lewis sat down again beside her and picked up her hand. "Yes," he said. "For awhile, I'm afraid, nights will be trials to be got through."

Emiline caught a note of desperation in his voice. No, not desperation. Desire. Desire, melancholy, longing. Longing for things to be as they had always been.

She turned to look at him. He had grown shaggy over the summer. His skin was brown from the sun, yet he appeared pale beneath the tan. His eyes were bright with unreleased tears. She recalled another time when she had seen this expression on his face, the first time he had driven her back to Cage Farm. Something is hurting him, she thought. Hester. What else could it be? Why, he's in love with her. She suddenly knew it. She recalled their past conversations, things he had said, his attitude, his tone of voice when he spoke of Hester. He's been in love with her all his life, she thought. Of course he doesn't want her to change. He wants her to be here for him the way she's always been, forever. Emiline felt a wave of pity. What must it be like, she wondered, to love someone that long and that hopelessly, someone so entirely unsuitable, someone impossible.

"Poor Lewis." She caressed the hand that was clasping hers. Then she raised her hand and drew his face down close to hers. She leaned forward and kissed his forehead. He raised his head slightly and placed his mouth on hers. She felt herself being drawn up into him so that she no longer had a body, no longer had a mind. She was pure being, floating out of herself and into him. He straightened, they looked at each other. He blinked his eyes as though to clear them.

Astonished as she was by that kiss, at the moment of their pulling away from each other, the world reinserted itself. The sensible world was stronger and pulled her with it away from her fantasy. "It is true," she said, trying to say it gently. "But even if it were not true, we have to give her up, Lewis. She's gone beyond us, beyond our understanding. Practically speaking, they'll take her from us. She needs more help than we can give her. What we have to do is see to it that a mentally ill, abused woman receives professional help. That's the reality."

She felt very sorry for herself. She felt sorry for Lewis. They had both lost Hester. She squeezed his hand.

They heard it together, a vehicle coming into the yard. They pulled guiltily apart and stared at the door. The motor stopped. A metal door slammed. Gravel crunched. Emiline held her breath as steps mounted the verandah, as a large shape loomed out of the darkness the other side of the screen, as a knock came at the door.

Lewis was the one who moved. Standing, he walked to the screen door and opened it.

Victor Cage filled the doorway. "I've come for Hester," he said. His voice was strangely calm, almost friendly. "Ma says she's here."

"She fell asleep," said Lewis. "We phoned your mother. You may as well leave her."

Victor must have come directly from the field. Smells of grain and earth entered the room with him. Glistening with sweat, his face was almost black from adhered dust and chaff. His eyes were black deep still pools. He never looked more like a devil, thought Emiline, who was now standing beside Lewis.

She felt stronger now that the play had started, now that she had an action to perform rather than sitting and worrying. She and Lewis were a team.

Victor looked past them, between their heads, his glance directed toward the sofa. He brought his gaze back to their faces, first one, then the other. He seemed to arrive at his conclusion. "Emiline can stay if she likes. But I'm taking Hester home."

"It got late," said Lewis, defensively. Emiline caught the note of apology in his voice. Her heart sank.

"I understand," said Victor, glancing again toward the sofa, then toward Emiline. "But I'm telling you to go and get her."

There was a silence. Emiline's eyes were transfixed on the screen behind Victor where a large yellow moth was making little pops like a ball against a tennis racquet on the inside of the fine mesh. What seemed like a long time was only twenty seconds. Then Emiline said slowly. "No, I don't think I will."

No one said anything for a further twenty seconds. It was as if they were actors in a play and each was waiting for another to remember his lines.

"She's sound asleep in the spare room," said Emiline. "Why disturb her? I'm sure she's all right until morning."

"She won't know where she is in the morning. She'll be mixed up."

Victor seemed to grow yet larger, more solid, as though as each second ticked past, he gained strength from the situation. This gain seemed to be in direct proportion to the loss of stature and strength of the other two. He looked at them closely. "What's going on here?"

Lewis stood as one paralyzed. Say it, say it, Emiline willed. Say the words of accusation that will destroy

Cage Farm. But Lewis said nothing, apparently could say nothing. It was as though all of his will had been sapped by Victor's overpowering presence. Must I say it? she wondered. She opened her mouth and she looked into Victor's face. His fierce lip curled with the surliness of his convictions, convictions that were immense even if mistaken, because they involved the great cycle of life itself. And she found that she could not say it. It was too monstrous a thing to put into words.

The sound of another motor interrupted the silence. It was coming closer. The three stood still, listening. The vehicle came into the yard at the back of the house. It stopped. They heard a door slam, then silence, then feet on the gravel driveway which connected the back and front yards. Victor turned and Lewis took a step across the threshold. Al was standing at the bottom of the verandah steps, looking up. Al, with his matter-of-fact face and manner.

"Everything okay?" he asked.

"Yes," answered Lewis. Everything's fine."

"Okay." Al stood a moment longer. "Just checking. Was on my way to the house when I saw a light on. Then I seen your truck there." He nodded at Victor. "Thought maybe something was up."

No," said Victor.

"Well, I'll be getting off to have a few hours sleep then. Likely, the boys in the bunkhouse are asleep already. We're all pretty beat. And weather like this, we'll be at it again at four in the morning."

They watched Al disappear into the shadows at the corner of the house.

Emiline was never to know why Victor suddenly acquiesced and turned on his heel. Was it Al's reminder of tomorrow's work demands, or the presence of several men on the place? Was he simply tired from a long day's labour?

"I'll be over first thing in the morning," he said from the edge of the verandah. "Make sure she's ready."

Emiline and Lewis stood together while Victor went down the steps and crossed the gravel to where his truck was parked. They heard his truck make the reverse sounds of his arrival. The motor leapt into play, the tires sounded close at first and then more distant, and, finally, the motor faded into the night. Only then did Emiline turn to Lewis.

He did not look at her. "What could I do?" he said. "He's her legal guardian."

"It's all right," she said. She could hear the defeat in her own voice. "Best thing, call it a day. Sleep on it. We'll both feel stronger in the morning. In the morning, we can call the police or whoever takes care of such things here. They'll know what to do." She placed her hand on his arm. Flinching, he shook it off. He strode over to the table, to the whisky bottle, and poured a large amount into his glass.

Emiline felt sympathy for him. He had had the chance to slay the dragon and rescue the damsel in distress, an opportunity of a lifetime for a romantic such as Lewis, and he had flubbed it. Emiline did not think that she would be able to help him with his demons this long night. Besides, she was suddenly extremely tired. She almost crawled up the stairway and made her way to the spare bedroom where she was to sleep in a second bed next to Hester. When she entered the room she saw in the moonlight that Hester was not in her bed. Her heart gave a wild leap before discerning a ghostly figure at the window. She breathed out a sigh of relief and went to stand beside Hester. The window overlooked the driveway. How long has she been standing here? wondered Emiline. Had she seen Victor arrive? Certainly, she had watched him leave.

Thank heavens she didn't come down when he was here, thought Emiline. I should have locked the door. It struck her. I've become her jailer, she thought, just like the others.

"Come on," Emiline said, "Come on to bed." She touched Hester's arm. Hester continued to stare down into the driveway, lit by the light of the white moon. Her lips were parted. Short panting breaths came out of her mouth. With one of the breaths, the word "Victor" escaped. "Victor," she whispered. "Victor," she repeated in a voice of longing and utter desolation, the voice of despair keening for the beloved departed. Victor. Victor. With every breath the word issued forth as though unbidden, as though part of her very breathing.

For a moment Emiline was stunned. Then her hands flew to her ears. "Stop it! Stop!" she demanded. But Hester would not, perhaps could not, stop.

Emiline felt frantic. What if Hester kept repeating that word forevermore? She must get her back to her bed. She must induce her to sleep.

Emiline's fingers curled around Hester's arm. She pulled her away from the window. Hester was like someone in a trance. She let herself be led, let herself be gently pushed down onto the bed, allowed her legs to be lifted up onto the bed.

Hester's face was wet with tears. The word coming from between her parted lips was less forceful now, more like a whisper or a sigh. Emiline lay down beside her, the two bodies pressed together on the narrow bed. Through the thin layers of their summer clothing, Emiline could feel the other woman's body. She was surprised. She had thought of Hester as being scarcely there. She had had an idea of Hester's body being constructed from sheer transparent materials, and now she discovered that Hester had substance. Hester was flesh, flesh and blood and bone and skin. Her flesh was palpable, pulsating with life, with mortality. Her skin was a fine, warm, soft pelt. Her smell was like that of Victor Cage, was of earth and grain, but with a difference. Hester's smell was clearly discernible as woman.

Hester was still in great distress, still breathing the name of the being who for her must be life. Emiline started stroking the tangled hair. "There, there, darling," she said in a low soothing voice. "There, there." Gently, she pulled Hester's body around to face her and gathered her in her arms. Hester's breasts and thighs were a pressure against her, Hester's tears wet her face. Emiline rocked back and forth. "There, there," she repeated over and over until Hester stopped uttering the hated word and slept.

chapter 15 Emiline was quick to wake up. A sense of doom, deep and bottomless, engulfed her. For an instant she did not know why she felt such blackness of soul. Then she remembered—Hester's utterance. To have it come, finally, the looked-for, waited-for, word. To have it be the wrong one. Hester naming her solitude. Victor.

Emiline knew instantly where she was, in the spare bedroom at Thorncliffe Heights. She remembered with a sense of incredulity all that had happened the day before. But it did not seem to be morning. Apart from the moon bathing the room in a silver glow, it was dark. But something had awakened her. A sound. She had heard something, something unusual. What was it? She listened intently. It sounded like cellophane crackling between hands, a very large amount of cellophane between very large hands, as if someone was removing cellophane from a wrapping and crushing it up before throwing it into the wastebasket. Then she smelled smoke. Smoke! She remembered that she had fallen asleep with Hester. But Hester was not beside her. She was nowhere in the room. Emiline's feet hit the floor.

Smoke was filling the room. Smoke was getting into her mouth. Her nostrils were dry and burning. Her eyes were stinging. She flew to the bedroom door. The door was closed but she pulled it open. It was as if a dam had burst. Smoke billowed into the room. She did not know whether to go forward into the hall or back into the room. She could jump to the ground from the window. At most she would break a leg, perhaps only sprain an ankle. But she must try and find the others. Hester.

"Hester!" she called. She screamed. And the others. Where were they? Out of the smoke and the flames appeared three figures, three bodies milling about, gasping and choking and groping their way in some sort of hellish nightmare as more flames licked up, casting an unearthly light onto the scene. Emiline discerned Lewis and his parents. Where was Hester?

From the top of the stairs she looked down on the fearsome sight of flames dancing their way up the staircase. At the bottom stood Hester, her wild hair framing her face. There was something so utterly primitive, so feral, in the way she looked up at them, Emiline's heart stopped in dismay. "Hester!" she screamed, and Hester turned and darted like a doe out the front door.

The staircase was crumbling at the outside edge, but near the wall it appeared to be still intact. Mr. McFadden, one hand across his face, the other guiding his wife, was already at the top of the stairs.

Emiline saw him take the hand from his face and gesture with it to her and Lewis, but Lewis was already pulling her in another direction. Coughing and choking, reaching out to the walls for a path before them, they made their way to a front bedroom window where they could climb out onto the verandah roof and relatively easily slide and slither to the ground.

In the nightmarish scene before her eyes, Emiline looked for Hester but could not find her. She looked for Lewis's parents. They were not to be seen. By this time Al and Millie and the hired men who had been sleeping in the bunkhouse were there.

Against a backdrop of leaping flames, against the sound of fire gaining momentum, she saw the bones and muscles of Lewis's face working. His mouth opened and what seemed to be silent screams issued forth toward Al, who was already running toward the door.

Lewis followed but both men were driven back by the flames. Someone had brought buckets of water from the well and had wet sheets ready. Lewis and Al swathed themselves and went back in.

The gathered men were attempting to keep the fire contained to the house, attacking with what water they had, sparks which flew onto outbuilding roofs, into tinder-dry straw.

Emiline watched stupefied with horror as the flames licked higher. A great sheet of molten orange and yellow flapped through the wooden frame. It was hot, hot. She had never felt such heat. It was like standing before an open furnace door, but intensified a thousand times. Lewis and Al. Where were they? Each second ticked off an eternity. Then she saw two silhouettes against the wall of red, two upright figures, each with a burden. Al had his slung over his shoulder like a sack of grain. Lewis had his in his arms. The bodies were placed gently on the grass. Al put his head down close to the two faces. Lewis searched frantically for a pulse. As the flames shot up bright as a midnight sun and overwhelmed the sky for miles around, people were already arriving from the closest farms. Before morning everyone in the district would be there, doing what they could to help in their neighbours' loss and grief.

Al and Millie, the hired men, the newly arrived neighbours were busy. A brigade had been organized. Pails of water from the river were passed along a line to danger areas. Luckily, most of the outbuildings as well as Al and Millie's house were a good distance from the fire and there was no wind to carry it. Emiline watched the scene in too great a state of shock to join it or even relate to it. Her eyes settled on Lewis, who stood helpless and lost before his parents' bodies. Where's Hester? she thought, suddenly remembering. Where's Hester?

It took Emiline's searching eyes a few minutes to find her, half-hidden, cowering beside the wall of a shed. Lewis must also have been looking for her, must have seen her at the same moment. He walked toward her slowly, as one in a daze. His fists by his sides were clenched. His body seemed clenched, as though in that way he was holding it together. When he reached Hester, with one hand he took her arm and pulled her up and away from the wall. With his other hand he raised her lowered head. He gazed down at her face. With a slow, resigned movement, he gathered her into his arms. She leaned against him. She seemed to be very frightened and very tired. Wrapping her still more closely in his embrace, he closed his eyes. They stood thus, absolutely still, for several minutes, while the grotesque ballet was performed around them, silhouettes darting and dancing against the backdrop of red and yellow flames.

Another vehicle arrived into the crowded scenario of confusion. The Cage truck came to an abrupt stop and Victor Cage jumped out. He strode directly toward Hester. "Hester." It was one short bark. Hester turned her face from Lewis's chest. She straightened and pulled away from him. She walked slowly, shoulders drooping, toward Victor.

Where are her shoes? thought Emiline. She shouldn't be out in the night without shoes.

Victor, with quick efficient movements, put Hester into the passenger side of the truck, slammed the door, rounded the hood, got into the driver's side and drove off. It did not seem to be a triumphant gesture so much as an inevitable one. The play had been played out, the story was ended. He was retrieving his wounded and leaving the enemy to the consequences of their folly.

chapter 16

This was a real town! Even though Emiline had been there for two days, every time she looked out of her hotel room window, every time she took herself out to the streets, she marvelled. She could not believe it—a real community of ordinary people, with streets of friendly-looking houses and picket fences and trees. And a main street lined with cars parked in a herringbone pattern of diagonal lines either side, and wooden sidewalks and real stores. There was even a Helen's Boutique. There was a drugstore with a soda fountain, a hardware, a movie theatre. Down at the end of Main Street were train tracks and a real train station. Over a block was a city hall and a public works. On the south edge of town was a dairy. Several gas stations with attached machine shops dotted the highway which arrowed through the town. Across from the train station was the three-storey hotel in which she was staying. In which she had been placed, she corrected herself.

And to think this had been here all the time, not thirty miles distant from the isolation of the farm.

I've been in solitary confinement, thought Emiline. A ghetto of the mind as much as anything else. But now I'm out! She breathed a deep breath of relief but she could not really exult. She would never be able to exult again. She had too much to answer for.

Emiline squinted down at the piece of paper in her hand which glared white in the midday sun. Four weeks now of blinding sun and dry heat. The farmers, the townspeople, wondered how long this was going to last. Good for harvesting, they said. But mighty uncomfortable for living, others said. Parched, everything's parched including me, a middle-aged lady in the drugstore complained. Dante's Inferno, the librarian who read a lot because she didn't have many customers, commented.

'412 27th Street.' That's what the man in the hotel had written down for her. At first, he tried to give her verbal directions—you turn left at the firehall and then go along until you come to a big brick house, you can't miss it, then you turn right and ... for, of course, he knew the Boyces, Sam and Elvira. Sam Boyce worked at the grain elevator, had for thirty-three years. Sam and Elvira had five kids, all grown up now. Amy was the youngest. The man, a nice man, with silky white hair and slinky arm bands, did not ask why she wanted to call on the Boyces. He did not probe for information. Perhaps he had already gauged her mental state. Likely it was clear to all that she had been through an ordeal. Everyone knew that she had been at Thorncliffe Heights at the time of the fire, although she could not be sure what they knew of the details. "They had that crazy girl there didn't they?" someone in the café had said. "What did they have her there for?"

Seeing that she was confused, the hotel man looked up 'Boyce' in the telephone book, a thin book, more like a pamphlet. He wrote the address down and put the book back beneath the counter. "It's easy as pie," he said. "Things are pretty well laid out in a grid here. We're not as complicated as Toronto."

Emiline had already learned that the town was arranged in square blocks sectioned by wide streets. She took a lot of walks. She had to get out of her hotel room. It was cramped, claustrophobic. She did not like being alone with her thoughts, she felt better if she was out amongst people. Forgive me, she wanted to say to the young woman who served her in the Chinese café. I should have known, she yearned to confide in the man who dispensed headache powders in the drugstore. She wanted to hire a podium and make a public declaration. 'It was all my fault. I took Hester to Thorncliffe Heights. I brought destruction on them all.'

She spent a lot of time in a small park with a pond and geese and red-winged blackbirds and bulrushes. She sat on the bench at the train station as though waiting for her train. She spent hours browsing in the small library, looking at merchandise in the shops, buying nondescript items at the drugstore. She looked closely at the faces that she met. Had this or that face been at the funeral? It had seemed like the whole county was there, overflowing the small country church, spilling out after the ceremony into the graveyard behind, circling the two coffins being lowered into the earth, listening to the words of the minister, "for a little while I will go amongst you ...." But she had been so distraught that day, a day the heat had poured down from a pitiless sun in a sky that looked like polished metal, she had been scarcely conscious of her own body, let alone of those who had crossed her line of vision.

Four-twelve was a two-storey white clapboard house with a peaked roof and a verandah edged with flowerbeds of asters and snapdragons in vivid exuberant colour. The lawn, browning now, was clipped. The dusty caragana hedge was trimmed. The place had a comfortable lived-in appearance, as might be expected of a house that had raised five children and Lord knew how many dogs and cats. Everyone in the country had dogs and cats.

Emiline went through the wire gate and clicked it shut behind her. She followed the walk up to the verandah steps. The closer she got to her destination, the slower became her movements, the more acutely did she question herself. Why was she doing this? Would she be able to say what she had come to say? Would she be able to ask the question? How would she put it? Did you ever see anything that would lead you to believe that Victor Cage took advantage ... that there was anything happening ... that things were not quite right .... All the various ways she could think of to frame the question were vague, but she doubted that she could put it in more specific terms. Ordinary people didn't think about such things, let alone talk about them. As she hesitated at the edge of the verandah, she knew that she had to try. If there was any chance at all that she might learn something that would absolve her of her crimes, she had to do it.

She crossed to the screen door. Through the mesh, she could see into a hall. The smell of fresh baking, something with butter and cinnamon, wafted out. She pressed a button to one side of the door. A figure came almost immediately from the back of the house. The door was opened by an attractive woman, rather thin, with soft grey hair and wearing a neat housedress. She had been wiping her hands on a floury apron and one hand still held the apron. Emiline looked closely at her face, trying to remember if she had seen her at the funeral. But, then, she had seen so little that day.

"Mrs. Boyce?" asked Emiline.

"Yes?" A little worried frown of inquiry creased the fine skin on the older woman's brow.

"Hello," said Emiline and put out her hand. The woman did not take it. Emiline pulled it back. "I'm Emiline Thomas."

"Yes," said the woman. Her voice was rather airy, but her eyes as she took in Emiline head to toe were shrewdly measuring. Emiline was wearing a cotton skirt, a sleeveless blouse and sandals. Giving no thought to her dress, she had thrown these things on because of the heat. The other woman's look made her wonder if she were dressed appropriately. "You're at the hotel."

Of course, thought Emiline. Everyone will have the story. "My train doesn't come through until tomorrow," she said, thinking that the whole town would know that detail also.

Mrs. Boyce said nothing, she seemed to be waiting for Emiline to speak. There seemed to be something decidedly hostile in her stance. Quickly, before she lost her nerve, Emiline asked, "Is Amy home?"

"Amy?"

Emiline thought for a second that she might deny knowing anyone by that name. It struck her, too, that perhaps Amy no longer lived here.

"Amy Boyce."

Mrs. Boyce hesitated. She was still holding the door open with one hand, leaving Emiline outside. "I don't know," she hesitated again.

Then, from the top of the stairs, which were to the side of the foyer, a voice, similar to Mrs. Boyce's but younger, called bouncily, "Someone for me?" Emiline turned her head up quickly. Amy, for surely this must be Amy, had stopped suddenly upon seeing her at the door.

"I'm Emiline Thomas," said Emiline.

There was a long moment of silence. She must know who I am, thought Emiline.

Amy came slowly down the stairs. "It's okay, Mom," she said to her mother, turning her head, but not her eyes, toward the facsimile of herself thirty years in the future.

Emiline was unprepared for Amy's appearance. After the stories, after Maggie's words about rolling in the hay, she had expected a rather coarse type, seductive and earthy, with makeup an inch thick. Here was a pale, willowy strawberry blonde with freckles, her hair pulled back in a pony tail and wearing shorts and halter on what looked like a chaste, untried body. Why she's a fresh-faced small-town girl next door, thought Emiline. What had been the outcome of her disgraceful past, the child she was supposed to have had? Or was that, too, just gossip.

At this juncture, Mrs. Boyce dashed back into the house. "I have cookies in the oven," she said across her shoulder.

Emiline caught and held the door open. "I've been living out at Cage Farm," she said. "I wondered if we could talk?"

Amy said nothing. Her eyes shifted away from Emiline's face. Emiline noticed that she did not fill out the cups of her halter top and that her feet were bare. She had long toes and pink toenails which looked freshly painted.

"I was hired as a tutor for Hester. I'm on my way back to Toronto." There was a pause filled with silence. Emiline forged on, "The train doesn't come until tomorrow."

Still Amy did not respond.

"There was a fire out there," said Emiline, growing more uncomfortable. "Oh, not at Cage Farm. At Thorncliffe Heights."

Amy's face revealed nothing.

"Hester Cage ..." Emiline stopped. People did not know, could not know, no one could know with absolute certainty that Hester had started the fire.

"Too bad about the McFaddens," Amy finally spoke. It came out as a whisper. "They were real nice people." Her calm grey eyes were directed to one side of Emiline.

"Yes." Emiline shifted her weight from her left leg to her right. Oh why had she not rehearsed this before coming? But she had not been able to think about it.

Whenever she tried to think about the events of the summer, her mind bounced away. As for the fire, it was a blur of movement and raging flames and intense heat. Perhaps all catastrophic events in one's life were like that, happening so quickly that ever after one wondered if they had really happened at all. And now, faced with Amy Boyce, faced with this *girl*, she was even less sure of how to phrase her remarks, how to put her question. But she must say something, something coherent. "I've been staying with some people out there," she started, "neighbours of the McFaddens."

"The Priestlys," interjected Amy.

"Yes." Why do I keep thinking that anything anyone does here is not known to the whole county, thought Emiline. "They were very kind," she said. Even going themselves to Cage Farm and retrieving my belongings, she thought. It must have been Mrs. Cage who had scooped everything out of the bureau drawers and into a cardboard box. The first thing Emiline had looked for was a long white envelope in which she had stashed her salary payments. She was relieved to find it amongst a jumble of nighties and underwear.

Probably the whole district knew, too, that she did not, could not, return to Cage Farm. How much people knew about the reason, Emiline could not be sure. Millie and another woman had been in the kitchen the whole afternoon, hearing every word and cry that was uttered. How explicit those words and cries had been, Emiline could not recall. "They brought me here," she continued, "after the funeral. But the train ... I wonder if I could have a few minutes of your time...."

"I'm pretty busy," murmured Amy. She looked at her pink toes.

Emiline could not let it go. She could not let Amy go without completing her mission. "The thing is, I'm not exactly sure what happened at Cage Farm this summer, that is ... the truth of it ..." Oh why did her voice keep trailing off? She willed herself to speak up. "... before the fire."

"I'm afraid I can't help you," said Amy. She looked up. Her eyes were clear. "I'm afraid you've wasted your time coming here."

"I thought, perhaps, since you were there for awhile ..."

"That was a couple of years ago."

"But you must know something about the situation there."

Emiline suddenly realized that the atmosphere had become tense. Amy seemed to have stopped breathing. The kitchen clatter had stopped. The moment hung, suspended.

Amy glanced across her shoulder in the direction of the kitchen. She took a step toward Emiline, then brushed past her and through the doorway, beckoning with a hand that Emiline should follow. She went down the front steps, down the walk, and stopped near the gate, causing Emiline, close behind, to also come to an abrupt halt. Amy turned. "I'm afraid I don't have time to talk. I'm real busy these days. I'm getting married. Next week. I haven't time to think about anything else. Tonight some people are having a shower for me."

Of course, thought Emiline. Other people have lives, plans, schemes, too. "Oh," she said, "how stupidly thoughtless of me."

"Every evening is some party or shower or something," said Amy. "And I've got me a good secretarial job. At City Hall. We've already got a nice little house in the new development west of town." She scarcely paused. "My guy, he works in the bank. He'll do good. Our house is white. I wanted a white house. We're gonna live in that white house and have a bunch of kids and live a good happy life together."

"I'm so happy for you." Upon impulse Emiline reached out and clasped Amy's hand. She squeezed it. It was cruel of her to remind this girl of what must have been a painful experience. She turned to go. " I wanted so to help Hester," she said, repeating the words that had become a litany of her suffering. "I wanted to do what was best for her. She was coming along nicely. She could draw pictures, she could print."

Perhaps it was the unshed tears in Emiline's voice which caused Amy to respond after all. "Oh, she could copy. She always could copy."

"She could learn," said Emiline. "I'm sure of it."

"She could mimic anybody. She was real good at that."

"Hester is a very special person." Emiline's voice was emphatic.

"Everybody knows," said Amy. "She's crazier'n a hoot owl. They should've had her locked up years ago. But Victor wouldn't have it. But everybody knows. That's why he advertised in city papers. No one from around here would take the job, and that's even with them not knowing about the fires."

"Fires?"

"She was always trying to burn things down. They kept finding new hiding places for the matches. But she always found them."

"Matches?" Emiline felt her skin tighten on her bones.

"She loved matches. She'd steal them until she got a whole lot, then she'd have a fire. She loved fire."

Emiline saw her night stand. She saw the white cloth, the flashlight, the package of cigarettes, the matches tucked in to one side. She had been told to be careful. She should have been more careful. She should have counted the matches. Stop it, she thought. Hester could have obtained matches in a dozen different ways. You have absolutely no evidence for thinking what you're thinking. You never noticed any matches missing. Still, she thought, you never counted them.

"I didn't know," she said.

"They didn't tell you?"

"No."

"That's why they never left her alone."

"No one told me."

"They didn't tell anyone. Victor didn't want anyone to know about fire. He would've told the others not to tell you."

"No one told me," Emiline murmured through numb lips.

"She liked to make things disappear. Things that had to do with blood. Maybe in her mind it was a sort of cleansing thing. Blood would set her off."

Emiline saw Hester's scratched arms. She saw long sharp fingernails scraping, tearing at flesh. She saw blood. "No one told me," she repeated.

"Blood upset her something terrible. And then if she had some matches, she'd try and burn the blood away. He should've told you."

"Yes," said Emiline. "I should have had that information."

"Victor was afraid they'd lock her up, if people knew. It's real dangerous in the country, having a person who starts fires. But he should've told you. Else how could you know what to watch out for?"

"Yes. How could I help her if I didn't have all the information?"

"You weren't meant to help her. Only to watch her."

"But I wanted to help her. And I could have. I could have changed the way things turned out. I know I could have gotten through to her, taught her something."

"You weren't meant to teach her anything."

"No," said Emiline. "I suppose not."

"She burned a towel once. And it wasn't even blood. It was berry juice. But quick as a wink she grabbed that towel and threw it into the cookstove. Before I could stop her. We both stood there and watched it blaze up. Then I put back the stove lid. We were alone in the kitchen. I didn't tell anyone. I thought I'd get merry old hell for letting it happen."

Emiline stared straight into Amy's face. "But you knew. You knew about the fire and blood, and the matches. Victor told *you*."

"He didn't tell me. Dane told me."

"Dane?"

"Oh, I always knew that Cage Farm was a weird place. Everyone around here knows that. Dad told me I was crazy to go out there. I only went because of Dane. We met at a dance."

"Dane?"

Amy was looking across Emiline's shoulder, into the distance, as though seeing something there that stirred a deep pool of memory. "Dane and me had real feeling for each other," she said. "We wanted to get married but Victor Cage put a stop to it."

Emiline's mind worked quickly in an attempt to sort out the gossip from the reality of what she was now hearing. She had been brought up in the belief that it was bad manners to pry. But she had to know. "The story I heard," she said, "was Victor ..." She could not continue.

"I heard that story, too, but I'd just as soon have something to do with a rattlesnake as Victor Cage."

Emiline recalled Dane's reactions the various times Amy's name had been mentioned. She would have liked to say, 'he still cares for you,' but thought better of it. It might be easier for Amy not to know. "But why didn't Dane leave?" she said instead.

"Oh, he wanted to. So did Maggie. Maggie hates it there. So does Mrs. Cage. But Hester won't let any of them go."

"Hester?"

"She keeps them all prisoners. If you ask me, I think she knows what she's doing, too. She gets that scheming look on her face. She's got a good thing going there. Queen bee. They all hop to her bidding. They're all scared of what she might do if she gets upset. Her fits or spells. The farm is a place for her to hide, otherwise she'd have to be put in an asylum. Oh, I admit it must've been a terrible thing, what she went through. But it's been made into an unholy suffering that they all have to worship. It's become the meaning of Cage Farm. So they have to keep it together. The farm. Victor's the one who's got them thinking that way. So even if they want to leave, they can't. They're under a sort of spell. And even though Victor is the boss, she's the one who controls Victor. She has such a hold on him, it's uncanny. It's almost like he worships her. All that work he does, it's for her. And what's more, she demands his worship and his attention. Did you ever notice how she gets real mad if he pays the slightest attention to anyone else? Mad and destructive."

Amy's voice in the telling of her story had gained momentum, as though once started she couldn't stop until she got it all out. Her tone had taken on a bitter edge, with something in it also of regret. Then she seemed to recover. She brought her eyes back from the distance to the side of Emiline's face. "I was nuts about Dane, but you can understand why I couldn't live out there, in that weird place."

"But, there's no real reason Dane can't leave," Emiline protested. "There's nothing real to stop him."

"There doesn't have to be anything real. It can be in a person's head. That's stronger than real. Especially at Cage Farm."

"You wonder," sighed Emiline, suddenly resigned. "She might be happier in an institution."

"That would be the end of Cage Farm. It wouldn't have any meaning without her."

"Maybe that would be a good thing. Then they can all leave."

"Anyway, this is all talk. Victor wouldn't have it."

Emiline half turned to go. She looked back. She saw this girl and Dane Cage as he had knelt in the straw that day with the kittens, his curls framing his vulnerable boyish face. "Did you ever think that you and Dane might get back together some day. I mean, before you met your new fellow? I mean, if Dane did leave the farm?"

Amy shook her head. "We have too much between us."

"Sometimes that brings people closer together."

"I stayed at Cage Farm longer than I should have because of Dane. Then when I got back to town, people blamed me, they said I was brazen. That was the word some of the church ladies used. It was hard. I was going to leave again. But then I lost it anyway, because of Victor Cage, because of the way he treated me. The doctor said it could've been caused by that."

Amy spoke as though, of course, Emiline would have heard the gossip, as, of course, she had.

Amy continued in an almost conversational tone, as though now she wanted to chat, as though by talking she could get the points of the story in order. "What happened only makes sense if we don't get back together. It's better for us to get into a new, happier life. It's better if we start off, cheerful like, with other people. And then there's Cage Farm itself. And Victor. And Hester. That've made Dane what he is. There'd always be that between us. He's lived twenty-five years with that. You don't get over something like that overnight. No, he'll always have a sort of darkness inside and I don't want to live with darkness. Oh no, there's too much between us. We could never forget. You have to start over."

Emiline thought what it must be like to be pregnant and unmarried in a small town. Amy must have been the target of so many cruel and unfair remarks. Because of such pressure, most girls in her position married the father even if they didn't want to. It was either that or leave town. Emiline could not help but admire this girl who had stayed, who had withstood the talk and risen above it, who would look the town in the eye and have a white wedding. She must have incredible strength, thought Emiline. This seeming wisp of a girl must have nerves of steel.

"Yes," said Emiline. "I suppose you're right."

Amy spoke with mechanical precision, as though she had thought the words to herself in every way, shape and form, and now was left with only the words, empty of emotion. "I don't want to have Cage blood in my kids. Every time I'm expecting I don't want to be thinking that I'm carrying the Cage genes. I don't want those things in my kids. Suicide, craziness, brain cancer."

Emiline took a sideways step. She had put this poor woman through enough. Still, if she was ever going to ask the question she had come here to ask, it had to be now. She opened her mouth but the words for asking the question would not come. How could she possibly ask this girl about such things. She, herself, could not speak of such things.

Amy's clear innocent grey eyes seemed to be staring into her own mind, looking at pictures she did not want to see, pictures that she had been successful at forgetting until this stranger had come along to remind her. "We never speak of Cage Farm around here," she said. "Dad won't hear of it. It upsets him something terrible."

Emiline backed away slowly, slowly stepped through the gate. "Sorry," she said. "Sorry. I'm sorry."

chapter 17

Sept. 10. Dear Vera: I'm so happy to hear about your forthcoming wedding. Roger sounds like a very special person. You say you're buying a little starter house. I know it will be very nice …

Sept. 14. Dear Vera: Great news. About Roger. He sounds great. I know you'll be very happy. People can be happy …

Sept. 17. Dear Vera: Hope this finds you well. As to the bridesmaid question …

Sept. 18. Dear Vera: I don't know how to tell you this but since I've already missed the start of fall term …

Sept. 21. Dear Vera: Thanks for your letter. And your concern. I know I've been tardy in my correspondence but all is well …

Sept. 21. Dear Vera: Thanks for keeping in touch. They gave me your letter at the post office …

Sept. 24. Dear Vera: No, nothing's wrong. I haven't forgotten my old pal…

Sept. 26. Dear Vera: How are you? I am fine …

Emiline's hand reached out. She picked up the sheet of hotel stationery and crumpled it into a ball with both hands. She tossed it onto the top of a mound of white paper balls already overflowing the waste paper basket on the floor near the writing table. She stood up and went out and crisscrossed the grid of streets.

The fields were full of ripe grain and there was a shop in town selling amber beads. Glass, thought Emiline staring through the showcase window. They resembled in colour everything that was going on around her, the country changing from green to various shades of brown. Sometimes on a sunlit day, she looked far into the distance from her second-storey hotel room window and saw a field with the light upon it that was exactly this same colour.

She kept meaning to leave but could not take the necessary steps which would take her to the train station. She could not understand this reluctance, no, not reluctance, impossibility. At first she thought that it had something to do with Lewis. Because of her guilt, the pain of her guilt, she thought that she would have to do something about him, but apologies, explanations, would be so inadequate as to be laughable.

As the days passed, she thought that maybe she wouldn't have to do anything about him after all. Maybe he would disappear. He knocked at her door once. She saw him coming. She was at the window as he was crossing the street. He looked up. She drew back behind the curtain. As his footsteps came closer, down the uncarpeted hallway, she huddled in a chair behind the door. His knock came. One, two. Pause. One, two, three. She held her breath until his footsteps receded, until they descended the stairs.

She envisioned his face with new long creases and sad eyes. She heard his voice as it had been at the fire, saw his lips close in a straight line as he let Hester go to Victor. "It wasn't her fault," he said. "That she wasn't what I wanted her to be. I should have understood her better. Victor was the one who understood her."

That was the last time she had heard his voice and, even then, he had been speaking not to her but to himself. She could not hear his voice now. She could not know what was in his head. She could not know what he was thinking. Perhaps his mind had suspended thought. She envisioned his mind as a red smear of pain, a blur that she could not enter. Now she must think for herself. In the past, at times he had relieved her from the task of thinking. He had allowed her another way of looking at things, for instance Hester. He had viewed Hester as a romantic dream. He had been wrong to do that, Emiline could see that now. But perhaps 'wrong' was not a good word, or at least a helpful one. He had been no more wrong than she in her insistence that Hester was normal. Both views had been dangerous. Both mistaken views had led to disaster.

She remained huddled behind the door and thought of their kiss. At the time it had happened, she had not been able to think. Now, she analyzed it as being unlike Bradley's peck, during which she had felt a sisterly response. Neither was it like what she had felt when confronted with Victor. She now recognized that as a mixture of fear and desire, of which she was thoroughly ashamed, not of the feelings so much as that such a man could have raised them in her. She was appalled that those two emotions should be so innately linked.

While for her the kiss had been a warm melting of herself into another human being through a meeting of a part of their bodies, she could not know Lewis's thoughts on the subject. She was sure that for now and for a long time to come his mind would not encompass anything but the catastrophe. His loss was so much greater than hers, his parents, of course, but Hester, too. Emiline understood him so much better since that terrible night. She understood that Hester had been a part of his life. His dream of her had been a part of who he was. Even when he was away, he knew that she was here. If he had never come home again, he would have been safe in the knowledge that she was at Cage Farm. He could have dreamed forever of his childhood and youth in the paradise of Thorncliffe Heights with nothing to disturb his dream. But the dream had been annihilated. He had been forced to wake up. Lewis was a man who did not like things to change, and everything had changed in a single night. In a few hours of a night, he had lost everything.

She thought about her own profound misreading of Hester. Not that she necessarily agreed with Amy's assessment. Amy's conviction likely was influenced by her bitterness toward Cage Farm, in general, and Victor Cage, in particular. Amy's belief that Hester not only wielded the power at Cage Farm but did so through conscious scheming on her part, could certainly be mistaken. Emiline believed that it was. She conceded, however, that Hester might have unconsciously held them all hostage. This was common in families where one member was sick or aged or otherwise infirm. But when she thought of Hester's delight in their walks, how she had twirled herself around in the field, held her face up to the sun, danced around the slow, knobby-headed calves, she was convinced that Hester was not a wily manipulator, not a profane seductress. Nor was she, Emiline had to honestly conclude, a pliant innocent.

Certainly, Hester had proven to be a force to be reckoned with, Emiline had to admit that. Far from being passive, at her centre Hester had an intense energy. It was Emiline's misunderstanding of this force and this energy that had instigated the disaster. She had thought her a child with an unformed mind, a clean slate on which could be written new thoughts, good thoughts. She had not understood that Hester's mind was fully formed, unmalleable, unalterable, calcified by its images and impulses, images that had been written there long ago with the indelible imprint of childhood experience. She had not understood that there was another side to Hester, a side with a will that must be done. She had not understood that Hester's will was not for the good of others, or even for herself, but for itself, and, therefore, could be destructive. She had not understood that Hester was dangerous.

She had failed because she had not been able to be with Hester on the inside. She had only been able to observe her from the outside and, thus, had not properly comprehended the effect on her of what she had seen, the head torn open, the blood of her father. I wanted to lead her out of her darkness and into the light, thought Emiline. I wanted to stop her suffering. I wanted to take it on myself. But I had no idea of the extent of it. And in the end, I caused her more suffering because I took her away from Victor.

Emiline thought of the scene at the spare bedroom window. She saw again the suffering in Hester's face when she turned. Hester must have thought that she had been abandoned by Victor, Victor, her only connection to this world. Victor and Hester, they were like the last two of a species. They understood each other. They were the only ones who did. He knew what was in her mind. He was with her on the inside, he was the only one who could be, who could properly understand her suffering. They spoke the same language, the language of silence. They were as one, whether their union was holy or unholy, Emiline would never know with certainty. She had to face that fact. She could never know.

I wanted to stop her suffering, thought Emiline, but Victor celebrated it. I wanted to take her suffering away from her, but Victor defended it as her identity. He viewed Hester as part of a larger story and he gave her the most important role in that story. And as it turned out, he was the hero, he certainly was her hero. She had spoken his name. He was the one with power to wake the sleeping beauty. Lewis did not want her to wake up. I tried to awaken her and failed. Both Lewis and Victor wanted Hester to remain as she was. I wanted to change her. But we all, each in our own way, wanted to control and possess her. My sin was as great as theirs.

Through these thoughts which turned round and round in Emiline's head like a torture wheel, she had an insight into what had happened that night at the window. She called for Victor, not me, she thought. In the final hour, I was invisible. I did not exist.

She thought again of how love had failed. Her love. There was something wrong with it. It was inadequate. That night, that terrible night when Hester must have been locked into her head with her unspeakable pictures, her love had not been enough to hold her. My body, the comfort of my body which I tried to give her, mourned Emiline, was not enough to create for her the illusion that she was not alone.

It was with a heavy heart that Emiline realized that her love had not been big enough to deal with Hester. But could anyone love Hester enough? Love, human love, had no meaning for Hester. She could not use it. It could not get through to her. And that could never be changed, Emiline knew that now. She could not help Hester to develop into someone who could love. Love was wasted on Hester.

The realization that love could be wasted shook Emiline to the core. For in spite of her failures, she had still believed in love. People might fail but love itself endured. Perhaps the adoptive parents had instilled that belief in her. They must have. Where else would she have gotten it? She had always believed that love is a good thing and that good must triumph. What she had not realized was the strength of a destructive element in the world and how large a love it would take to bear that element and turn it into good. Even if she put all her optimistic belief and compassion and love into place, these qualities in her were those of a mere mortal. What was required here was something more. There are limitations to human love, decided Emiline.

But then as she thought of these things across the days that turned into weeks, she began to think that limitations to love were not necessarily an inevitable conclusion to the story of the human heart. She began to think that the more difficult a love, the greater expansion of the heart it demanded and the greater the opportunity for growth in the individual. She began to think that any love was not wasted because of what it allowed the person who loved.

During those weeks when her raw bleeding wounds turned into scars, she thought of them as wide ugly scars, Emiline lost track of Lewis. She doubted that he was still in town. She certainly would not be, if she could help it. But why couldn't she help it? She had no place else to go, she decided. No one to go to. She could not go back to her former life or to Vera. She would be like a soldier returning from a war that the others had not experienced, so could not fathom. She went out with great reluctance, in case Lewis was still around. I skulk, she thought. I sneak around like a prowler. She hid behind a wall of tinned goods in the general store and heard the gossip at the till.

"Didja hear about Victor Cage buying Thorncliffe Heights?"

"Decent of him when you think the mess he's getting."

"But the land's good."

"Heard he got it cheap. Lewis didn't want to have anything to do with it."

"Can't say as I blame him."

"How did he feel about selling it? His father built that house."

"The house is gone."

"The lawyer arranged it. Lewis told him to sell to the highest bidder. I'm sure he never wants to set foot on the place again."

"There's a man who'll never be the same."

"Can't be, not when you see the two parents go at once like that."

"And in such a terrible way."

"A shame."

"A real shame."

"What started the fire?"

"No one knows."

"It coulda been a lit cigarette."

"This time of year everything's so dry."

"I heard the McFaddens kidnapped that crazy Cage girl."

"Why would they do a thing like that?"

"I don't believe that."

"She wanted to go home. She was raving something terrible the whole afternoon. Why was she still there at midnight? She shouldn't've been there. She should've been home in her bed."

"You never know what sorts of queer things people will do."

"Millie said it wasn't the McFaddens kidnapped her. It was that other one, the babysitter from the east."

"No wonder. She's from Toronto.

"Maybe the McFaddens belonged to one of them religious cults."

"That's nonsense."

"There's the one where they torture people to drive out evil demons."

"That was in Saskatchewan."

"Could be here, too."

"I still don't believe it."

"The McFaddens always seemed like such decent people."

"They *were* hoity toity."

"Pride goes before a fall."

The post office was another well where people gathered to draw up bucket after bucket of information. There, as everywhere else, Emiline felt that she was without presence.

"Victor Cage is building a house out there."

"Where?"

"Thorncliffe Heights. It's gonna be a dandy. Big rooms, high ceiling."

"That'll be a change for him. Cage Farm is such a dark hole."

"There'll never be another Thorncliffe Heights."

"It was such a beautiful place."

"And a happy place. I used to like going out there. When I was a kid, I'd go with Mom. Mrs. McFadden had sewing bees for the Red Cross. I'll never forget."

"I know what you mean. It was real peaceful there."

"What'll happen to Cage Farm?"

"Victor'll keep the land. I suppose the house'll go to wrack and ruin, another ghost house on the prairies."

So Thorncliffe Heights was to rise again. Emiline wondered what the new house would be like. She wondered about Victor Cage's version of paradise. It was certain to be quite different than the McFadden's. From what Amy had said it might be a pagan version, with Hester as the worshipped idol. Victor might even change the name to Cage Farm.

"Why does Victor need a big house like that? It's only him and his sister now."

"Too bad his ma can't be around for the new place. After all those years in that pokey house at Cage Farm."

"But she always did want to spend her last years with that sister in Saskatchewan."

"I heard Dane's left too."

"Where did he go?"

"Dunno. The city maybe."

"Somebody told me he might go to that agricultural school down at Olds."

"I heard that, too."

"Maybe it's true."

"And Maggie's in Edmonton. Somebody saw her there."

So Cage Farm was no more. Soon it would be deserted. The people, except for Victor and Hester, had already gone. Soon the remaining two would move into the new house. Emiline could not know what had happened at Cage Farm after the fire. No one could know that except the Cages and they would never talk. There was gossip, of course. People speculated that Victor no longer needed Maggie and Dane now that he could afford to hire itinerant labour. Emiline heard Victor's, "we all belong to Cage Farm," and Dane's, "we have to keep the farm together." Was it possible that since Cage Farm would no longer exist, since there was no longer a farm to keep intact, they were free? But what of the new place? Might not the bondage have been transferred there? Something must have happened. Perhaps the prisoners had taken advantage of the upheaval to demand their liberty. Emiline liked to think that the three had taken their lives into their own hands. She liked to think that they had rebelled, that they had changed Victor's story, that they had chosen their own destinies. She liked to think of seeds planted—the hair comb, her talk of the outside world and freedom. But she had to acknowledge that, in the end, Hester, rather than she, had freed them. Her destructive force had freed them all. As for Hester, it seemed to Emiline that Victor had been right when he said that freedom had no meaning for her. She existed in her head, she was locked in there, she was lost to her own mind. It would not matter where she was as long as she was with Victor.

"So Victor gets saddled with that retarded sister of his."

"He's devoted to her."

"Millie'll be there. Her and Al are staying on."

"That's what I heard, too. Al says he's too old to change."

"And where would they go? At their age."

"With them two, Victor'll get along fine without the others."

"You've got to give Victor Cage a lot of credit. The way he took charge. The way he took care of his ma and his brother and sisters, and even that crazy one."

"And they didn't have two sticks to rub together."

"He's got money now. The crops've been good."

"He's a hard worker."

"And he didn't get hailed out five years in a row like some of us."

"He must live right."

"I always say, in the end people get what they deserve."

They don't know me, thought Emiline, looking in the mirror above the sink in the tiny hotel bathroom. Why would they? I never came to town. And even if I had, I've changed so much. I scarcely recognize myself.

Gone was the attractive girl with soft cheeks and a bright expectant appearance. In her place was a woman with bones close beneath the skin and sad drooping eyes. The new face was one of shadows, hollows beneath the cheekbones, deep eye sockets. The mouth was taking on a grim edge. Sometimes this woman forgot to comb her hair. Sometimes she didn't bother to bathe.

When she went out, she marvelled at the town's order, the precise hedges, the trimmed lawns, the flowerbeds, now full of dying nasturtiums, pansies, and late blooming sweet peas. The Chinese café served up ghastly coffee, but it was wet and usually hot. Once, when she was sitting in a booth pretending to read a newspaper, she looked up and saw Lewis, sitting in the open section of tables, turning over loose pages of white paper. Wasps coming in from the cold circled his head but he did not appear to see them.

Before she could look down toward her newspaper, he turned his head and spotted her. Their eyes met in shocked silence. She was prepared to let the moment pass without taking action, but he stood up. The wasps rose with him. He moved as though he had just awakened from a deep sleep. There was an element of anguish in his smile, and his eyes darted as though, in making contact with hers, he might start something in which he had no wish to become involved. He brought the wasps to her table.

At the beginning of their friendship, Emiline had decided that their relationship depended on their situation and not on any ongoing reality of their lives. When the incident that had brought them together was over, their connection would be over. While they were making polite social gestures toward each other—how are things, didn't know you were still in town—when she looked at him across the small table, she realized why she had thought that. She had not tried to enter into his inner space. She had not tried to know his solitude. She had not cared enough to try, and so his life, with its sadness and tears, was unknown to her.

That explained her misinterpretation of his motives, how she had failed to recognize the power over him of his romantic dream. But how could she have been so unaware? Now that she gave it some thought, it had been so obvious, in his appearance, in his every gesture, even in the way he moved, and in the subject of his study. How could she not have predicted his indecision, that when it came to any real action, he would be inadequate?

The waitress came to the table and poured them more coffee. It was while she was staring at the amber stream from pot to cup that she realized the difference between the solitude of Hester and that of Lewis. She had not been able to enter Hester's inner space even though she had put all of her energy into the endeavour because Hester could not respond. She did not contain the human element necessary for sharing herself.

In this thought, Emiline was able to see that she and Lewis might find consolation in their shared sadness and guilt. They had both betrayed the ones they loved most dearly. They knew this about each other. Their losses, which were part of their individual solitudes, could be part of their connection. If they could forgive themselves and each other they might find a way to live.

Emiline's insight and realization happened in slow motion as Lewis drifted over to her table, then got up and slowly drifted out of the café, carrying his dissertation like his collapsed life in his hands.

She realized the task before her. She must find love again within herself. She must believe in the strength and largeness of that love. She must do it for Lewis. Lewis needed her to try. She must help him to try. She must help him. She was the only one who could help him.

It was a matter of getting out of one story and into another, getting out of a dark story and into a brighter, more cheerful, one.

Emiline got up from the table, slowly. There was no hurry. Lewis would be waiting for her some place, if not here, there, if not today, tomorrow. When they found each other again, then they would decide their future. As she batted a wasp away from where it was hovering before her face, she decided that their life together had already begun. At its centre was a devious, even uncertain, interpretation of happiness. She thought it would be enough. In any case, it would have to do.